"You want to see how he is, don't you?"

That was certainly true. Julia hadn't climbed down the ravine, had the wind knocked out of her and taken an unplanned mud bath just to have Cameron die on her. She went to the back of the ambulance and took the paramedic's proffered hand. He helped her inside and returned to work, adjusting gauges and checking IV lines.

Cameron lay on the stretcher. She took a few awkward steps toward him in the confined space. He tried lifting his head, but his movements were limited by a restrictive collar. Nevertheless, he smiled. That same devastating smile she remembered shining on her from the podium of a Riverton College classroom, not even diminished now by a background of nasty lacerations.

The medic pointed to Julia. "Professor, meet Miss Julia Sommerville, one-woman mountain rescue team."

"Actually, we've met before." He stared intently at her before adding, "Moon Pie?"

Dear Reader,

Hopefully once in a lifetime each of us will find a place that feels like home even when it isn't. The Blue Ridge Mountains of North Carolina have been the home of my heart since I first visited there thirty-five years ago. That's why I had to write about two characters who find love and happiness in the mystical, magical mountains.

Julia and Cameron returned to the small valley town of their childhoods for different reasons—Cameron to reconnect with the folklore of the hills, and Julia to lend support to her family after a heartbreaking suicide left them floundering. Neither Cam nor Julia intended to stay. Neither expected this particularly splendid autumn would inspire them with so much pain and so much promise. Tragedy brought them back, but the love of a little girl and each other made them stay.

I love to hear from readers. You can visit my Web site at www.cynthiathomason.com, e-mail me at cynthoma@aol.com or write to me at P.O. Box 550068, Fort Lauderdale, FL 33355.

Cynthia Thomason

HER SISTER'S CHILD
Cynthia Thomason

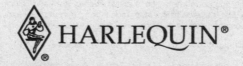

TORONTO • NEW YORK • LONDON
AMSTERDAM • PARIS • SYDNEY • HAMBURG
STOCKHOLM • ATHENS • TOKYO • MILAN • MADRID
PRAGUE • WARSAW • BUDAPEST • AUCKLAND

ISBN-13: 978-0-373-71419-3
ISBN-10:   0-373-71419-X

HER SISTER'S CHILD

ABOUT THE AUTHOR

Cynthia Thomason writes contemporary and historical romances as well as an historical mystery series. She has received the National Readers' Choice Award, nominations for the *Romantic Times BOOKreviews* Reviewers Choice and the Golden Quill. She and her husband own an auction company in Davie, Florida, where she is a licensed auctioneer. They have one son, an entertainment reporter, and a very lovable Jack Russell terrier. Learn more about Cynthia at www.cynthiathomason.com.

This book is dedicated to my "Buddy"
of nearly thirty years, who longs, as much as
I do, for a waterfall to appear around
the next mountain curve.

PROLOGUE

THE SOUND of the front door closing roused Tina from a drowsiness brought on by having drunk too much wine. She glanced at the clock by her bed. 2:18 a.m. Wayne had promised to be home by midnight, but Tina had known he wouldn't be. She reached beside the bed, picked up the bottle she'd set there a few minutes ago and tipped it to her lips. It was the last swallow and it tasted bitter. She dropped the empty to the floor, rolled it under the mattress and heard it clink against the other one she'd hidden there a couple of hours ago so her daughter wouldn't see it.

Wayne's heavy boot connected with the partially opened bedroom door, swinging it wide. He stood a moment, squinting against the soft light of the bedside table. "You still awake?" he asked unnecessarily.

"You promised you'd be home hours ago," she said.

He closed the door, strode awkwardly to the middle of the room. "Don't start, Tina. I'm beat." He slipped his T-shirt over his head, tossed it onto a chair and un-zipped his jeans.

"Where have you been?" she asked, knowing she wouldn't believe the answer.

"I told you. I met my brother at the pool hall. We had some wings, played a few games."

"Until two o'clock in the morning?"

"Yeah, until then." He stepped out of the jeans and threw them on top of the shirt. She caught a whiff of something floral and cloying.

"Daryl sure smells good these days," Tina said.

Wayne crawled between the sheets. "I'm going to ignore that. There were women at the bar."

"I want you to tell me where you've really been all this time."

He rolled onto his side. "Turn out the light."

She sat a little straighter, the effects of the wine making her dizzy and nauseous. But she couldn't give in now. All evening she'd planned this confrontation. No, she'd planned it for weeks and tonight it was going to happen. She jostled his shoulder. "Wayne, we need to talk."

He tensed, but didn't turn toward her. "Fine. You talk. But I'm going to sleep."

A single tear slid down her cheek. She wiped it away. "I'm miserably unhappy."

He yawned. "What else is new?"

"No, I mean this is serious. I…"

"Go to sleep, Tina. We'll talk in the morning."

She trapped a sob in her throat. "This can't wait until morning."

"It's gonna have to." He punched his pillow hard. Tina flinched. "Now either go to sleep or leave me alone so I can."

She waited at least a minute, hoping he would move, say something else, look at her. He didn't. The clock read 2:22 a.m. when Wayne began snoring.

Tina got up, smoothed her nightgown down her body with damp palms and went into the bathroom. Grabbing the sink for support, she looked at her reflection in the mirror. When had she grown so old? So sad? So worn-out from the task of living each day?

She stumbled in bare feet to the living room and took an envelope from the old oak desk scarred with cigarette burns. She'd sealed the envelope a couple of hours ago. Somewhere in the back of her mind was the faint hope that she wouldn't need the note, that something would happen to change her mind. Foolish hope. That's all it was. She picked up a pen and wrote "To Wayne," and leaned the envelope against a picture of her and her daughter on the fireplace mantel.

She walked into the tiny second bedroom of her run-down cottage and stood by Katie's bed. The child slept peacefully, unaware of the tears flowing down her mama's face. Lately, Tina knew, Katie's dreams had been the only place the little girl found true contentment. Kids sensed when something wasn't right, when their worlds were about to crumble, when a parent could no longer be counted on to fix the problems in their lives. Tina had disappointed Katie too many times.

She leaned over the bed, brushed a few tangles of golden blond hair off Katie's brow and kissed her cheek. "I'm so sorry, baby," she said. "But everything is going to be better now. I promise."

Tina took one last long look at her daughter's face before she left the room. Wayne would do the right thing. At least she could depend on him to do what he needed to for Katie.

She walked through the house, feeling weightless, free, sure of her course for the first time in years. She went out the rear door and headed toward the lake. At the edge of the water, she stopped and looked back at her house. The roof over the small porch sagged from neglect. The shed still lay in ruins from the last tornado, its sad contents rusting on red clay where only weeds survived. Nothing in Tina's life was ever fixed. It all simply rotted away, little by little, day by day. But she could stop the decay from destroying her daughter. At least she could do that.

She looked up at the Tennessee sky sprinkled with a thousand stars and stepped into the water, still warm from September's Indian summer. She walked straight ahead, enjoying the feel of her gown rippling around her ankles, her calves, her thighs. The worn flannel was as soft as a petal, clinging, protective. When the water reached her breasts, she spread her arms, inviting the earth's most basic element to claim her, opening herself to the calm that awaited.

Water lapped at her chin, her nose. She opened her mouth and let the lake flow in until the stars disappeared.

CHAPTER ONE

JULIA TURNED OFF her shower and heard the phone ringing. She grabbed a towel. "Oh, great." With just thirty minutes to dress, hail a cab and travel ten blocks to an off-Broadway theater for a Friday opening matinee, she didn't have time for conversation. Nevertheless, she raced to her nightstand and picked up the portable.

Caller ID displayed her mother's name. Julia considered not answering, but she couldn't do that. It wouldn't necessarily be bad news. Her mom didn't have a problem *every* time she called. Although since Julia's dad died a year ago, it seemed as if she did.

She draped the towel around her body, sat on the bedspread and punched the Connect button. "Hi, Mama. What's up? I'm kind of in a hurry…"

There was a moment's pause, then a trembling sob from Cora.

"Mama, what's wrong?"

"W…Wayne's here," she said.

The stutter alerted Julia that her mother was either nervous or upset. This could be a long call. Tucking the phone into the crook of her neck, she walked to her dresser and took out some underwear. "What's he doing there?"

"He—he brought K-Katie."

Oh. Well, that was okay. Julia slipped on her panties

and reached for a bra. "That's wonderful," she said. "You must be excited to have Katie for a visit."

"It's not a visit," Cora said, her words coming slowly.

Alarm raised goose bumps on Julia's arms. "Mama, where's Tina? Is she there?"

"No." A quaking sob stopped Cora's speech.

Julia gripped the phone more tightly and spoke deliberately. "Tell me, Mama. Where's Tina?"

There was no answer, only a rustling sound. The next voice Julia heard was Wayne's. "Hey, Julia, it's me." Julia had never gotten along with her sister's live-in boyfriend, a man she considered a Neanderthal.

"What's going on, Wayne?"

"I don't know how else to tell you, but Tina's dead. She killed herself."

"What?" The towel fell to the floor. Julia sat heavily on the mattress, feeling as though a vicious clamp were squeezing her chest.

"It was pretty awful," Wayne said. "When she wasn't in the house yesterday morning, I went outside and saw her body floating in the lake. She still had her nightgown on."

Pretty awful. How could he summarize this horrendous news with such an idiotic description? Her sister was *dead.* She meant something to people, maybe not to Wayne but to Julia. And Cora. And certainly Katie. *Katie.* Julia tried to draw a deep breath but only managed to push out two words. "She drowned?"

"Yeah. She left a note like suicide victims do. The police found footprints leading to the lake. She must have just walked into the water." He paused a moment before adding, "I don't know, Julia. Tina hadn't been feeling too good lately."

Julia blinked hard, releasing hot tears onto her cheeks. "Wayne?"

"Yeah?"

"Is Katie there—can she hear you?"

"Well, hell, Julia, she knows. There wasn't any way to keep it from her. The cops were everywhere. And the ambulance…"

"Where's Katie now?"

"We're at your mom's store. She's sitting at the snack bar coloring. She's okay."

You idiot. "Put Mama on."

Julia had to strain to understand her mother through the incessant buzzing in her own mind. Nothing made sense. Tina was often emotional, but this…it was unthinkable. "Y-you've got to come h-home," Cora said.

"Of course, Mama."

"I can't take any more."

"I know."

"We've got to raise K-Katie. It's what Tina wanted. It's why W-Wayne brought her here."

"We will, Mama. We'll take care of her." Julia had run out of air, out of strength. She clamped her hand over her mouth to stifle a cry.

"When will you get here?"

Julia bit her bottom lip. "I'll leave for the airport as soon as I pack a few things. I'll get the first stand-by seat to Charlotte."

"Hurry, Julia."

"I will, Mama. I'll see you soon."

"W-Wayne's going back to Tennessee, but he doesn't know how long he'll stay in the c-cabin. He's giving me his c-cell phone number."

Big of him. Julia choked back an accusation that

Wayne had never been much of a father to Katie. She kept quiet because this time he'd done the right thing. He'd brought Katie to Cora, where she'd be safe and loved. Julia knew that, and, with her last breath, so had Tina.

She put down the phone, pulled her suitcase from the closet shelf and tossed clothes inside. As she was zipping it up, she remembered to grab the prescription her doctor had given her a few months ago. The pills were intended to be a quick, temporary fix. She needed them now more than ever.

A LITTLE AFTER 10:30 p.m. Julia called her mother from the car-rental agency at the Charlotte, North Carolina, airport. When she heard her daughter's voice, Cora broke into tears again. "Where are you, Julia? Are you almost here?"

"Yes, Mama. I'm at the airport. I'll be home in a few hours."

"I'll wait up for you."

Julia knew it wouldn't do any good to advise her mother to go to bed, to remind her that she wouldn't arrive until nearly 2:00 a.m. Cora didn't sleep well under the best of circumstances and surely her anxiety level was at the breaking point now. "If you want," she said. "Is Wayne still there?"

"Oh, no. He left. He said he'd t-try to send something for Katie's support when he found a decent job."

Gee, thanks, Wayne. "How is Katie?"

Cora sniffled, muffling her answer with the tissue Julia could picture in her hands. "She's hardly said a word, the p-poor thing. But she's sleeping now in Tina's old room."

Julia ached for all of them but especially for eight-year-old Katie. Past resentments that no longer seemed to matter had kept the sisters apart, so Julia had seen her niece only on rare occasions when they all gathered at Cora's house. She'd always found the girl quiet and respectful. Julia had attributed her demeanor to a creative, intelligent mind. Like a lot of kids, Katie preferred reading and drawing to playing outside. Only now did Julia think that introspective behavior might have signalled a deep emotional problem. Julia would have to watch her carefully.

"Did you tell her I was coming?" she asked Cora.

"Yes, I told her."

Julia concentrated on how she could help Katie get through this tragedy. In the time she had, she would certainly try, but she wondered how much could really be accomplished in the one month leave of absence she'd arranged from her job at *Night Lights Magazine*. "I'll see you soon, Mama."

"Drive carefully." Cora sobbed. "You and Katie are all I have now. I couldn't b-bear it if anything happened to you."

Cora had managed to turn a simple motherly word of caution into a dire warning. But it was an easy three-hour drive into the mountains with little traffic. "I'll be careful," she said.

Two hours after she left Charlotte, Julia watched the landscape change from the flat, straight panorama of central North Carolina to the gently rolling swells of the Blue Ridge foothills. The highway was bordered by trees that in the daylight would show the first splendor of autumn, though now, in the middle of the night, the colors were all blended shades of deep charcoal. Fall had always been Julia's favorite time of year. She felt sad now thinking that it might never be again.

An hour later, she turned off the main four-lane highway onto the narrow road that wound through the picturesque small town of Glen Springs. Julia's lights flashed on the wooden placard that announced its name and its population of a rarely fluctuating 3,312 people. The town was quiet, its residents nestled into their flower-decked cottages and charming bed-and-breakfast inns.

She drove down the main street and turned onto Whisper Mountain Road, where Cora's General Store was located directly across from Whisper Mountain Falls, one of the area's most popular tourist destinations. After a two-mile winding climb, she turned into Cora's gravel lot and pulled behind the store to the split log cabin where she'd grown up. Before Julia had even turned off the car, Cora stepped through the screen door onto the wraparound porch and opened her arms.

A FEW HOURS LATER, Cora and Julia sat at the pine table in the kitchen, each with her hands wrapped around a steaming mug of coffee. Cora seemed remarkably calm, as if the sleep she'd managed to get had renewed her ability to cope. "Should we check on her again?" Cora asked when she'd taken a sip of coffee.

Relieved by her mother's improved emotional state, Julia allowed herself to believe she might not have to stay in Glen Springs for as long as she'd thought. "I looked in on her a few minutes ago," she said. "She's sleeping. That's probably the best medicine for her right now."

"We'll have to see about school, I suppose," Cora said.

"Of course. It's hard to imagine Katie in the same classrooms where Tina and I…" She stopped when the biting pain returned. "Anyway, I'll bet some of our teachers are still there."

Cora sighed. "Prob'ly so. Nothing much changes around here." She looked out the window. "Except the leaves. You can always count on the leaves changing."

Julia glanced outside. The first twinges of gold and red colored the trees. One good cold snap and riotous color would descend in all its autumn glory. As would the tourists. Right now, Julia didn't think she could face an onslaught of customers, but life had to go on. Cora still had to survive on the store's income. And now, thanks to that worthless Wayne, so did Katie.

"We'll give Katie a few days," Julia said, returning to the topic of her niece's schooling. "Let her get used to being here with you. See how she handles Tina's…" Again, she couldn't talk about her sister. Was Cora actually coping better than she was?

Cora shook her head. "Look at us. Tiptoeing around Tina's name as if just saying it will shatter us."

"I know. We've got to stop that. Katie will need to talk about her mother and we'll have to let her." She sipped her coffee. "Did you get any more information from Wayne?"

"Just that it happened after he came in for the night. He said everything seemed fine when he got home. Tina was in bed. She must have gotten up after he fell asleep. He didn't know anything was wrong until he couldn't find her in the morning and then saw a note telling him to bring Katie to us."

Julia frowned. She'd always doubted anything that came out of Wayne's mouth. "Did he mention any signs that Tina was troubled?"

Cora's shoulders slumped. "You know Tina. She had

more highs and lows in her life than these mountains have hills and valleys. I loved her with all my heart, but I couldn't make her happy. I doubt anyone could've. Not even Katie." She reached across the table and patted Julia's hand. "She wasn't my easy girl to raise, Julia. You were. You've always been the strong one, the one I could depend on."

If you only knew. Julia anticipated what her mother was about to say next. Whenever Julia returned home, Cora always strongly suggested that Julia remain on Whisper Mountain for good. But that wasn't why Julia had gone to college and gotten her journalism degree. She'd studied hard and worked long hours at the store so she could get away from here, from the isolation and the cold and snow.

And to get away from Tina and the bitterness between them that had started one autumn when Julia was a sophomore in college. That resentment had continued to the present day, or at least until the day Tina died. This morning, Julia felt only overwhelming pity for her older sister and, God help her, guilt over the tragic, lonely way her life had ended.

And she hadn't thought much about Cameron Birch for years. The handsome, charismatic assistant professor who'd taught American Literature during her sophomore year in college had eventually faded from her mind. Cameron, the man who'd opened her eyes to the beauty of the written word. The man she'd adored. The man Tina had set her sights on the moment she discovered her sister idolized him.

Cora stood and carried her mug to the coffee machine. "You want a refill?" Cora's voice reminded Julia that her mother hadn't yet begged her to stay.

"No. I'm fine."

Cora filled her own cup. "What were you thinking about just now? You seemed far away."

"It's funny, but I was thinking about Cameron Birch. You remember him?"

"Your college professor?"

Julia nodded.

"Sure. A nice-looking young man. His grandfather lived up the road at the top of Whisper Mountain. Cameron used to visit as a teenager. They'd come into the store for supplies." She smiled sadly. "Old Josiah's gone now. Died a while back. I'll bet you don't remember your Professor Birch from those days."

That was almost true. Julia had been a little girl when Josiah Birch used to come into Cora's with his grandson. Julia had barely noticed the gangly, grinning boy trailing behind the old man from the top of the mountain.

After those childhood encounters, she never gave Cameron Birch a thought until she walked into that classroom at Riverton College years later and there he stood, all grown up, wearing jeans and a blue denim shirt, his acorn-brown hair slightly mussed and falling over his forehead. He absolutely stole the air from her lungs that day and it was a full term before she took another normal breath.

Cora returned to the table. "It's the oddest thing, you mentioning Cameron. This is the second time his name has come up this week."

Julia stared at her. "Really?"

"This must be old home week on the mountain. Rosalie said that Cameron had inherited Josiah's place and was coming back to stay for a while."

"Where did Rosalie hear that?" Julia asked.

"At the coal supplier's. She overheard the manager talking about an order Cameron had placed for the winter."

Julia faked nonchalance with a shrug of her shoulder. She'd never admitted that she'd been completely infatuated with Josiah's grandson, or that part of her heart had broken when she learned from a former classmate that the gorgeous Professor Birch had married. "I haven't seen him in years," she said. "The last I heard he was married and teaching at North Carolina State."

Cora nodded. "He wasn't from around here. His family lived in Raleigh." She tapped her finger on the tabletop. "I know what brought him to your mind today," she said.

Julia flinched, sitting back in her chair. "What?"

"Tina had a few dates with him at one time, years ago. It's strange how a tragedy can make the mind conjure up all sorts of details from the past. I'd always hoped those two would get together."

Julia swirled the contents of her coffee mug. "I'm sure that's it. Why else would I think of Cameron?"

A soft shuffling caused both women to shift their attention to the door. Katie stood in the entrance, one hand fisted around the folds of her white nightie, the other curled and rubbing her eye. Tousled blond curls fell over her shoulders like spun silk in the morning sun. She looked like an angel, a sad, heart-weary angel.

Julia went to her and got down on one knee. "Hello, Katie."

The child's voice was barely a whisper. "Hi, Aunt Julia. Grandma said you'd be here today."

Julia gently finger-combed hair from Katie's cheeks. "Of course, sweetheart. We Sommerville women have to stick together, don't we?"

Katie's expression didn't change. She stared at Julia, then dropped her gaze to the floor. "I guess."

"I can't believe how big you've grown," Julia said. "I haven't seen you since Christmas."

Cora got up, opened a cupboard and carried a bowl to the table. "Do you want some breakfast, honey?"

"Okay." Katie sat in a chair, folded her hands in her lap. "Daddy's gone, isn't he?"

Cora opened a cereal box. "For now, yes. He had some things he had to do."

"He has to pick up Mommy's ashes."

Cora dropped the box on the floor. "What?"

"He said she was cre… I don't know the word."

Cora grabbed the handle of the refrigerator to steady herself. Her eyes glittered with fresh torment and something else—fury. "D-damn your f-father," she cried. "I told him I wanted a traditional service to bury my daughter properly here on the mountain. He's taken that away from me."

Julia's momentary hope that Cora had found the strength to face this tragedy for Katie's sake vanished. She looked into her niece's eyes, saw the fear reflected there. She took the girl's arm and led her onto the back porch. "Look at the trees, sweetie. It's beautiful this morning. We'll have breakfast out here."

She went back to get Katie's cereal, poured herself a glass of water and took her prescription bottle from the pocket of her robe. She swallowed the tiny pill and brought a sobbing, trembling Cora to a chair before facing the fact that a few weeks might not be enough time for any of them to heal.

CHAPTER TWO

JULIA ENTERED the kitchen on Tuesday morning and headed for the coffee machine. She filled a mug that had been left for her on the counter and smiled at her mother. "Thanks for letting me sleep in."

Cora glanced at the kitchen clock. "8:45 a.m. is hardly worth thanking me for. Besides I have a good idea how many times you got up during the night."

Julia took her first sip of fortifying caffeine, walked to the back door and looked onto the porch where Katie sat in an old bent twig chair, her eyes cast down on a book. An empty bowl and glass were on the rustic table beside her. "At least she ate her breakfast," Julia said. "That's encouraging, even if she's still not sleeping well."

"Nightmares again?" Cora asked.

Julia nodded. "I doubt she remembers them, though. She cries without fully waking up." She sent her mother a concerned look. "Did you bring up the subject of taking a bath yet this morning?"

"I mentioned it. Katie just shook her head and said she didn't need a bath yet. She said you'd help her wash when you got up."

Julia mentally counted the days since Tina's death— again. "It's been a week. I understand her reluctance to get into water now, but this can't go on. Phobias that affect children at Katie's age can last a lifetime."

Cora sighed. "I guess you may be right about Katie needing to see a professional."

Relieved that Cora had come around to her way of thinking, Julia sat across from her mother. "I know you were hoping to avoid outside influences at this early stage of her grief. But we have to face the fact that family may not be enough to see Katie through this." She sighed, staring down into her mug. "Especially when one of those family members is me and I've been conspicuously absent for too much of my niece's life."

"Stop blaming yourself for the alienation between you and Tina," Cora said. "Your sister didn't do anything to bridge the gap, either. Anyway, you saw her and Katie on holidays. That's more often than many estranged siblings get together."

Cora's absolution didn't make Julia feel better. Now that it was too late, she wished she'd tried harder to reconcile with Tina and reestablish the relationship they had enjoyed as kids. But first there had been Cameron, then Wayne, then Tina's refusal to share the responsibility for family problems...

Julia shook her head, dispelling the same old destructive thoughts that had kept the sisters apart for years. It was pointless to dwell on regrets. Julia would deal with the past later. Now she had a frightened, grieving little girl on the porch who needed her help. "I'll check with the elementary school today," she said. "They must have a counselor who deals with children's trauma."

"While you're at it, see if you can find someone who can help the older generation."

Julia had suggested many times that Cora seek help

for her grief over her husband's death. "You've been dealing better with Dad's passing lately, haven't you?"

"I was. But this...I don't know if I can do it again."

"Yeah. It's a lot, Mama." Julia paused, her mind struggling to focus on Cora's problems, but refusing to abandon Katie's. An idea suddenly occurred to her. "About that bath situation..."

"What?"

"I've got an idea." Remembering the prescription she'd tucked into her jeans pocket, Julia said, "I've got to go into town and I think I'll suggest a shopping trip for Katie that just might make her decide a bath isn't so bad, after all. At least maybe it will be a first step." She returned to the back door and waited for Katie to look up. "Hey, sweetie."

"Hi." Katie sat placidly.

"I've got to go into Pope's Drugstore today. You want to come?"

Katie chewed the inside of her cheek. "I guess."

"Bring your bowl and glass inside. We'll get you dressed and go."

Katie shut the book and reached for her dishes. It was a start.

LINUS POPE, the pharmacist and owner of Pope's Drugstore came around the counter where countless prescriptions had been filled for Glen Springs residents over several decades. He stuck out his hand when Julia approached. "Well, look who's here."

Julia shook his hand. "How are you doing, Mr. Pope?"

His eyes were kind when he said, "I should be asking you that."

Julia managed a smile. "You heard?"

He squeezed her hand. "Word travels fast in Glen Springs, both good and bad. Margaret Benson came in the other day and told me." He passed a hand over thinning gray hair. "A terrible thing, Julia. Just terrible. Especially coming on the heels of Gene's passing. You ladies have my deepest sympathies."

"Thanks."

"How's Cora holding up?"

"About as well as you'd imagine."

"I know she's thankful you're home." With considerable effort because of his arthritis, Mr. Pope got down on one knee and pulled a lollipop from the pocket of his smock. "Nice to see you again," he said to Katie. "I was wondering if a pretty little girl would come into the store today and take this treat off my hands."

Katie waited for Julia to give her the thumbs-up before accepting the gift with a quiet "Thank you."

The pharmacist stood, placing his hands on his hips. "Can I help you find anything?"

Julia handed him the prescription she'd brought from New York for her antidepressants. Mr. Pope glanced at the doctor's handwriting. It seemed for a moment as though he might comment on the meds, but he wordlessly folded the paper and slipped it into his pocket.

"You can point us in the direction of bubble bath," Julia said, grateful for his discretion. Mr. Pope had known her since she'd been born and no doubt wondered why she was taking the medication. Perhaps he assumed she'd just gotten the prescription to help her deal with Tina's death. That was fine. He didn't need to know the truth.

He pointed down a narrow aisle. "All the bath accessories are over there. You girls have a look." He raised a corner of the prescription from his pocket. "I'll have this ready in a few minutes."

Julia put her hand on Katie's shoulder and guided her down the row of shampoos and scented bath oils. When they came to the children's section, she stopped and affected a great interest in the assortment of colorful plastic bottles. "Look at all these choices," she said. "Which one do you like best, Katie?"

The child tentatively pointed to a bottle shaped like a duck. "That one, maybe."

Julia took it from the shelf.

"No, that one."

She replaced the duck, reached for a fairy princess bottle on the top shelf and unscrewed the cap. Holding it down for Katie to smell, she said, "What do you think?"

Katie sniffed. "It smells good."

Julia tested it. "Wow, sure does. I think I'll buy it. Nothing makes me feel better than a good long soak in tons of sweet-smelling bubbles. How about you?"

Katie hunched one slight shoulder. "I never had a bubble bath."

Julia disguised her shock by loading her basket with other items from the shelves. "Then we'll definitely have to remedy that. We'll buy some of these kitty-cat soaps, and one of these pink spongy things and this shampoo."

Julia set the basket on the counter while Mr. Pope filled her order. "We still have a few minutes," she said to Katie. "Want to have a drink?"

"Okay."

They went to the soda fountain and Julia helped Katie onto a stool. While she waited for the clerk to take their order, she ran her hand along the smooth Formica surface where, over her lifetime, she'd enjoyed hundreds of vanilla Cokes. Nothing had changed at Pope's ice cream and drink fountain. The mirror behind the shelf of soda glasses still had a crack in it. The chrome napkin holders still gleamed. Straws dependably popped up when a customer lifted the lid of the heavy glass dispenser.

And almost as predictably, Julia's past came flooding back. She vividly recalled when she and Tina were kids, three years apart, and they'd sat on these very stools, sharing a drink and laughing about something that had happened at school. Or when they'd left the matinee at the Glen Springs cinema and waited at Pope's for their father to pick them up. Or years later, when they'd been sitting here during Julia's sophomore year at Riverton College and the dashing new professor from the English department had stopped at the pharmacy to pick up a few things for his grandfather who lived at the top of Whisper Mountain.

When Cameron Birch had spotted his student at the fountain, he'd come right over to say hello. Although tongue-tied with nervous excitement at seeing the handsome Professor Birch right here in her hometown, Julia had somehow managed to introduce him to Tina without stumbling over both their names. And that night she'd gone to Tina's bedroom and gushed to her sister about how gorgeous his hazel eyes were, how intelligent he was and how she couldn't sleep at night because he'd taken up permanent residence in her mind.

And a week later, the larger-than-life Professor Birch showed up at the cabin behind Cora's General Store to pick Tina up for a date. And everything changed.

"What can I get you?"

Julia looked up at the young man behind the counter.

"Two vanilla Cokes," she said, and smiled at her niece, whose eyes were the same beautiful blue as her mother's. She handed Katie a straw. It was too late for her to make amends with her sister, but she prayed it wasn't too late for her and Katie.

AN HOUR LATER, Julia parted the bathroom curtains. Glorious late morning sunshine sparkled on the tile floor and porcelain claw-foot tub. She looked over her shoulder at Katie, who stood silently watching her. "Isn't that better? Sometimes, like on a day like today, I really hate those curtains."

Katie shrugged. "I guess."

Over the last days, Julia had noticed that Katie often responded to direct questions without emotionally committing herself to the answers. *I suppose…I guess…Maybe…* These were the responses Katie gave when asked her opinion. It was as if she qualified every answer so she could amend it quickly and simply if circumstances indicated she should. Julia wondered what had made her so unsure of herself. Growing up, Tina had always displayed more than her share of confidence. Apparently that trait hadn't been passed down to her daughter.

Julia turned on the tap and tested the temperature of the water flowing into the tub. She reached behind her back. "Hand me the bubble bath, sweetie."

Katie took the bottle off the vanity and passed it to Julia.

"Unscrew the cap," Julia said.

"No, you do it. I don't think I'm going to take a bath right now."

Julia complied, filling the cap with liquid and pouring the entire amount under the faucet. Frothy bubbles spread over the water. "Look how beautiful," she said. "I think you should add another one." She handed the cap to Katie and was relieved when the child stepped close enough to the tub to pour in the contents.

Julia swished her fingers through the bubbles. "You have to feel this, Katie," she said. "It's like touching air you can see."

Katie reached forward, poked a couple of bubbles and then scooped a small mountain of them into her hand.

Julia stood. "You know, I could be the first person to enjoy this bath, but I rather thought you might like to be."

Katie made a fist, shooting bubbles into the air above the tub. "I don't know…"

Interrupting her, Julia said, "But if you go first, I have a really big favor to ask."

Katie's eyes widened. "What is it?"

"Well, we just got Grandma's favorite lady's magazine in the mail and I want to read it. I realize that we girls like our privacy when we bathe, but since the light in the bathroom is the very best in all the house, I was hoping you'd let me stay in here with you and read. I promise to be very quiet."

Katie looked from Julia to the rising water. Her eyes showed a bit of sparkle, just enough for Julia to hope the bubbles might be working some magic. "It would be okay if you want to," she said after careful consideration.

"Great!" Julia pulled a magazine out of the basket Cora kept in the bathroom and sat on the commode lid. "Why don't you undress, and I'll just start reading."

Fifteen minutes later, most of the bubbles were gone and Katie had been scrubbed clean with the exception of her face and hair. "I think I'm done," she announced.

Julia looked up from the magazine. "Almost." She

picked up the bottle of children's shampoo from the side of the bathtub and flipped open the lid. "Still have to wash your hair, don't you? And I haven't finished this article." She reached for a plastic cup she'd brought in earlier. "Can I wet your hair with this?"

Katie nodded, but her eyes widened with the first sign of alarm. "It's going to be all right, sweetie," Julia said.

Katie closed her eyes tightly and threaded her hands between her knees. Bending her head forward, she said, "Hurry, okay?"

Julia leaned over the tub and poured the first cupful over Katie's head. Water sluiced down her forehead and the sides of her face. Katie trembled but remained silent. Julia slowly emptied the contents of another cup, decided Katie's hair was wet enough and reached for the shampoo.

Katie began to scream. Her face more than a foot above the water, she cried that she couldn't see, couldn't breathe, that she was drowning. Each frantic word was punctuated with shrieks of sheer terror. Her panic ripped through Julia. She dropped the cup, grabbed her niece and lifted her partway from the tub. "It's okay, sweetheart."

Katie reached up, wrapped her arms around Julia and held on. She buried her face in the crook of Julia's neck. With bathwater soaking her skin and clothing and her own tears mingling with her niece's, Julia crooned words of comfort into Katie's ear. "I'm so sorry, sweetie. You're going to be all right. I won't let you go."

Moments later, the cries subsided. Katie sniffled loudly. "Do we have to wash my hair?"

Julia drew a normal breath. "No, we can wait for another time. But when we do, we'll do it another way. If you look up at the ceiling, not at the tub, the water will run down your hair and your back, not into your face. I promise you won't feel so scared."

The child considered the advice for a moment and said, "Aunt Julia?"

"Yes?"

"Why didn't my mommy look up at the sky when she went in the lake? Didn't she know that the water wouldn't have gotten her then?"

Julia hugged Katie close again and said, "Oh, baby, I don't know why she didn't look up. I know we both wish she had, though. Maybe it was just too much water all at once, not like the shallow bit in this bathtub."

Katie arched back, looked at Julia with eyes glistening with tears. Still, a subtle hint of a smile curved her lips. "You're all wet, Aunt Julia."

Relief flowed through Julia. She laughed. "I guess I am." Plucking her damp blouse from her chest, she said, "See? A little water never hurt anybody."

Katie sat down in the tepid water, pursed her lips in a determined line and stared at the ceiling. "Okay, you can do it now," she said.

A minute later, Katie had clean hair and Julia couldn't stop thinking about her sister, who, in her last moment of life, with her child sleeping a few yards away, didn't look up.

AT CLOSING TIME, six o'clock the next night, what had started out as a picture-perfect autumn day ended with dark thunderheads blanketing the mountains and lightning illuminating the valleys between the tallest hills. Julia and Cora carried rocking chairs in from the store's front porch and removed hanging baskets from the eaves before the storm could send them tumbling down the mountain. Fighting a near gale-force wind, Julia turned tables upside down on the porch floor and advised her mother to seek shelter. "I'm almost done," she hollered to Cora. "You and Katie make sure the windows in the store are closed. I'll be right in."

Cora ducked inside just as the first fat drops of rain hit the shingle roof over the veranda. By the time Julia secured the last of the outside decorations, the wind had driven the downpour sideways, pelting the wood slat floor and dampening her clothes. She ran into the store, closed and bolted the door and took the roll of paper towels Cora handed her. Wiping her arms and legs, she said, "This is what we used to call a toad strangler."

"And how," Cora said, her worried gaze fixed on the closest window. "It's nights like this I really miss your father. We'll probably lose power before this one's over." She lifted a lacy curtain panel and peered out at the pitch-black evening sky.

Julia placed her hand on her mother's shoulder. "Come away from the window, Mama. You know it's not safe to be near glass when there's wind and lightning."

Cora started to walk away, but stopped and went back. "My goodness, Julia," she said. "I think I see headlights coming up the mountain. Who would be fool enough to be out on a night like this?"

Julia joined her at the window. "Someone caught on Whisper before they realized the storm was going to be this bad is my guess."

"I'll wait by the door to see if they pull in to ride it out." She looked over her shoulder at Julia. "You and Katie go in the back room and get those old lanterns and oil your dad kept there. If this person passes us by, we'll still have time to make it to the cabin before the worst of it hits."

Julia took Katie's hand. As they went into the store-room, Julia noticed headlights veering into their lot. A few seconds later, the front door opened. A gust of wind sent the chimes above the entrance into a jangling frenzy, which was followed by a rumbling bellow of thunder.

And then the door was closed, reducing the wind to a steady ominous howl. The sound Julia heard next made her heart pound and her hand freeze around the glass chimney of a hurricane lantern. She wasn't pre-pared for that strong baritone voice from her past.

"Hi, Mrs. Sommerville," the man said. "Some night, isn't it?" Silence stretched for a few seconds until he added, "I bet you don't remember me."

Cora gasped. "For heaven's sake. Cameron Birch?"

He chuckled. "In the dripping flesh, and am I ever glad you're still open."

Julia tucked the lantern into the bend of her elbow and pressed it against her chest to keep from dropping it. Making her way to the storeroom entrance, she stood on the threshold. Her curiosity urged her to peek around the door frame, but her feet felt glued to the floor.

"Who's out there, Aunt Julia?" Katie asked from be-hind her.

"I'm not sure," she lied. "Probably someone looking to get out of the storm." She leaned against the open door and listened.

"We were just talking about you the other day," Cora said.

"We?"

"My daughter's here with me."

Cameron coughed. His voice was raspy when he said, "Tina?"

Julia held her breath, fearful that the mention of her

sister might send Cora into tears. But she calmly answered, "No. My younger girl, Julia's visiting for a while."

"I remember Julia," he said. "She was a student of mine when I taught at Riverton. Smart girl. Got excellent grades, as I recall."

"She has a job in Manhattan now," Cora said. "She's a reporter."

"Good for her."

Julia heard footsteps and assumed Cameron was choosing supplies. "Is she married?" he asked after a moment.

"No," Cora said.

Katie tugged on the end of Julia's blouse. "Why don't we go out?" she asked.

"We will," Julia said. "In just a minute. But for now I need you to be very quiet."

Katie dropped her hand. "Okay."

Thunder rumbled over the rooftop, and Julia missed the next words spoken. When the sound faded she heard Cameron say, "I had just started up to my grandfather's place when the storm hit. I was hoping to buy enough supplies from you to get by until morning."

"Pick out what you need," Cora said. "But you might want to wait until the weather clears before you continue up the mountain. This road is slippery in a rainstorm. You can stay in the cabin with us till it's safe."

That's just great. Julia wasn't really thrilled with the idea of the four of them sitting in the cabin parlor talking about old times, which in retrospect were alternately tragic and embarrassing. But then an even worse picture formed in her mind. Cameron's wife was probably out in the car. If he accepted Cora's invitation, it would be the *five* of them huddled together until the storm passed.

How cozy would that be, especially after she'd relived all those old memories the past few days.

Julia released the breath that had been trapped in her chest when Cameron declined. "Thanks anyway, but I can make it to the top. I've got four-wheel drive on a Jeep that can plow through anything and I think the rain's letting up some now."

Julia heard the rustle of paper and assumed Cora was filling a sack with supplies. She was thankful when the cash register drawer opened and closed, indicating the transaction was finished. "Nice seeing you again, Cameron," Cora said. "How long you planning to be on Whisper?"

"I'm not sure. A while. My grandfather left the cabin to me when he died. This is the first chance I've had to come up here."

"We'll be seeing more of you then," Cora said.

"Definitely."

Wonderful. Julia winced. She didn't look forward to running into Cameron and his wife. Although, thinking rationally, she'd been over Cameron for years. So why was she reacting like a love-struck college coed now?

"You be careful now," Cora called just before the door closed.

Julia stepped aside and let Katie precede her into the store.

"What took you two so long?" Cora asked. "You won't believe who was just…"

"I heard."

"I guess the rumors about him coming back to Whisper were true," Cora said. "Imagine Cameron Birch walking in here after we were discussing him the other day."

"Yeah, imagine." The lanterns still in her arms, Julia walked toward the rear of the store and glanced out the back door. "Well, come on. If we're going to make it to the cabin, we'd better go now."

Cora checked the lock on the front entrance and started to follow, but the squeal of brakes and the grating of twisting metal stopped her.

"What was that?" Katie asked, clutching Julia's arm.

Julia dropped the lanterns on a nearby worktable. Her heart raced. She recalled only two times in all the years she'd lived on Whisper Mountain when she'd heard that sound. She looked at Cora's stricken expression. "Oh, God, Mama," she said. "He's gone through the guard-rail."

CHAPTER THREE

JULIA GRABBED a yellow slicker from the hook by the storeroom, slipped her arms through the sleeves and hurried to the counter under the cash register where her parents had always kept a flashlight. Shoving the light into the waistband of her jeans, she headed for the front door. Cora followed, talking incessantly, her anxiety clear. "I t-told him not to g-go out in this weather. I w-warned him, Julia."

"I know, Mama," Julia said, pulling the vinyl hood and securing the snap at her chin.

"You c-can't go after him!"

"I'll be all right. I'm just going to cross the road and look down in the ravine. Maybe he's fine and I'll see him climbing up toward me."

"But, but what if he's not climbing out? What if you don't see him?"

Julia paused, her hand on the doorknob. "We can't just ignore this and leave him at the bottom of the falls. I need you to stay focused, Mama. Call 9-1-1, tell them what's happened."

Cora nodded and walked toward the phone.

At the door Julia stopped when she heard Katie sobbing behind her. "Don't go out there, Aunt Julia. It's raining and you'll get all wet."

Julia took Katie's arms and held them tight. "I'll be fine, Katie. Nothing is going to happen to me. I've been down that ravine more times than I can count."

Katie sniffed loudly. "In the dark?"

"Dark, light, all kinds of weather." She kissed the top of Katie's head. "I have to do this, honey. People could be hurt down there and we don't know how long it will take the police to get here. I want you to be a brave girl and wait with Grandma. Will you do that for me?"

Katie pinched her eyes closed and nodded. "You'll hurry though, won't you?"

"You bet I will." She gave Katie what she hoped was a reassuring hug and stepped outside. A strong wind propelled raindrops as heavy as pebbles against her face. Fighting a gust, she shouldered the door into its frame, testing the latch to be certain it took hold.

Julia flicked the switch on the flashlight and aimed it left and right. She had a fleeting, hopeful thought that she might encounter travelers out on this wicked night, someone she could flag down to help her. Instead, all she saw was dense rain in her beam of light. Within seconds, her jeans were plastered to her legs and her tennis shoes were soaked through.

Julia hugged her arms to her chest and started walking up the mountain road, knowing that was the direction Cameron had taken just minutes ago. She aimed her light at the guardrail, a thin strip of galvanized metal that had originally been erected by FDR's Works Progress Administration during the Great Depression. Over the years, the rail had been inspected often, mended many times, but never replaced. And, ironically, considering what had just happened, always considered by the locals to be "good enough."

She had progressed about a hundred yards when she spotted the breach, a mere ten-foot gap in the otherwise continuous flow of gray posts and barriers. Just ahead of the hole, her flashlight caught the ominous shimmer of an oily substance on the road, probably an engine leak from a vehicle belonging to a negligent local.

Julia quickened her pace. She reached the edge of the ravine and pointed her flashlight to the bottom. A tight pain squeezed her chest when she realized that the Birches' car had gone over at the steepest decline. With her meager light, she saw nothing resembling a vehicle but she heard the fury of the waterfall rushing over the rocks, gaining power from the rain and its one hundred-foot drop from the mountain ledge where it tumbled from the Glen River.

The thundering falls ended some forty feet below in a frothy pool of water that drew tourists from all over before it gained momentum again and flowed to the bottom of Whisper Mountain. Julia knew that, right now, the swollen pool would be roiling, struggling to accommodate the downpour that could cause it to overflow its banks. And somewhere near that angry cauldron lay Cameron's car, perhaps submerged, perhaps not. There was only one way to find out.

Julia tucked the flashlight under her arm, aiming it down to light the path ahead of her, and grabbed hold of the nearest tree. And then, as she'd done many times before, but never in conditions like this and never in the dark, despite what she'd told Katie, she began her descent. She lost her footing again and again, the tread of her sneakers no match for slippery patches of mud and leaves as squishy as wet sponges.

She wished she'd remembered to bring gloves. Tree

bark and shale bit into her hands as she reached for anything solid to steady her downward climb. Her heart hammered as the ravine seemed to swallow her up. Strange sounds assailed her—night creatures scurrying to safety, raindrops beating on the underbrush, water rushing everywhere, blending with the frantic buzzing in her own brain. A mixture of rain and sweat ran into her eyes. But she kept going until, perhaps no more than ten minutes after she'd begun her climb down, she reached the bottom and noticed a dim glow near the base of the falls.

She took the flashlight from under her arm, drew a deep breath to fortify her for what she might see and aimed it at the light. With an overwhelming sense of relief, she realized she was staring at Cameron's headlamps, half buried in mud and brush, but proof that his vehicle hadn't plunged into the pool—yet.

"Professor Birch!" Julia hollered his name as she advanced toward the driver's window. "I'm coming to help you!" She flicked rainwater from her eyes and struggled to catch her breath. *Good grief, Julia, Cameron Birch won't care if you use his first name.* She continued over the soaked ground, her heart pounding harder with each labored step.

When she reached the Jeep, she relaxed slightly. Somehow Cameron had managed to steer down the embankment without losing complete control and rolling over. She held on to the roof and hit the rain-streaked window. "Cameron, answer me. Are you all right?"

When she didn't get a response, she used the sleeve of her slicker to clear a circle in the mud-streaked glass, wiped her eyes and peered inside. Shining her light into the interior, she saw her former professor unconscious, his safety belt fastened, his head slumped over the wheel. She slammed the window hard with the heel of her hand, and then immediately regretted the action. The SUV slid forward toward the rushing water, maybe only a foot or two, but the motion left the headlamps buried deeper in mud.

Julia yelled louder. "Wake up, Cameron! I've got to get you out of there." She walked around and shone her light in the passenger window. "Mrs. Birch, are you in there?"

The seat was empty. She aimed the beam at the back and saw where boxes had been stacked for transport. There was no one else in the vehicle. Julia returned to the driver's side and tested the door. Miraculously, it opened. Cameron's head slipped off the steering wheel. His arm fell out of the SUV. And the Jeep inched farther down the muddy slope.

Julia grabbed the door and held on, as if by sheer force she could stop the forward motion. "Wake up, Cameron!" she screamed. She pulled on his arm. "You've got to get out before you go in the water."

Still receiving no response, Julia had the horrifying thought that perhaps she was trying to revive a dead man. "No!" she shouted. "You can't be dead." She pinched his jawline between her thumb and forefinger. "Wake up!"

When a long, low moan rewarded her, Julia renewed her efforts to get Cameron out of the vehicle. She reached over his body, felt for the seat belt release and freed him. Next she twisted him so his back was toward her. "Okay, that's good," she said in an even, level voice, meant to soothe herself as well as the victim. "We can do this, Cameron." She slid her hands under his arms and pulled with all her strength. The next moments were a blur. Cameron groaned. The Jeep rolled forward. Julia fell back onto the ground, and Cameron landed on top of her. Air rushed from her lungs.

Pushing her feet against anything solid she could find, she scooted them both back from the car until they were clear. And then, with Cameron heavy on her chest, she raised her head and watched in numb shock as, with a huge sucking sound, the SUV plunged engine-first into the churning pool. Seconds later, only the faint red glow of taillights and the weak gleam of a chrome bumper were visible above the water.

Shaking off the horrifying realization of what nearly had happened, Julia tried to scramble out from beneath Cameron's limp body. But he was like lead pressing on her breastbone, and she succeeded only in sinking farther into the mud. She turned his head to the side, felt his faint breath warm on her cheek. "Cameron, wake up. Please. You're okay. We're both going to get out of this, but you have to help me."

She concentrated on the details of the first-aid course she'd taken years before and tried not to panic. "Keep the victim still and quiet," she said. "Keep him warm. Elevate his legs. Check for broken bones." A ripple of inappropriate laughter bubbled up from her chest. "Yeah, right." One arm was pinned to her side and her fanny felt as if it were mired in freshly mixed cement.

Her strength waning, Julia gave up struggling. She was stuck underneath Cameron until help came. Wiggling around only pushed them both farther into the depression she'd created when they landed on the wet ground. Minutes seemed to stretch into hours as she lay there. To keep her mind occupied, she talked to the unconscious man on top of her. "I'll bet you wish you'd taken Mama's offer to stay with us," she said. "I didn't think it was such a good idea at the time, but now I sure wish you had." A minute passed before she spoke again. "When are the rescuers going to get here?" She almost jumped out of her skin when she heard a response.

"Hey, Jules, you okay down there?"

Recognizing the voice of the class clown of her Glen Springs High graduating class who went on to join the Vickers County firefighters, Julia laughed almost hysterically. "Is that you, Bobby?"

"Yep, it's me, MoonPie."

She never thought she'd be so glad to hear the nickname Bobby had given her in grade school. "Well, hurry up and get down here!" she hollered.

"That's the plan. Just hold on. We're on our way."

Seconds later, Bobby Cutter and two other rescue workers rappelled down the slope in a fraction of the time it had taken her to cover the same distance. Bobby and one fireman rushed to her side, while the other waited for a fiberglass backboard to follow them on ropes into the gully.

Bobby leaned over her, flashing a brilliant light in her face. "So how'd you manage to get yourself in this situation, MoonPie?" he asked.

She couldn't see his expression and that was just as well. If she'd detected a smart-ass smile on his face, she'd have found enough strength to slug him—once she got out from under Cameron. She frowned up at him. "Just get us out of here, Bobby."

"Will do." He ran his hand down her arm while his buddy examined Cameron. "Do you think anything's broken, Julia?"

"No. I'm fine, but I'll be even better once I know that this guy on top of me is okay."

Bobby switched to rescue mode. He helped the third member of his team position the board next to Cameron, then asked if the victim could be safely lifted. The rescuers' voices blended together in a flurry of well-rehearsed commands and evaluations.

And Julia lay back, waiting patiently, relieved to be turning the task of rescuing Cameron Birch over to the experts, at last.

THE TRIP up from the ravine proved much easier than the one going down. Of course, it helped that Julia was tied securely to a two-hundred-pound fireman who attached them both to a pulley controlled by a team at the top. With his arms around her, she let the pulley do all the work, and if it hadn't been for her concern over Cameron, she might even have enjoyed the ride.

The rain had finally stopped, and Cora and Katie stood at the edge of the road when the fireman set Julia on the pavement. She tried to take in all the details of the scene at once. A half dozen emergency vehicles, red lights flashing, lined the road. Barricades placed a hundred yards in either direction from the breach in the guardrail kept traffic from hampering the efforts of the rescue team. A news helicopter circled overhead, its bright light illuminating the ravine where efforts to bring Cameron to the top were still ongoing.

Julia assured waiting EMTs that she was fine, and traded her slicker for a blanket Cora had brought from the cabin. The storm had left behind a brisk, clean breeze, signaling the first cold snap of the autumn season, and Julia shivered in her woolen cocoon.

"Will he be all right?" Cora asked her.

"I hope so, Mama, but I don't know. He was still unconscious when the rescuers got there." She recalled the skill and confidence with which the three men went about their job. "I'm sure the guys are doing all they can," she said.

She looked down at Katie, who was huddled in a worn parka at least two sizes too small for her. *New winter coat* jumped to the top of the mental shopping list Julia had been preparing for her niece over the past several days. "And how are you, sweetie?"

"Okay. I was worried about you, though."

"I know, but I told you I'd be all right." Julia tucked a strand of wispy hair inside the hood of Katie's jacket. "I'm a mountain girl, remember?"

Katie nestled close to Julia's side. When Julia put her arm around her, she said, "I guess I'm one now, too."

Julia smiled at her. "You know, I guess you are. And you're going to make a fine mountain girl. I can tell."

When a stark light shone in her face, Julia blinked and squinted. "What's going on?"

A woman approached her, walking in front of a man with a large camera balanced on his shoulder. "Cut the light, Benny," she said. She stuck her hand out to Julia. "I'm Margo Wright from Channel Seven News. From the details I've gotten from onlookers, I figure you're the hero of the hour."

Julia minimized the comment with a shrug. "Hardly."

The reporter moved her fist in a circular motion, indicating the camera should start rolling. "Don't be modest, Miss…" She flipped a pad open and took a pencil from her pocket. "Would you spell your name, please?"

Julia did. Though the last thing she wanted to do was be interviewed when she didn't even know Cameron's condition, she understood what it was like to be on the reporting side of the camera—not an easy job with an uncooperative subject.

"I understand the victim is a professor from North Carolina State University," Margo said.

"That's right."

"What was he doing on Whisper Mountain?"

"You'll have to ask him that," Julia said.

"Okay, but you can tell me what happened down there."

Julia kept the facts simple and brief. "His car rolled over the edge and I pulled him out before it submerged in the river."

Katie gasped. "Did you really do that, Aunt Julia?"

She hadn't allowed herself to piece together those frightening moments until now, though she was quite certain the entire panic-filled episode would stay in her mind forever. "I guess I did."

"Tell me what you were thinking as…"

Julia no longer heard the reporter's voice. The rescue guys had just appeared, the tops of their protective headgear the first signs that they were finally coming out of the gully. One man on each side leveled the board while Bobby guided it up. Julia broke away from the reporter and rushed to meet them.

With efficient calm, the rescuers relayed information to a team of paramedics who'd come from a waiting ambulance. Cameron was transferred to a wheeled stretcher and taken to the emergency vehicle. Julia grabbed Bobby's arm as he followed the medics. "Will he be all right?"

"I think so. He's kind of busted up, but he was starting to come around about halfway up the mountain." Bobby patted her arm. "You done good, MoonPie. And by the way, it's nice seeing you again, even if the circumstances that brought you home aren't the best."

"Thanks, Bobby. And you done good, too."

Bobby walked off toward a woman who offered him a cup of coffee, and Julia suddenly felt as if her legs would no longer hold her. She didn't want to talk to the reporter again. And she hoped she wouldn't be questioned by the police right now. Searching out Cora and Katie in the crowd, she said, "Let's go home. Tomorrow will be plenty of time to sort all this out."

A paramedic stepped from the back of the ambulance. "Hey! Which one of you is MoonPie?"

Julia grimaced but slowly raised her hand. "I guess that would be me."

The medic waved her over. "Can you come here? The patient says he won't go to the hospital until he talks to you."

Julia hesitated, but Cora urged her forward. "Go on. Cameron probably wants to thank you."

"It's not necessary."

"You want to see how he is, don't you?"

That was certainly true. Julia hadn't climbed down the ravine, had the wind knocked out of her and taken an unplanned mud bath just to have Cameron die on her. She went to the back of the ambulance and took the paramedic's proffered hand. He helped her inside and went back to work, adjusting gauges and checking IV lines.

Cameron lay on the stretcher. She took a few awkward steps toward him in the confined space. He tried lifting his head to see her, but his movements were limited by a restrictive collar. Nevertheless he smiled. That same devastating smile she remembered shining upon her from the podium of a Riverton College classroom, not even diminished now by a background of nasty lacerations.

The medic pointed to her. "Professor, meet Julia, Glen Springs' one-woman mountain rescue team."

"Actually, we've met before," Cameron said. He stared intently at her and added, "MoonPie?"

She exhaled and shook her head. "It's a long and very uninspiring story."

"I think I'd like to hear it."

"Someday, maybe." She sat on a bench built into the side of the ambulance and leaned toward him. "How are you feeling?"

"Alive. Thanks to you."

"Don't mention it. All in a day's work."

"I'll bet." He slowly reached out his left hand and stroked her cheek with his fingers. "You've got a little smudge there."

For the first time she was aware of how she must look. She glanced down at her mud-caked jeans. Her hands were splotched with ravine debris and she doubted she'd ever get her fingernails clean again. She lay her hand where his had just touched and felt a flush of heat. If her face looked even half as bad as the rest of her, well, she didn't want to think about it.

"So, are you all right?" he asked. "You weren't hurt?"

"No. It takes a lot more than a freaky autumn sprinkle to take me down."

He smiled again. "Not even a half-crazed driver plunging off a mountain?"

She laughed, relieved he seemed okay. "Nope, not even that. But don't feel so bad. I saw an oil slick just before where you breached the rail. I don't think the accident was *all* your fault."

The paramedic lifted Cameron's right arm and placed it on his abdomen. Julia flinched when she saw the bone threatening to poke through the skin covering his wrist.

Cameron winced in pain.

"Sorry, Professor," the medic said, setting a splint under his forearm and wrapping gauze around it. "I've got to stabilize the injury before we take off."

Cameron watched his practiced motions. "Do you think it's broken?"

"I'm not the doctor, but I think it's safe to say this arm is going to be out of commission for a while. It looks like you've got a compound fracture and my guess is you're going to need surgery and external fixators to patch it up."

Cameron frowned. "That doesn't sound good."

The medic taped gauze to Cameron's wrist. "Could be better, I'll admit. Do you remember how you damaged your wrist this badly?"

Cameron snickered. "The last thing I recall is feeling like a pinball inside my Jeep, complete with some pretty weird sound effects."

Finished with his temporary immobilization job, the medic called to the driver in front of the ambulance. "I've got him ready to roll, Rick."

Julia got up from the bench. "Well, I guess that's my cue to leave. Good luck, Cameron."

"Wait, Julia…" Cameron stared at her as if he were unexpectedly at a loss for words. "I haven't really thanked you," he finally said.

"Sure you did. We're square."

The medic looked at her. "Actually I was going to suggest that you come to the hospital, too. You need to be checked out."

She shrugged off his concern. "That's not necessary. I'm fine, really."

"It's a precaution," he said. "There's another ambulance waiting to take you, but since you two know each other, I guess it would be okay if you rode with the professor here. He doesn't have any family in the area and would probably appreciate the company."

Cameron stared up at her.

She looked at him but spoke to the paramedic. "He has a wife. I'm sure if you call her…"

"No, I don't," Cameron said.

"You don't?"

"Divorced." He raised his eyebrows in a placating way. "I'm all alone here, Julia. It would be nice if my rescuer agreed to hold my hand."

Suddenly feeling light-headed, Julia sat back on the bench. Maybe she was experiencing repercussions from the night's trauma, after all. Or maybe she'd just heard news that she hadn't had time to process yet. "I'm not really the hand-holding type," she said.

He gave her an earnest look. "Okay, no hand-holding. But I'd appreciate it if you'd come along. At least until they know what they're going to do with me. I've been gone so long from the mountain, I don't know anybody else to call."

Before she could decline again, Bobby Cutter appeared at the back of the ambulance. "Everybody okay in here?"

Cameron answered for all of them. "I'm trying to get Julia to come to the hospital with me. She needs to be examined, too."

Bobby shook his finger at her. "You're going, MoonPie. No arguments. I don't want you doing something stupid and girlie like staying here and fainting on me."

Outnumbered, she sat against the ambulance wall

and fastened the seat belt. "Fine. I'll go. But ask my mother to come to the hospital to pick me up in an hour or so. And tell her to bring some clean clothes."

Bobby slapped the door of the vehicle before closing it. "Will do. My job here is done."

Cameron raised his good arm. "Just one more thing."

Bobby paused. "Yeah?"

"How'd she get the name MoonPie?"

Bobby laughed. "You can blame me for that. Julia loved those damn cakes. Had 'em in her lunch box every day so I just started calling her that. I think Cora must have bought them by the caseful. And then, one day, she just decided to stop eating them." He stared at Julia. "Why was that, Julia?"

She rolled her eyes. "For heaven's sake, Bobby, that's ancient history. Nobody cares anymore."

"I care," Cameron said.

Bobby gave her a what'd-I-tell-you look. "Anyway, I guess Julia didn't want to hurt Cora's feelings by telling her not to put any more pies in her lunch, so she started secretly swapping them for things like carrots and grapes and celery. But by then the name 'MoonPie' had stuck."

Julia shook her head. "Exciting story, isn't it?"

Bobby chuckled. "Julia's the only person I've ever known who'd give up a MoonPie for a bag of carrot sticks. The first woman on Earth content to trade down."

"Not anymore, Bobby," Julia said. "I learned my lesson."

Bobby laughed again and shut the ambulance door.

When Julia glanced at Cameron, she noticed his expression had changed, become more reflective than amused. "What?" she said.

"You've just given me my first Blue Ridge Mountain story," he said. "A Girl Called MoonPie." The ambulance lurched forward. Cameron sucked in a deep breath and looked at his arm. "Too bad I can't hold a pen to write it down."

CHAPTER FOUR

ONCE SHE'D LET the hospital staff coat her hands with antiseptic ointment and cover them with gauze, Julia was able to convince the emergency room nurse that she'd suffered no more ill effects from her trek into the ravine than minor cuts and bruises. The minute the doctor signed her release papers, Julia hurried to the admitting area, sounding as though she were walking on squeegees instead of shoes and leaving an embarrassing trail of mud flecks. She was going to make some maintenance people very unhappy tonight.

The receptionist at the admitting desk was the same middle-aged woman who'd assigned Julia to an examination room earlier. When she looked up from paperwork and saw her again, she wrinkled her nose. "Oh. They didn't give you a hospital gown?"

"They tried, but I've got clean clothes coming..." she glanced at her wristwatch, which was still smeared with mud, and wiped the face "...any minute now." She started to lean on the counter but thought better of leaving a residue for this woman to contend with. "Can you tell me where Cameron Birch is, please?"

The woman pointed to a set of double doors. "In there. Exam room eight if he's not down for tests. I'll have to buzz you in." Julia squished her way along the row of curtained-off areas until she found Cameron's and peeked around the drape.

He roused, slowly lifting his eyelids. "Hey. Come in."

She moved to the side of his bed and stood looking down at him. Trying not to reveal her shock, she glossed over the dark purple bruise that had formed on his forehead and the scratches on his face and arms. Plus, he had a cumbersome half cast secured to his wrist. "So, when are they springing you?" she said.

"Not until tomorrow, maybe early afternoon."

"And what have they poked and prodded tonight?"

"I've had an EKG, a chest X-ray, a CAT scan. All I've heard about is my wrist X-rays, and the paramedic was right. The orthopedic surgeon thinks about two hours of surgery in the morning ought to do the trick. And then I'll have a network of miniature antennae sticking out of my arm for six weeks."

"Well, look at the bright side. You might not have to invest in a satellite dish to keep up with *Grey's Anatomy*."

He smiled. "And there's one more silver lining to this cloud. My handwriting's never been any good, and now I have an excuse."

His offhand comment took her back ten years. She remembered her surprise at discovering this minor flaw in the otherwise seemingly perfect professor. His comments on her assignments had been practically illegible, and when each paper was returned, she'd spend several minutes trying to decipher his scratch marks.

"…for the bandages on your hands?"

His voice returned her to the present. "Sorry. What did you say?"

"Your hands? Why are they bandaged?"

"A couple of giant-sized splinters mostly, from some inhospitable oak trees in the ravine." When she saw the concern on his face, she added, "Nothing I haven't experienced many times in the past."

He released a long breath and shook his head. "Geez, Julia, when I think about what you did, what almost happened down there…"

She held up her hand. "Don't go in that gully again, Cameron. It's over, happy ending and all."

"But there has to be a way I can thank you."

She smiled. "You did. Ten years ago. You gave me an A."

"You *earned* an A." He pushed himself up with his good elbow, the movement obviously causing him pain. He tried to be cavalier about it with a forced grin. "I might have cracked ribs, too. But, anyway, about showing my appreciation, I may have to thank you twice since I have to ask one more favor."

"Oh?"

"I'll need a ride to my grandfather's place when they let me go."

His request dumbfounded her in light of his injuries. "You're not thinking of staying alone on top of the mountain while you heal, are you?"

He shrugged his shoulder, then winced. "Sure. I'll manage." He must have sensed the doubt in her eyes, because he added, "I need some time on that mountain, Julia. I've planned it for months. I've taken a sabbatical from the university." He drew his lips into a determined line, pulling in a deep breath. "I think Whisper Mountain will heal me, broken bones and all."

She wondered what he meant by "and all," and decided that maybe it was Cameron's spirit that needed mending. She stood. "Okay, I'll pick you up tomorrow afternoon." She jotted a phone number on a pad by his bed. "Just call the store when you're ready."

JULIA COULDN'T STOP thinking about Cameron. Restless and impatient, she strode to the automatic doors of the waiting room, stepped into the cool night air, came back, then sat in three different chairs while staring at *CNN* on the television. Mostly she wondered what could have gone wrong in Cameron's life that made him admit to needing this time on the mountain.

She thought about her own life, as well, and the months before she'd finally seen a doctor. She'd never been able to identify one isolated problem that had eventually sent her to him for help. She'd only known that something hadn't been right in her life, and she wasn't successfully dealing with it. A major part of her downward slide had been the breakup of a five-year relationship. She'd believed that Kevin had been *the one*. She'd pinned her hopes on him. Her future, her friendships and her weekends. They'd been inseparable for at least three years, one rarely seen without the other, two like-minded souls content to imagine a lifetime together.

Until suddenly she was the only one imagining.

When she'd lightheartedly brought up the subject of making their relationship permanent and legal, he'd found nothing funny about it. Nor anything remotely serious.

Julia looked up at the clock in the waiting room. 10:15 p.m. Had her mother forgotten about her? It was too late now to bring Katie out. Julia walked to the wall of windows and stared at the near empty parking lot. And her thoughts returned once more to Cameron.

Had he been the one to initiate divorce proceedings

with his wife? Had she disappointed him, or had it been the other way around? Had the breakup been amiable? Julia supposed some could be, between two rational people who decided that ending a relationship would result in improved lives for both.

She recalled the day she'd gotten the prescription for antidepressants. Kevin wasn't the only reason she'd seen a doctor. There had been problems at work, frantic calls from her mother, no calls from her sister. And nearly everyone Julia knew in Manhattan was on some kind of antistress medication. Pills were the big city quick fix that many people relied on.

Headlights veered from the main road and traveled up the drive to the hospital entrance, saving Julia from a potential bout with her conscience. She watched the approaching car closely, hoping to identify it as her mother's dependable old Ford. "Thank goodness," she said, when Cora pulled up to the drop-off area, and she went outside to meet her.

Cora got out, handed over a bundle of clothes, stared at Julia's hands and gasped. "Oh, my heavens, Julia."

"It's nothing, Mama. The hospital staff overreacted. I can remove these bandages in the morning." Too tired to control her impatience, she asked, "Where have you been?" She looked down at her soiled garments. "I feel like I've been wearing this stuff for weeks."

Cora frowned and Julia felt bad. She didn't mean to take her foul mood out on her mother. She considered going inside to a restroom to change clothes but decided she wouldn't bother now. "Did you lose power at the cabin?"

"No, but I had to make arrangements for Katie," Cora

explained. "The time just got away from me, and I didn't want to make her come along this late."

Julia put the clothes in the backseat and did the best she could to dust dried particles of mud from her jeans. "I'll just wear these home now." Once in the car, Julia asked her mother "So what did you do with Katie?"

"I put her to bed and called Rosalie. She was happy to watch her while I came for you."

Julia made a mental note to thank the neighbor who also helped out at the store during the busy season.

"Unfortunately, Rosie had to pick up her supper dishes first," Cora said. "She was running late because the TV kept showing bits about the accident."

Julia settled into the seat and closed her eyes. All at once her bones felt as if they were melting into little puddles around her. She rested her head back and said, "Oh."

"You were on television. That lady reporter talked about what happened and they showed you." Cora pulled out of the hospital parking lot. "I wish they'd let you go in and comb your hair first."

"Yeah, that would have been nice," Julia said absently, knowing a comb wouldn't have helped much.

"So how is Cameron?" Cora asked.

Julia looked over at her mother. "Pretty banged up. He's having surgery on his wrist tomorrow morning. Tonight, he mostly had tests."

Cora nodded with understanding. "They do that these days. Make sure the ticker's working right, your blood pressure's normal, all that stuff, before you go under the knife. I suppose it's good they take such care."

Through Julia's haze of exhaustion, Cora's voice seemed to drone on in another dimension. "I suppose," she said.

"I guess he's going back to Raleigh now that he's had the accident."

"Actually, no. He's asked me to pick him up tomorrow and take him to his grandfather's place."

Cora looked at Julia and quickly returned her attention to the road. "He's staying up there?"

"That's what he said."

"Pure foolishness."

"I kind of thought so."

"What time will you get him?"

"In the afternoon. He's going to call the store when they release him."

"I'm glad it's not the morning," Cora said. "I told Katie you were taking her to the elementary school to see about getting her enrolled."

Suddenly alert, Julia sat up straight. "You did?"

"Yes. She needs normalcy in her life, a schedule."

Julia couldn't argue. "How did she react?"

"She said she didn't need to go to school. I hope you can find a way to change her mind, Julia. Your idea with the bubble bath seemed to work well the other day."

Julia sighed. "I'll think of something, Mama."

AT NINE O'CLOCK Thursday morning, while she waited for Katie to get dressed, Julia called the Vickers County Medical Center to get an update on Cameron's condition. The operator switched her to the second floor station where a nurse reported that Cameron was currently in surgery. She suggested that Julia call back in an hour or so.

Julia tried to put her concern for Cameron out of her mind as she and Katie drove down Whisper Mountain and headed for Glen Springs Elementary. Katie hadn't spoken a word, so Julia attempted to break the ice. "I'm excited to see the school," she said. "I was very happy there as a student."

Katie stared out the window.

"Did you enjoy school in Tennessee?" she asked.

"It was okay."

"Were your teachers nice?"

"I guess."

Julia drummed her fingers on the steering wheel. "You know, one thing about living behind the store is that you don't get the opportunity to meet other kids. We're kind of isolated on the mountain. I suppose that's why I always looked forward to school."

Katie knotted her hands together.

"I'll bet you miss your friends in Tennessee."

Katie turned her head, stared out the side window. "I have you and Grandma."

Julia gripped the wheel tighter. *Oh, baby. But I'm not always going to be here.*

The principal of Glen Springs Elementary was a staid though seemingly competent individual who said he'd spoken to Cora and he understood the circumstances that made Katie's enrollment unique. While Katie waited in the outer office, he assured Julia that the staff would do everything in their power to make her niece's assimilation stress-free. Then he instructed his secretary to send Katie into his office.

Her eyes downcast and her hands fisted at her sides, Katie walked stiffly to the wooden chair on the other side of the principal's desk.

Mr. Dickson interlaced his fingers on top of his desk, smiled and said, "So, you're Katie."

She didn't respond. Julia wasn't surprised. It was a rhetorical question.

"We're very happy to welcome you as a Glen Springs Chipmunk," he said.

Katie stared at her hands. Her feet, a clear six inches above the floor, began to swing.

"You can start tomorrow." The principal waited for a reaction, predictably received none, and prompted, "How does that sound, young lady?"

Katie turned to Julia. "I don't need to go to school," she insisted.

"I was hoping that perhaps you'd want to, honey," Julia said.

"I don't. I want to stay with you and Grandma."

Julia smiled. "We're okay for a lot of things, but we can't help you learn everything you need to know. You have to have a real teacher for that."

Mr. Dickson added his sensible argument. "And the government requires that you attend school. You wouldn't want your aunt and grandmother to get in trouble for keeping you out, would you?"

Katie stared up at him, her eyes crinkling in determination. "I can homeschool. Lots of kids do."

Julia couldn't help admiring Katie's quick wits. Unfortunately homeschooling wasn't possible for her niece. Once Julia returned to Manhattan, Cora wouldn't have time to oversee lessons with her responsibilities at the store. "There are always options, Katie," she said. "But I think we should try this one first."

When Katie started to protest, she said, "And tomorrow will be just right. It's Friday. You can attend one day and have the whole weekend to tell us about your class and the kids you met. What do you think of that idea?"

Katie didn't appear to think much of it at all, so Julia tossed in one more selling point. "And after school, we can stay late, visit the library and take out some books."

Baby steps, Julia. One inch at a time and eventually a foot is gained.

"We could do that, I guess," Katie said.

Julia stood, extending her hand to Mr. Dickson. "We'll be back tomorrow. In the meantime, if you would consult the school's guidance counselor about Katie as we discussed, I'd be grateful."

"Certainly. We'll see you ladies in the morning."

When they left the school five minutes later, Katie took Julia's hand. "What are we going to do now?" she asked.

Julia paused, considering the answer. "Excellent question. I'm thinking we should go to the mall, have a snack at the food court and buy you some new clothes, maybe some especially sparkly things." She smiled down at Katie. "Just in case Friday goes well, we have to be prepared for Monday."

And then I'll pick up Cameron at the hospital and see if he's come up with a better option for his situation, she thought. Before starting her car, Julia called the hospital on her cell phone. The second floor nurse assured her that Cameron had come through the surgery just fine and was resting in the recovery room.

WITH SEVERAL shopping bags in the backseat of her rented Toyota and ice cream still sticky on their fingers, Julia and Katie headed up Whisper Mountain. Julia pulled into the gravel lot of Cora's General Store and parked next to the cube van belonging to Sunny Vale Bakery. "Have you ever met Oscar?" she asked Katie.

"No."

"Then you're in for a treat, maybe literally, although you'll have to save it for after dinner now."

The store was crowded for a weekday afternoon. Cora had a line at the cash register, and Rosalie was helping customers pick out native-made jewelry from the glass showcase. A couple sat at one of the booths in the snack bar chowing down on Cora's famous hot dogs, "the best on Whisper Mountain," according to the sign on the store's front porch. Of course, nowhere could the customers read that Cora's hot dogs were the *only* ones offered, since the store was the only stop between the town of Glen Springs and the top of the mountain.

A middle-aged man with thick salt-and-pepper hair looked up from a display shelf where he was stocking prepackaged goodies labeled with the Sunny Vale trademark, a bright sun rising over a meadow. "Hey, Julia," he called. "Good to see you."

"Same here, Oscar." She walked over, gave him a quick hug and stepped back so he could see Katie. "I'd like you to meet my niece."

The man smiled at Katie. "I heard there was another golden-haired Sommerville lady here," he said, his old-country accent as charming as always. Oscar Sobriato was proud of his Italian heritage. He rubbed his thumb over his chin and gave serious consideration to the items he'd arranged so far. "I wonder what this little one would like, hmm? Do you suppose she wants a MoonPie?"

Julia laughed. Oscar had been on this route for only five years, but legends were passed down forever on Whisper Mountain. "I know her to be a cookie fanatic," she said.

"Pick out what you like," Oscar said, waving Katie closer to the goodies. While Katie studied her choices, Oscar took Julia's arm and led her down the aisle. Placing his thick, soft hands on the sides of her face, he said, "I'm so sorry, Julia. I remember when you were here for your papa's funeral. Such a short time ago, and now Cora can't even bury her daughter in the family tradition."

"Thanks, Oscar. Folks have stopped by all week. That has helped."

He folded his arms. "How are they doing—your mama and the little one?"

"Okay, I guess. Katie is so quiet. That really worries me. And Mama…" She tried to give the impression that she wasn't overly concerned about Cora. "Well, Mama is Mama. She's sad but trying to cope."

Oscar glanced over at the cash register. "She's got a strong constitution, that one."

Julia's eyes widened. *My mama?*

Oscar thumped his chest. "And a heart as big as this mountain. She loves with it and grieves with it, and always takes care of those around her."

Julia followed his gaze, tried to see her mother as Oscar did. She supposed she could agree with the heart part of his description, but the rest of it was up for debate. When she looked back at Oscar, she realized his attention hadn't wavered from Cora.

"But she looks tired," he said. "And too thin." He patted his own round belly. "She needs to eat more. Pasta, some hearty Italian sausage. And a few napoleons wouldn't hurt, either." He shook a finger at Julia. "You see to it, okay?"

"Okay." As she walked back to Katie, Julia watched her mother with the customers. She smiled as she always had, but the gesture was void of any real feeling. She engaged in small talk, but her voice sounded flat, toneless. All the Sommerville women had blond hair, but Cora's lacked any sign of a healthy luster. Her blunt cut hung straight to her shoulders and was streaked with coarse gray strands that made her pale face appear washed-out, older than her fifty-eight years. An idea occurred to Julia. There had been an aisle at Pope's Drugstore for Katie. And there was one for Cora, too.

Julia settled Katie at a booth with a coloring book and crayons. When the last customer paid his bill, she went to the register. "Has Cameron called, Mama?"

"No, not yet. But someone was here from the towing company. He said they were going to try to bring Cameron's car up from the ravine later on today. But he figured it was a total loss."

Julia sighed. "I thought it would be." She looked at her watch. "It's almost one o'clock. I think I'll just drive over to the hospital and see if he's ready to go."

"Okay."

Julia waved at Katie and smiled at Oscar, who was taking his sweet time stacking muffins and cupcakes on the shelves. Had he always given Cora's General Store such special attention? Julia was suddenly quite certain that Oscar found more to like at Cora's than just the invigorating ride up the mountain.

HAVING FOUND OUT Cameron's location from the receptionist, Julia took the elevator to the second floor and headed toward his room. Her pulse increased with each step down the quiet hallway. Though she hadn't fantasized about Cameron for years, just hearing his voice in the store last night had awakened familiar emotions. And imagining him at the bottom of the ravine had propelled her to risk her own well-being in an effort to save him.

She stopped outside Cameron's door when she heard

a voice with a clear take-charge attitude. "You simply can't handle your immediate medical needs by yourself, Mr. Birch," a woman said. "Those fixator insertion points must be cleaned and dressed daily until your doctor says otherwise."

"That's nonsense," Cameron argued. "I've had a wrist operation, not open-heart surgery."

"But it's your right wrist, and you're right-handed. You can't manage your care with your left hand." The woman sighed. "And need I remind you that you also have a concussion and two cracked ribs. Even simple movements in the next few days will cause you pain."

Cameron groaned. "Isn't there a form I can sign that allows me to accept responsibility for myself? I promise you, Miss Winston, I won't hold the hospital liable for anything that happens to me once I walk out this door." His declaration was followed by a whistled intake of breath. Julia's own breath hitched in sympathy with his obvious stab of pain.

"Your doctor won't release you until we've established home care, which, unfortunately is proving quite difficult considering your remote locale. None of our regular attendants will commit to traveling that mountain road. It's known to be quite dangerous in iffy weather conditions." She paused. "I guess I don't have to remind *you* of that."

Julia stepped into the room just as Cameron tossed his head back on the pillow and stared at the ceiling. "This stalemate is ridiculous," he said. "I can take care of myself. I don't need anyone to make that drive every day just to…"

He turned his head, spotted Julia and pushed himself upright. Just as they had so many years ago, his green-gold eyes seemed to penetrate her to the core. Breaking eye contact, she caught her first glimpse of Cam's "antennae," the system of fixators sticking out of his wrist, as well as the thick gauze and sling supporting a contraption that looked more like a throwback to medieval times than an example of modern medicine. When Cameron fell back against the mattress, Julia realized he wasn't going to pull off any sort of macho display.

"Thank goodness, Julia," he said. "Will you tell this well-meaning hospital administrator that you are taking me home, and that you will see that I am appropriately tucked in and medicated?"

Miss Winston seemed relieved. "Are you a health-care professional?" she asked Julia.

Cameron darted a quick warning glance at Julia and followed it with a blatant lie. "Of course she is…"

"No, I'm not," Julia admitted before he could say anything more. "But I did agree to take Mr. Birch home today. I'm staying on Whisper Mountain myself for a while, so it's no problem. I'm not concerned about making the drive."

Cameron arched his brows. "There, you see? I'm all set. No worries."

"I'm sorry, but you still need medical care. I'm waiting for one more home-care person to report back to me. If she doesn't agree to make the trip daily, then you'll have to come into the hospital every day or make arrangements for more accessible accommodations."

Cameron shook his head. "I can't do that."

Miss Winston picked up a cell phone, which had been sitting on her clipboard. "Then we wait."

He blew out a long, frustrated breath. "There has to be something we can do."

Julia inched to the doorway. "I'll come back later when all the details have been worked out."

He nodded. "You might as well."

She started to leave, but he called after her. "Wait, Julia, don't go."

She turned around, saw that his eyes reflected a certain confidence that hadn't been there a moment before.

"How long are you going to be in Glen Springs?" he asked.

"A few weeks."

"Will you have some extra time while you're here?"

"I'm not sure. I have a lot on my mind."

"I understand," he said. "But maybe you could spare an hour or two a day? If you would agree to be my home health-care person, I could be released today."

She blinked, swallowed, tried to ignore the tingle of panic working its way down her spine. And then she sputtered her response. "What? No way."

CHAPTER FIVE

No way? Cameron certainly hadn't expected that response. But maybe he should have. His approach had been rather blunt. He didn't know what had brought Julia home. Maybe he was interfering in a family situation. But there had to be a way he could talk her into shuffling some of her time on the mountain to help him.

Despite the shooting pain in his chest, Cameron propped himself higher in the bed—one-handed, like he'd have to do everything for the next couple of months—and tried to think of a way to convince her to hear his deal, the one he was just now formulating in his mind. He reached behind him, plumped the pillow so it supported his back. "Would you at least consider it?" he said.

"I don't need to. I'm not a nurse. I don't know the first thing about taking care of a person with your injuries."

Cameron pictured the cute college sophomore he'd known ten years ago. Julia Sommerville had been a good student, one of the most rewarding to teach. She'd been eager to please, attentive, a strong participant in class discussions. He remembered her as she'd been then, her pale hair swept into a ponytail or held back with some sort of wide band. She'd had a ready smile and an enthusiasm for the written word that almost matched his passion.

This new Julia, the Manhattan version, looked different, more sophisticated, but that was to be expected. Time and circumstance changed everyone. Her hair was styled in a modern layered cut that brushed her shoulders and curled delicately at her jawline. She wore minimal makeup. Designer jeans fit meticulously to her slender legs and she had on a loose-fitting silky blouse that draped what he couldn't deny was a tempting figure. She wasn't the girl who'd parked her bicycle outside the Liberal Arts building and wore Riverton College sweatshirts. But these were all outward changes. Inside she still had to be the same bright, sweet young woman he remembered, didn't she? And he wasn't asking for a lifetime commitment, just a little kindness between neighbors.

Miss Winston's cell phone rang. She walked toward the door and answered it. When she disconnected, she looked at Cameron and shrugged. "We're out of options. Our last candidate just told me she couldn't fit you into her schedule. If you lived in town…"

"But I don't." Cameron waited for Julia to react to the latest announcement, but instead she turned away from him and faced the window. He said, "Could you leave us alone for a few minutes, Miss Winston?"

"Certainly." She started out the door, but stopped and addressed Julia's back.."The floor nurse could show you what has to be done."

Julia remained impassive, her attention fixed on an indeterminate spot outside the window. Miss Winston spoke to Cameron. "You let me know what you decide." She went into the hall to give them privacy.

Cameron spoke softly. "Julia…"

She turned. "Look, Cameron, don't try…"

"One of the nurses told me that a woman called twice today to ask how I was doing. It was you, wasn't it?"

"Yes, but don't read anything into a couple of phone calls. I was trying to plan my day since I'd made a commitment to you."

He smiled. "Of course. It's just that the Julia Sommerville I remember would be concerned about another person's welfare, and I was sort of hoping you were concerned about mine."

"Of course I'm concerned."

He chose a less direct approach. "I know you're here visiting your mother. Cora said you live in Manhattan."

She seemed to relax, perhaps believing that he wasn't going to pressure her. "That's right. I'm only in Glen Springs to take care of a family matter."

"Right. You said a few weeks. Funny. That's all I need." He leaned toward her, hating the feeling of desperation that had gripped him. But she was his only option for now, and he had to convince her to help him. He had no reason to expect her cooperation, nor did she have an obligation to give it. She'd done far too much for him already. But he'd come this far. He'd taken a year's sabbatical from the university, not only because the time off would allow him to pursue a longtime dream, but because he needed these months on Whisper Mountain. He needed to forget Louisa and the betrayal that had destroyed their marriage.

He had nothing to lose, so he gazed at Julia and put his immediate future in her hands. "You saved my life," he said. "I can't imagine the courage it took for you to climb down that ravine." He chuckled, tried to ignore the stab of pain that accompanied it. "Heck, I don't even know that I'm worth saving, but you did it."

She exhaled, looked away from him. "You've already thanked me."

"I know, but I still need you." He waited for her attention to shift to him again and said, "You heard the administrator. You could do what needs to be done for me over the next few weeks. And I'll tell Miss Winston to keep looking for someone else. Maybe you would only have to come to the top of the mountain a few days..."

She sighed. "A few days. A few weeks. It doesn't matter. I'm an entertainment journalist, Cameron. I critique plays and movies and art exhibits. I don't know the first thing about nursing. Good grief, my home first-aid kit consists of a tin of Band-Aids."

Cameron's frustration level hitched up another notch. Maybe Julia wasn't his only hope for finding home care, but she certainly was the one person who could get him out of the hospital today and to the top of the mountain where he could start investigating other possibilities. So he presented her with another option. "I would pay you, of course."

She shot him a warning look. Her spine straightened. Her hands clenched, and he figured he was screwed.

"You must have expenses in New York," he said, using logic to dig himself out of the hole he'd created. "An apartment, a car. I don't know what journalists make these days and I don't know your situation, but when I was investigating that career for myself, I remember thinking that making ends meet would be difficult."

She didn't argue.

"I can give you the going rate for health care, whatever that is. I would think fifteen dollars an hour or so." He tried to read her reaction in her downcast eyes and the slight lowering of her stiff shoulders and allowed himself to hope. "Julia, please. Can we give it a try, at least? If it doesn't work, I won't pressure you to stick with me. And I'll be a model patient."

Her lips turned upward in the first sign of a grin. "I doubt that." She looked at the ceiling, back at him and headed toward the narrow closet in the corner of his room. "Are your things in here?"

"I suppose."

She opened the door, took clothes from a plastic bag and lay them on the foot of his bed. Frowning, she said, "I should have thought to bring you something clean to wear."

He grinned at her. "I don't have anything clean to wear. It was all in my car."

"Oh. Of course."

"From what your friend the firefighter told me, everything I brought to sustain me for my first few days on Whisper Mountain went under the waterfall. Somehow I don't think much survived."

"That reminds me. They're pulling your car out today, but—you're right—I don't think much will be salvageable."

"I have things coming from Raleigh soon," he said. "Office supplies, books, files, winter clothes…" He stopped and stared at her as she brushed dried mud from his jeans. "Does this mean what I hope it means?"

Her hand stilled and she stared at him. "We'll try, Cameron. That's all I'm promising. I'll take you up to your grandfather's place, but first we'll stop at Wal-Mart so I can get you some basic supplies."

He lay back against the pillow, smiling. "Just underwear and toiletries," he said. "I can get everything else

I need at Cora's. Whisper Mountain Falls souvenir
T-shirts and shorts will last me until my things arrive."
He leaned over the side of the bed. "Miss Winston!
Draw up those release forms!"

CAMERON MAY HAVE THOUGHT they'd come to an understanding, but an hour later Julia still didn't have a clue
what had possessed her to agree to be his private nurse.
Of course there was the matter of money, a darned good
enticement since she could use the extra cash to buy
things for Katie. She hadn't had time to sublet her
Manhattan apartment for the weeks she would be gone.
And while her editor at *Night Lights Magazine* had
been sympathetic about the tragedy in her life and
given his consent for her to miss work, he'd made it
clear that her pay would be suspended until she returned.

She'd left her Chevy Cavalier in the garage parking
space that cost three hundred a month, wondering for
the millionth time why she even kept the twelve-year-
old automobile when she hardly ever used it. Security
meant different things to different people, and Julia
supposed that dented, scarred sedan was her safe
haven, her assurance that she could escape her life
whenever she wanted to. So she kept up her payments
to State Farm and wrote checks to Louie's Downtown
Garage.

But perhaps the most visible sign that Julia may have
lost her mind when she agreed to nurse Cameron was
the small mountain of supplies an orderly brought into
the hospital room. Cameron's release was delayed
an hour while a nurse showed Julia everything she
would have to do to clean and dress his wounds, take

his blood pressure and pulse and record his temperature on a daily chart.

"You'll do fine," the nurse told her. "Many of the county's home health-care workers for these temporary assignments are laymen like you with minimal training, and they do a good job." She handed Julia two boxes containing alcohol, gauze, tape, cotton swabs and other miscellaneous items. "If you have any questions, just call the hospital and ask to be directed to this floor. Anyone who answers can help you." She smiled at Cameron. "I don't think we'll forget the patient who slid down the ravine to get our attention."

From the gleam in the nurse's eyes, Julia suspected she'd freely given Cameron her attention for reasons that had nothing to do with his wild ride. And why not? Once Julia had been completely smitten by him. Not now, though. So much time had passed and circumstances had changed dramatically since that autumn of her sophomore year. Today she could view Cameron objectively. And she did so as he sat in the obligatory wheelchair, his light brown hair mussed, his face shadowed with two days' growth of beard, his hazel eyes practically twinkling since he'd gotten his way. And, objectively speaking, Julia had to admit he was still a very handsome man, though perhaps not the ideal she'd once believed him to be.

She looked away from Cameron and held the supplies against her chest. "I'll just take these boxes with me while I pick up my car."

"That'll be fine," the nurse said. "I'll wheel Cameron down to the front entrance and we'll meet you there."

Minutes later, Julia's rented Toyota Corolla was on

its way to Wal-Mart. Cameron sat in the passenger seat staring out the side window. "I never grow tired of it," he said out of the blue.

She glanced at him. "Of what?"

"The leaves turning. It's the magic of a Blue Ridge fall."

"Yes, it's nice. We have a similar magic in Central Park, you know."

"I'm sure you do, but here…" He pointed up. "It's just started at the higher elevations. The birch and beech trees are always first, followed by maples and hickories. You can see a hint of crimson already." He turned to her. "If we're lucky, we won't have another storm, which would rip the leaves from the trees before they're ready to fall. This could be one of the most beautiful seasons ever. It's getting off to a late start, but that only means the color will last longer."

Julia considered his prediction. She'd always appreciated the season, like everyone else, but she'd never calculated the change in terms of elevation and tree varieties. And she'd never really thought about conditions that made one year's season better than another's. Mostly, she'd equated autumn with increased tourism and the possibility of bigger tips for serving more hot dogs at the general store. It was those tips that had enabled her to go to Riverton College after delaying her admission for only one year.

She pulled into Wal-Mart and turned off her engine. "Did you make that list?"

He handed her a paper, scowling at his handwriting. "Sorry. That's practically unreadable. I'm suddenly left-handed without any practice."

She skimmed the list, sounding aloud the scribbled words. Cameron was specific about brands and labels.

She smiled, not finding that surprising. "Six packs of briefs?" she said.

"I don't know when I'm going to do laundry again. I don't even know if Gramps had a working washing machine when he died. I need to buy enough to last a while."

She mumbled the rest of the description. "Size thirty-four, Hanes Classic, preshrunk." Good heavens, she was blushing! Ten years ago, who would have ever thought she would be reciting her American Literature professor's underwear particulars. She quickly shoved the paper into her purse.

Flinching as he twisted on the car seat, he reached into the pocket of his muddied jeans and pulled out his wallet. Digging out a credit card, he said, "At least this survived." He held it up to the light. "You might have to wipe it off to make the metal strip work. If not…" he flipped the wallet open again "…here's some slightly muddy cash."

She took the bills, stared at them, and handed them back. "I can't tell if these are ones or hundreds. I'll put the purchases on my credit card and you can pay me back."

Fifteen minutes later she returned with three bags of essentials, which she put next to the medical supplies in her trunk. She got into the car. "You okay?"

"Fine. I can go in Cora's with you."

"No, you can't. The nurse said no walking around to-day. You still could have a reaction from the concussion."

"That's silly. I'm perfectly capable…"

She glared at him. "Cameron, you said you'd be a model patient. We've been away from the hospital for half an hour and you're already giving me a hard time."

He put his left hand up in a gesture of surrender. "Okay. You win."

She pulled out of the parking lot and headed into Glen Springs. She made a quick stop at Pope's Drugstore to drop off Cameron's prescriptions for pickup the next day and turned onto Whisper Mountain Road. They'd just started up the steep incline when Cameron said, "I knew your sister back when I taught at Riverton. How is she?"

Julia's hand slipped, and the car veered sharply to the left. Her front tire scraped the rocky embankment at the side of the road. "Shit."

He clutched his rib cage with his good hand. "I just went off this road last night, Julia. I was sort of hoping to make it all the way to the top today."

She closed her eyes for a second and gripped the steering wheel until her knuckles hurt. "Sorry."

"Was it something I said?"

He didn't know about Tina. She hadn't told him why she was here. Everyone else in Glen Springs knew, but naturally Cameron wouldn't have heard the details. The pain over Tina's death was a constant heartache for Julia. She couldn't imagine that someone in the small town wasn't aware of her grief. But Cameron wasn't responsible for his remark. He didn't know.

She took a deep breath but kept her eyes straight ahead. "Well, yes, it was something you said."

He waited a moment, obviously pondering the last moment of conversation. "All I did was ask about Tina."

"I know. Tina's why I've come home."

"Oh? I remember her leaving years ago."

Of course you do because she left you, just like she

left Mama and Daddy, the general store, the mountain. Me. None of those things had fulfilled Tina's wishes. None of them were good enough, exciting enough. She'd found Wayne. And a life that she thought would have her reaching for the stars ended at the bottom of a Tennessee lake.

Julia followed a curve in the road. Cora's General Store sat just a half mile ahead. She checked the rear-view mirror. No one was behind her, so she slowed to a crawl. She looked over at Cameron and said, "There's something you should know."

He tensed, leaned forward.

"Tina died last week."

He jerked, straining against the seat belt. "What?"

"She drowned in a lake behind her house."

"Oh, my God. That's why you're here." After a long pause he said, "Look, if you don't have the time to help me, I understand. I had no idea."

"It's okay. It happened over a week ago. We're not having a service. I've agreed to help, so we'll see how it goes."

He was silent another moment and then said, "Do you remember introducing me to Tina at the drugstore?"

Julia lied. "Vaguely."

"After that, we went out a few times."

"I know. I'm sorry to have to tell you. Blurting it out like that was insensitive, but—" she pulled into Cora's parking lot and faced him "—you should know since we're here and Mama's still grieving."

"No, no, it's okay. I'm just sorry for imposing on you at this time. This has to be devastating for your parents."

She turned off the car. "It's just my mother now. My dad…well, that's another story."

He yanked on the handle and stepped onto the gravel surface.

Julia stormed around the hood and confronted him. "Where are you going? Get back in that car."

"Sorry, Julia." He winced in pain but walked around her. "I promise this will be the only time I defy your orders."

She frowned at his back. "Right."

"I've got to go in there. I remember Gene from when I was a kid. He always helped me pick out fishing tackle. And now Tina. I have to pay my respects to your mother."

What could she do? Julia clamped her mouth shut and followed him inside.

When Cora saw Cameron, she came from behind the counter and hurried toward him. "Oh, you poor boy. Look at those rods. How are you feeling?"

"I'm okay."

She gently took his arm and led him to the drink cooler. "Pick out what you want, Cameron, and then we'll have to get you out of those dirty things." She glanced over her shoulder at Julia. "How could you let him wear these clothes?"

Julia crossed her arms over her chest. "I went to all the men's clothing stores in the hospital, Mama, but I couldn't decide which fanny-revealing gown to get him."

Cora opened the cooler door. "She's a smart-alecky one, my daughter."

Julia couldn't tell if Cameron wanted a drink or not, nor could she hear his response because she headed to the snack bar, where Katie was painting with watercolors. But, to Cameron's credit, he wisely selected a bottle while apparently informing Cora that he intended to buy a few things to wear. The two of them went to the clothing rack and began choosing garments and layering them into a pile on the counter.

Julia sat opposite her niece. "Hi. You okay?"

Katie continued sweeping a brush over the roof of a coloring book house. "Yes. Who's that man? Is he the one who crashed his car last night?"

"That's him, all right."

"Those things coming out of his arm are creepy."

"Yeah, a bit creepy, I guess. But they have to stay there until his broken bones are healed." She noticed that her mother and Cameron had stopped stacking T-shirts. Cameron's head was lowered, an attempt to close the distance between his six-foot-plus height and her mother's short stature. Cora's expression had sobered. He shook his head slowly, curled his left hand over her shoulder. She nodded, wiped one finger under her eye. And then she reached for the stack of clothes and carried it to the cash register.

"Julia, Katie, come help," she called. "These clothes need to be rung up and folded, and this poor man needs food."

"Guess we'd better get to it," Julia said, sliding out of the booth. Katie reluctantly put down her paintbrush and followed. Cora introduced Katie to Cameron as her granddaughter.

Cameron smiled. "Hi there."

"Hi."

He spoke to Julia. "She's yours?"

Katie lifted wide eyes to look at Julia. "Why don't you get some paper bags from under the counter?" Julia suggested. "We'll need a few of them."

Katie scurried behind the cash register.

"She's my niece," Julia said.

Cora cast a pitiable gaze on the child. "Katie is T-Tina's daughter. Mine to raise now."

Cameron's brows lifted as he apparently tried to grasp the full extent of the tragedy. His voice barely a whisper, he said, "Wow. Where's her father?"

At the mention of Wayne, Julia grabbed a loaf of bread off the shelves Oscar had recently arranged, shifted it to the crook of her elbow and stuffed other items against it. "Your guess is as good as ours." She continued to grab and stuff everything in sight. "He dropped Katie off here and split. As far as I'm concerned, we're all better off for it."

Cameron tried to take some of the crumpled load from her arms. She only squeezed it tighter. "I take it Katie's father isn't your favorite person," he said.

"Hey, look." Katie pointed toward the road. "I'll bet that's your car."

Everyone rushed to the window, where they saw a tow truck slowly advancing past the store with the barely recognizable form of a mud-crusted Jeep hitched to its tow bar. Cameron took hold of his injured arm, hurried outside and shouted to catch the driver's attention.

Cora took the food from Julia's death grip and began plumping the bread back into shape. "For heaven's sake," she said. "His car's already crushed. Do you have to do the same thing to his food?"

Julia ran to the door. "That man is crazy. If he's lucky, his food will be the only thing I crush."

Cora stopped, her hands wrapped around the loaf. "What are you talking about?"

Julia called over her shoulder as she went outside, "For a supposedly smart man, Professor Birch sure can be an idiot!"

CHAPTER SIX

THE TOW TRUCK DRIVER pulled his rig onto the narrow shoulder next to a rocky outcropping along the base of the mountain wall. Cameron went immediately to the back of his Jeep and wiped mud from the windows.

Julia reached him before the driver had climbed out of the cab. She grabbed his left arm. "Stop that right now."

He paused long enough to glare at her. "I have to see what's left of my truck." He peered inside a rear window. "And my stuff."

"We're not supposed to be thinking of your Jeep right now, Cameron. We're supposed to be concerned with broken ribs, a concussion and the surgery you had just a few hours ago."

"They're cracked, not broken," he said.

Refusing to relinquish the hold she had on him, she added, "Get back to my car now, please."

"I will, I will. Just give me a minute."

The driver sauntered around to the back of the Jeep to join them. "What's going on here?" He stared at Cameron's arm contraption and released a low chuckle. "You the guy who was driving this thing?"

Cameron frowned. "'Fraid so."

The driver jutted a thumb at the boxy vehicle he'd just hauled up from the ravine. "You were lucky to make it out with just your arm in a sling, buddy. Hate to think what would have happened if it had rolled over."

As Cameron surveyed his Jeep as if he were looking upon his firstborn child, Julia realized that he had something in common with a lot of men that she'd never have expected—a love affair with his wheels.

"She'd have made it through," he said, slapping the top of the Jeep in a man/car bonding ritual. "Turned over on me once in the Rockies. The roll bar saved us both."

The driver nodded solemnly. Apparently few words were needed to communicate the wonders of a four-wheel-drive dinosaur. He peered into the interior of the driver's side. "Air bag didn't work, though," he pointed out.

"She doesn't have one," Cameron said as he came around the Jeep. "This is an early '98 model. Came out just before drivers' bags were required." He stared in the passenger window. "Guess the other bag didn't open, anyway, so the driver's bag probably wouldn't have if I'd had one."

This was ridiculous. Julia was once again questioning her sanity in agreeing to help Cameron do anything beyond rising from the mucky bottom of the ravine. She never should have ridden in the ambulance. And she shouldn't have agreed to pick him up at the hospital. And she certainly shouldn't…

"Can we open the cargo door?" Cameron asked the driver, breaking Julia's mental litany of recent misjudgments.

"We can try."

"Ah, gentlemen," Julia interrupted. She spoke to the driver. "Do I need to point out that you are parked on the side of a curving mountain road?" To Cameron, she said, "And four hours ago, you were still in a

hospital recovery room and you are due your medication in exactly—" she glanced at her watch "—eight
minutes, or that wrist is going to remind you in a
most excruciating way why those rods are sticking out
of it."

Cameron looked at her. The driver looked at her.
Neither argued. When they looked at each other, they both
had the same reaction. "We'd better hurry," Cameron said.

"Sounds like it," the driver agreed. He yanked on
the cargo door. Aided by the force of gravity, it flew
open, a corner banging against the pavement. Cameron
reached inside and pulled out a standard-sized leather
shoulder bag. "My laptop." He stuffed the bag under his
sling, ran his left hand over the outside. "It's dry. Damn.
It's dry. It's fine."

Julia felt an accompanying rush of exhilaration.
This was a triumph she could understand. His laptop had
survived the fall, its hard drive still protecting the valu-
able files inside. To a journalist, a writer, this was nir-
vana. "No kidding?" she said. "That's wonderful."

"You bet it is." Cameron handed her the bag. "I wonder what else stayed dry."

The driver shook his head. "Not much. There was
only a foot or two of the rear visible when I got down
there." He opened the passenger door, releasing a stream
of brown water onto the road. Cameron watched with a
pain in his face that had nothing to do with his injury.
But he quickly recovered and rummaged through the
rest of his belongings. He managed to retrieve a pair of
heavy shoes befitting a lumberjack's lifestyle and a
serious backpack, one supported by a metal frame.

"Great," Julia said. "Now you can go hiking."

Cameron hoisted the pack onto his left shoulder. "I

know. I can't believe how lucky it is that I put these things in the back of the Jeep."

She stared at his broken wrist since everyone else seemed to have forgotten about it. "I was kidding!" she said.

But the man at her side eyeing the surrounding mountains *wasn't*. He appeared to be planning his next expedition into the wild. At that moment, Julia realized there was a side of Cameron Birch she never would have predicted. The shabbily elegant professor with a voice like maple syrup and the contemplative soul of Robert Frost was actually an intellectual, smaller version of Paul Bunyan.

She smiled to herself. The image, while unexpected, was not without its appeal. She shouldered the laptop, picked up the shoes and pointed to her car. "Cameron…"

"Okay." He asked for Julia's cell-phone number and scribbled it on the back of a business card the driver produced from his shirt pocket. Then he thanked the man for stopping and suggested he keep Julia's number handy, since his phone was no doubt stuck somewhere in the mire of Whisper Mountain Falls.

"I'll call my insurance company and have a rep take a look at the Jeep," Cameron said. "In the meantime, if you think she can be cleaned up and made to run again, I'd sure like to know your opinion." He patted at the Jeep with almost reverent affection as the driver closed the cargo door. Then he nodded decisively. "She'll be back. I've got confidence in her."

"You might be right," the driver said. "These old workhorses can take a lot of punishment."

Cameron hugged his right arm close to his chest and wrapped his left hand around the protected elbow. His face paled. When he looked at Julia, she saw the pain etched in the fine lines around his eyes. "Maybe we'd better get going," he said.

"Gee, I wish I'd thought of that." She automatically grabbed his left elbow and guided him to Cora's lot where the Toyota sat. Once he was in the car, she went into the store to get his supplies. Katie helped her carry them out. "Do you want to ride up the mountain with us?" Julia asked her. "I'll be a few minutes settling Cameron into the cabin, but we'll be back here in time for supper."

Katie contemplated her answer. "Can I bring my paints?"

"Sure."

"Okay."

She ran back inside to get her things. Moments later they were all headed up Whisper Mountain, the Toyota's engine laboring because of the steep incline and the added weight of passengers and equipment. With each curve, Julia sensed Cameron's concern. "I know," she said. "The Jeep would be handling this climb like we were on a level race course."

He half smiled. "Pretty much. But this car would hit the guardrail and bounce back onto the road, instead of plowing through it, and right now—" he closed his eyes, leaned his head back "—I have to say I wish I'd been in the Toyota last night."

Julia took pity on him. "Just a few minutes and you can have your next dose of Vicodin."

"Vicodin? That's what I'm taking? I never thought to ask."

"Yes. It's what the doctor gave us. He prescribed a couple weeks' worth."

"That's addictive."

"It can be. But only if you abuse it."

"I don't want to take anything addictive. Maybe Gramps left some Tylenol in the cabin."

"Tylenol?" She speared him a quick glance and looked back at the road. "You've got to be kidding. You have to follow the doctor's orders and take something strong enough to dull your pain. Something meant for simple body aches won't do it."

"But…" He blew out a breath, rubbed his elbow. "Yeow. Maybe one more dose won't hurt."

Julia had feared that she'd become addicted to her antidepressants, though her doctor had assured her that by following the recommended dosage, it was unlikely. "Becoming addicted is the last thing you should worry about," she said. "Easing your pain is the first. Your prescription is for two weeks, so you might as well get used to the idea of letting modern medicine help you through this."

"Mommy took pills sometimes," Katie said from the backseat.

Julia glanced at her in the rearview mirror. "She did?"

"Daddy called them her happy pills, but I guess some days she forgot to take them. She wasn't always happy."

Julia's hands tensed around the steering wheel. For the first time, she wondered about the similarities, not the differences, that existed between her and Tina. For the past few years, Julia had believed that she and Tina were opposites in almost every way. Tina was wild, adventurous, self-centered. Julia had always thought of herself as stable, conscientious, studious. Growing up, the two sisters had seemed to have evolved from separate gene pools, with Tina ultimately more like their mother, with mood swings and moments of high anxiety, and Julia more like their father, a genial man everyone could depend on.

Yet she and Tina had both experienced emotional highs and lows and both had resorted to medication. But ultimately Tina hadn't been able to cope. What had been her breaking point? When had she stopped taking her "happy pills" and succumbed to the ultimate escape? Julia shivered, realizing that her comfort zone of believing she and Tina were nothing alike no longer existed.

She let her thoughts fade to the back of her mind when she realized Cameron was staring at her. He rolled his eyes to the backseat and mumbled, "Poor kid."

"Yeah," she said. *Poor all of us.*

Cameron stared out the front window. "There it is, just as I remember it."

They'd reached the top of Whisper Mountain, where thick pine trees and beeches and elms, their leaves tipped with fall colors, shielded a tin-roof cabin Julia had never seen before despite her years on the mountain. She pulled up to a welcoming porch that spanned the front of the wood-sided structure and parked on a blanket of pine needles.

Cameron got out of the car and walked to the base of three steps that led to the entrance. He studied the porch, seeming to concentrate on every little detail one by one, from the pair of rush-seat rockers to a well-aged wooden sugar bucket filled with garden implements.

Julia and Katie came up behind him. Julia motioned to a front door with cheerful gingham curtains covering its top windowpanes. "Do you have a key?" she asked Cameron.

"No need," he said. "There has only been one key in

existence since the cabin was built." He climbed to the porch, awkwardly tipped an old crockery jug and pointed down. "And there it is."

Julia scooped up the key and held it out to him. "Do you want to do the honors?"

"No, you go ahead." He rubbed his forearm over the sling. "As anxious as I am to go inside, I'm slightly more interested in taking that medicine."

A sheen of perspiration had appeared on his brow. He was well past the time for his next scheduled dose of painkillers. She opened the door and let him in. He sought out the nearest chair, a comfortable glider cushioned with what appeared to be down-filled pads. He released a long breath when he sat.

"You did too much today. I'll get the bottled water and your pills from my car," she said.

He nodded. "Thanks." He bit his lower lip, squeezing his eyes shut for a moment. His voice uncharacteristically hoarse, he said, "Julia, you've been great..."

She smiled to herself. "No, I've been a nag, but it hasn't done either of us much good. Promise me you won't move."

He chuckled. "That's an easy promise to keep."

She went to the car and returned with the boxes of medical supplies. Cameron swallowed two pills without hesitation. Julia had never taken Vicodin, but Kevin had when he'd pulled a muscle in his back playing basketball. Julia remembered that it had worked fast and effectively.

By the time she'd brought in most of the supplies, Cameron was resting comfortably and Katie was painting at an old wooden farm table that looked as if it had withstood many seasons and countless meals. Julia took a moment to examine the cabin and acquaint herself with the amenities, or lack of them, that Cameron would have to adjust to in the next few days.

The central focus of the living room was a large stone fireplace with a thick pine mantel. Drawn to it at once, Julia inhaled the scent of wood smoke and noticed that a fire seemed to have been recently built. "Has someone been here?" she asked Cameron. She knelt to inspect a log with burnt edges. "I think this fireplace has been used in the last couple of days."

Cameron sat forward. "Impossible. No one has been here in a year."

She looked more closely at the log. "That's strange. This piece of wood was extinguished before it burned itself out."

"Could have been that my grandfather left it that way. He never wasted anything, especially wood."

"I suppose." She walked away from the fireplace and checked for other heat sources in the room. Discovering only an ancient radiator, she determined the fireplace was more than a decorative addition to the house. It was an essential part of surviving the winters.

A winding set of stairs led to a second floor, presumably the bedrooms, and a door opened to a small kitchen off the main room. Julia carried in the food they'd bought at Cora's and was relieved to see fairly modern appliances, including a microwave oven. Apparently old Josiah recognized the value of convenience in his later years.

The back door of the house opened onto an herb porch. Small pots lined a wooden shelf that spanned the four walls. Unfortunately, most of the plants had died from lack of attention. Bunches of dried, harvested herbs hung from the ceiling, however, and their brittle leaves would make excellent seasonings.

Besides a rickety ladder-back chair, the only other significant item on the porch was a stacked washer and dryer. Julia smiled, remembering Cameron's excessive purchase of briefs and decided he would be glad to see the gleaming appliance. She looked out the screen enclosure and spotted a latched door that opened to an underground cellar. A deep coal bucket and shovel on the ground next to the door indicated that the basement held the house's main source for heat, the coal furnace.

When she returned to the living room, Julia had determined that Josiah Birch's cabin was an uncomplicated yet sufficient dwelling that had everything it needed and nothing it didn't. And since Josiah had lived in the home into his late eighties, and left only when forced to spend the last two days of his life in a hospital, the cabin had obviously served him well.

Cameron smiled at her when she walked by and nodded in Katie's direction. "I asked if I could see her painting, but she seems a little shy."

Julia placed her hand on Katie's head. "Won't you let Cameron see your picture?"

She swished her brush around in a cup of water and smeared more paint onto the bristles. "Maybe when it's done," she said.

"There you go," she said to Cameron. "Spoken like a true artist. We'll have no viewing until it's time."

"What else does she like to do?" he asked quietly.

"She colors. And reads. She loves books."

"Really? When my things come from Raleigh, I may be able to interest her in some of the literature. I can read to her."

"That would be nice," she said, keeping her voice low. "She needs attention right now. I think Katie has been a somewhat solitary child most of her life."

Cameron nodded, his focus on the little girl. "That's a shame. And now the loss of her mother."

If you only knew the truth about Tina's death, you would understand just how great a loss it is. "I've got one more load to bring in," Julia said. "I'll be back in a minute."

She walked outside, climbed down from the porch, and stopped dead. A tall, gaunt, almost spectral-looking man with a beard that reached his chest and gray clumps of hair brushing his shoulders came around the corner of the cabin. He stared at Julia as intently as she did at him. For a moment, she actually wondered if this willowy, somehow fragile individual were human or the embodiment of one of the ghostly mountain legends she'd been told as a child. She trapped a scream in her throat while a vision of the half-burned logs in the fireplace came back to her. No specter she'd ever heard of needed to light a fire to stay warm.

She thought about calling for Cameron but decided against it. The visitor posed no imminent threat, and what could a one-armed man do to protect them, anyway? It was best to keep Katie and Cameron in the cabin.

After they stared at each other in shocked silence for several seconds, the man looped his thumbs through the straps of his denim overalls, spat a stream of tobacco into the dirt, and said, "'Afternoon. Who are you?"

"I should be asking you that," Julia said as she backed toward the steps with an awkward, uneasy step.

The man narrowed his eyes and peered at her. "What's the matter with you? You scared?"

Julia hoped her answer expressed a confidence she

didn't feel. "No. Why would I be scared?" She darted a quick glance around their heavily forested surroundings. Driving up Whisper Mountain, she hadn't passed a house in more than half a mile. No surprise. She knew that no one besides Josiah lived this far up. The only vehicle within walking distance of the cabin appeared to be hers, and this man stood between her and escape. "How did you get here?" she said to the stranger.

"My pickup."

"Where is it?"

"Out back. I been here since last night."

At least something made sense. "The fireplace," she said aloud.

"What?"

"Did you stay inside?"

"Of course. It rained like the dickens. I'd have floated away if I'd slept outside." His jaw worked before another brown stream splattered next to the bottom porch step. "Now I'm just waiting on the boy. What are you doing here? You belong to the boy?"

Julia had no idea what he meant. "The boy? What boy?"

"Josiah's boy. He called me from Raleigh, said he was coming back to the mountain."

"Are you talking about Cameron?"

The man sputtered a chortle of laughter. "Of course I'm talking about Cam. Though I guess he ain't a boy no longer."

"No, he isn't."

He remained at the foot of the steps and closed one eye to better aim the other at Julia. "Are you his new one?"

"His new what?"

"Woman?"

"No!"

"I never met the old one, but Josiah didn't like her much. Said it wasn't his business, though, who the boy picked. But he didn't like her just the same."

Realizing that this man obviously had a relationship with Cameron and his grandfather, Julia relaxed her guard. She leaned against the porch rail and said, "Look, Mr...."

"Just call me Marcus."

"Fine, Marcus. I guess you haven't heard, but Cameron had an accident yesterday."

The man's jaw finally stopped moving. "An accident? I sure didn't hear that. Is he okay?"

"He will be."

"Hope he didn't go to the hospital. They only make it worse in there."

"Well, yes, as a matter of fact… But that's not the point. He's here now, and I'm just…"

The man walked around her and headed up the stairs, looking quite spry for a senior citizen of sixty… seventy…one hundred… Julia didn't have the slightest idea how many years that beard had been growing. But he cupped his hands around his mouth and hollered with the strength of a twenty-year-old, "Boy! Come out here!"

Julia tried to shush him, realized that was like attempting to stop the water from flowing at Whisper Mountain Falls, and gave up.

From inside the cabin, she heard Cameron's voice, weak but brimming with excitement. "Marcus? Is that you?" A moment later, he appeared on the porch with a grin. "Good to see you, you old son of a gun."

Marcus scrutinized Cameron's fixators and sling. Finally, he shook his head. "I knew it," he said. "You've been standing up talking when you should have been sitting down listening, haven't you, boy?"

Cameron laughed. "Not this time."

A serious scowl settled on the old man's face. "How'd it happen? Is there anybody I got to see about avenging a wrong?"

"No, no. It was purely an accident." Cameron gave him an abbreviated version of the details, with special emphasis on Julia's heroic rescue, and finished by introducing him to her. "This is Marcus Hempstead," he told her.

"We've sort of met," Marcus said, extending his hand. "That was a brave thing you done, getting Cam out of that Jeep, lady."

Julia's face warmed. For some inexplicable reason, she was humbled by this mountain man's praise.

"Julia is Cora and Gene Sommerville's daughter," Cameron said.

"I knew Gene," Marcus said. "Good man. Sorry he's gone. I never stopped in the store, but I used to see Gene at the Home Depot when he was stocking up on firewood for the winter."

Julia was certain she'd never seen Marcus before. "Where do you live?"

He pointed to a crest in the distance, which Julia remembered was dusted with snow long after the last flakes had faded from the other mountains. "On Snowy Top. I don't get over to Whisper all that often, especially now that Josiah's passed."

Cameron lowered himself into a porch rocker. "I guess nobody's ever gone missing here on Whisper Mountain," he said.

Marcus thought a moment. "Not since 1976. There was that family camping on Stone Creek Ledge, and their boy up and disappeared."

Julia was suddenly caught up in the mysterious conversation. "What are you talking about?"

Cameron smiled up at her. "Marcus is a journaler," he said.

"Journaler? Do you write for a newspaper?" she asked.

Marcus chuckled. "Nope. I'm not a *journalist*." He pointed to the second rocking chair, suggesting that Julia sit. She declined and instead upended the crock that had hidden the key and sat there. Marcus took the rocker.

Cameron corrected the misconception about Marcus's profession. "I meant that Marcus keeps a journal about his activities, which includes his special talent of finding people who are reported missing in the mountains."

Julia stared at Marcus. "Wow. Does that happen often?"

He shook his head. "Only about fifty, sixty occurrences in my lifetime."

"And did you find any of the missing people?"

"I found a few of them. Even found one fella that didn't want to be found."

"Why not?"

Marcus laughed. "Remember me telling you about that old cuss, Cam?"

Cameron nodded.

"He wanted to lie low 'cause he'd robbed a half dozen banks in Asheville. I discovered him and his loot in Briarwood Cave at the base of Snowy Top."

"What did you do when you found him?" Julia asked.

"I kept my rifle trained on him, except for the one shot I fired to alert the sheriff." He gave Cameron a nearly toothless grin. "I lived for three years off that reward money. Of course, that was in the sixties, and things are different now. Today when somebody goes missing, there are swarms of searchers, park rangers, private citizens, sometimes even the FBI. I'm getting up in years so I don't come in on the search until they ask me, usually when all the professionals and psychics and the like have given up. That doesn't happen much anymore. I haven't been on a search in a good many years now."

He delivered a well-aimed stream of tobacco juice over the porch rail and set the rocker pitching. "It's just as well. The finding of bodies instead of living souls was beginning to break my spirit." He stared into the distance and shook his head slowly. "These mountains can be unforgiving if you don't respect them."

"Did you bring your journal like I asked you?" Cameron said.

"It's in my truck. I'll get it for you and then I got to leave soon. Only left my hounds one day's worth of food."

Cameron's eyes sparked with what could only be the flow of creative juices. "Wait till you see that journal," he said to Julia. "Marcus knows these mountains like the entire Blue Ridge had been etched in his mind. He knows how many paces a person has to walk from Thorny Creek to Misty Cove. He's given names to all the places the rest of us take for granted. He knows every tree and bush and what it's called and if a person can survive on its fruit. He knows which creeks have good drinking water. He's drawn his own maps and they're better than any you'd buy at the store. He…"

"That's enough going on about nothing, Cam." Marcus stood. "My journal is only good if you're looking for somebody. Otherwise, it's pretty dull reading."

"You're wrong," Cameron protested. "I told you that when I asked you to bring the journal to me. Your writings should be archived, preserved."

"Well, you can have it now, for whatever you want to do with it. Those findings aren't much good to me these days." He stepped down from the porch and tapped the side of his head. "Besides, all them things I wrote down are in here, anyway." He stepped off the porch and headed toward the corner of the cabin. "Can't imagine what you think is so all-fired important in my old scribbles."

When he'd disappeared around the side to retrieve the journal for Cameron, Julia tilted the crock and leaned back against the rough exterior wall. "That's one interesting man and an incredible story."

Cameron settled his hand on her arm. "He's only one."

His touch was warm, supportive. Liking the feel of it too much, Julia mumbled a response. "What do you mean?"

"That's why I'm here, to record the writings of people just like Marcus. Poets, chroniclers, storytellers, those who preserve the legends of the hills. Even people like you, a girl called MoonPie, who came from Whisper Mountain and wrote her way to New York City."

He looked down at his useless arm. "But I can't drive to interview these people. And I can't type to record their thoughts." His grasp on her arm tightened. A moment later, he said, "Julia, I know you've got a lot going on now, but..." He paused, keeping his gaze on her face.

She sensed where he was headed with this, and despite many misgivings was intrigued. "What are you trying to say, Cameron?"

"Do you think you could help me with it? Drive me a few places, input data on my computer—in essence, be my hands?"

Julia raised her face to stare at him with wide eyes. Cameron shook his head, slowly withdrew his hand from her arm and leaned back. He hadn't intended to ask Julia for anything more. Geez, she had enough on her plate. Besides, when he'd decided to come to Whisper Mountain, he had planned on isolation. And yet he'd just pleaded with this woman he barely knew to work alongside him day in, day out.

And now he didn't have any doubts that asking Julia to participate was the right thing to do, the completely natural thing, despite all the plans he'd made in Raleigh. He'd expected to come to the mountain to be alone, think through the last despairing year of his life and then bury the memories, and himself, in research until his mind didn't let him dwell on anything else. But Julia, his personal Florence Nightingale, had her own memories to bury. Perhaps they could help each other.

So he looked over at Julia, smiled, and said, "So what do you say?"

She blinked rapidly several times. "Where did this idea come from?"

He shrugged. "I don't know." That was true. "It just seems right." That was true, too.

"Well—" she paused "—well... it sounds fascinating, but I can't. I just couldn't."

He looked through the window at Katie, where she still sat at the table painting. "I understand." The disappointment that settled in his gut shocked him. His next words surprised him even more. "Katie's going to school, isn't she?"

"Yes, but…"

"When she's not in school, you could bring her here. I'd be glad to help with her if you think I can."

She stared beyond her car to the trail that led away from the mountaintop. "There's Mama, the store…"

He nodded. "I understand you want to help her. But when you're in Manhattan, doesn't she run the place by herself?"

"She has help, but she's also got to adjust to having Katie."

"And we already determined Katie could come here when she's not in school." Cameron's excitement was building.

Marcus returned with the journal. "Don't let me interrupt. I'll take this inside and see if you've got any grub."

Julia waited for him to cross the porch. Cameron thought she might continue her argument, but she didn't. He drew a deep breath and began to anticipate that, with a little more persuasion, she might agree.

"And you're a natural," he added. "You're a writer, and my guess is you're not writing anything now." He grinned at her. "I know what withdrawal from the keyboard can do."

"Cameron, I told you, I write criticism mostly. I don't know if I'm capable of doing what you need."

"I remember your writing, Julia. Ten years ago you were already very accomplished. I'm not worried. And a lot of this work will be research to start, and then compilation and commentary—not so different from what you do now." She started to shake her head, so he increased the logic of his argument. "And you've always liked American literature, haven't you?"

"Yes, you know I have."

"Well, this is our country's literature at its rawest, most basic, most emotionally revealing, written by individuals who have lived hard and experienced few rewards. I want to understand the people of the Blue Ridge through their own words, unfiltered and, in some cases, uneducated. This is an opportunity to delve into the real grit of American thought and uncover community traditions that link the past to the present in the southern Appalachians."

He took a breath, letting the fire of his enthusiasm simmer for a moment. Then, aware that he still had Julia's attention and the wheels of decision-making seemed to be turning, he pressed on. "And besides, you're from the area so you know your way around, even better than I do. This region must be in your blood, more than it is in mine since I grew up in Raleigh." She still didn't speak, so he continued. "And I'll pay you. Fifteen dollars an hour, for the home health-care and now this. I'd have to pay someone else to drive me around, so why shouldn't it be someone with knowledge of the Blue Ridge and talent with words?" He pointed his index finger at her. "That's you, Julia. The perfect package, as far as I'm concerned."

He looked away from her and gripped the arm of the rocker. Damn. Julia was everything he'd just said, and it suddenly hit him that he not only *needed* her to help him, he *wanted* her to.

How great would it be if he saw that youthful, eager spark of creativity he saw in her his first year of teaching? If she could experience the pride he felt in the humble surroundings of people just like his grandfather? Folks who, in many ways, were still pioneers and whose clarity of understanding often surpassed university-trained minds. He could picture Julia and him sitting before the fire here in his grandfather's house, their conversation flowing as fast and energetic as a rain-swollen mountain stream, their minds blended in a common thread, their purposes united. Their heads together…

He swallowed, tried to change the direction of his thoughts but couldn't. Their heads together, close, intimate… The intellectual image he'd imagined was mutating into something else entirely, and Cameron wasn't prepared for its possible significance.

He coughed, looked at her and saw an emotion in her eyes that reflected his own. She was right there, on the precipice of accepting his challenge. He leaned toward her. "Say yes, Julia."

She stared at him. "I don't know. I'll have to talk to Mama."

"Of course."

She stood. "I'll fix you a sandwich now, let you rest while I take Katie home. Then maybe later, I'll come back…"

"Great!"

She scowled at him, but it wasn't an expression of anger. He guessed that above all else she was irritated by her own desire to give in and accept his offer, to admit that he'd whetted her intellectual appetite. "To see how you are," she snapped. "Maybe I'll have made up my mind. Maybe not."

"Deal." He grinned and was rewarded by a reluctant smile.

"If Marcus left any food behind, I'll make you that sandwich now. Then you're on your own for a few hours."

As she went into the cabin, Cameron looked at his watch. A few hours couldn't come too soon.

CHAPTER SEVEN

WHAT'S REALLY going on here? Julia asked herself as she followed the twisting path down the mountain. *You shelved Cameron from your life when he proved to be blind to your feelings and asked out your sister. You told yourself that everything you'd believed about him wasn't true—that he wasn't the sensitive soul you'd imagined him to be. That he was like every other man who'd drifted up Whisper Mountain and set his sights on Tina only to discover she was as elusive as a mountain breeze.* "And now you're actually considering letting Cameron into your life again?" she said out loud. "You must be nuts."

But she knew that this time was different, and that scared the wits out of her. This time he wasn't her professor and she wasn't a naive coed who allowed her idealized version of a man to fill her waking thoughts and her nighttime dreams with fantasies. Now she'd realized that Cameron was three-dimensional. He wasn't perfect. He hurt, made mistakes, took chances, suffered, and—this was the problem—approached his life with even more passion than she'd suspected. He was real, and in ways she'd never thought about before, this was what could make him even more dangerous to her emotional well-being than he'd ever been as an ideal.

"What are you talking about, Aunt Julia?" Katie asked. "Your face looks funny."

Aware that she'd actually spoken some of her thoughts aloud, Julia glanced over at her niece. "Funny? How?"

"Like you're kinda happy but kinda scared, too."

Wow. How true. They arrived at the general store, and the steadily increasing whisper of the falls that could be heard from almost anywhere on the mountain had become the cacophony of unbridled energy cascading over granite walls. For Katie's sake, Julia forced Cameron to that dark part of her mind where he'd dwelled for many years and focused on her niece. "No, sweetie, I'm fine," she said.

"You are too scared," Katie said. "And I know why."

Julia parked and turned off the car engine. "You do? Okay, why am I scared?"

"You're worried about me going to school tomorrow."

Julia smiled. Leave it to an eight-year-old to put things into perspective. "I wasn't really so worried about that," she said. "But I'm thinking maybe you are."

Katie stared down at the coloring book and tin of watercolors in her lap. "It's okay if you don't get up in time to take me," she said.

Julia covered Katie's hand with her own. "Of course I'll get up," she said. "You can count on it."

"Sometimes Mommy didn't."

"What? Your mommy didn't get you ready for school every day?"

Katie shook her head. "Sometimes she didn't feel good, and I would wake up after the sun was way high, and I'd go in her room and tell her I was late for school. She'd say it was okay, that I didn't have to go that day and she'd write me a note."

Julia crossed her wrists over the steering wheel and stared out the front window. *Oh, Tina, what happened to you? When did you stop being the mother this child needed?* She sighed, looked at Katie. Nothing could be done about her sister's failings now. Tina had always thought of herself as the center of whatever universe she lived in. This was just another example of how that belief affected the lives of people around her. "Did that happen often?" Julia asked.

"Not when the principal called. Then Mommy would get up on time for a while. And one time a lady came to our house. She asked me to leave the room, but I listened at the door. She told Mommy she had to do better. Mommy got mad at her and I went to her room to find the alarm clock. I thought if I knew how to use it, I could wake up by myself and keep the lady from coming back and being angry with Mommy." Katie shrugged both slender shoulders. "But I couldn't find it."

Julia leaned over and hugged her niece. "I don't want you to worry about that here, sweetie. I have a very dependable clock, and it will wake me up in plenty of time to get your breakfast and help you get ready for school." There was no need to tell Katie that for the past few months, she'd seen many more sunrises than she'd missed, making an alarm practically obsolete in her life. She couldn't remember the last time she'd slept eight hours straight.

Katie drew back and stared into Julia's eyes. "So I guess I'm going then?"

"Yep. And tonight after supper, you, Grandma and I will pick out your clothes and put your supplies in your new backpack and decide what you want to have in your lunch bag. Then when we get up tomorrow, we won't have anything to do but fix your hair really nice and bundle you into the car. How does that sound?"

"Okay, I guess." She started to open the car door, but turned back. "Aunt Julia?"

"Yes?"

"Next week, if I'm still going to school, can I take cupcakes one day?"

"Maybe. Why do you want to?"

"Because in my old school, kids brought cupcakes on their birthdays and everybody sang."

"Oh, my gosh." Julia pictured her hand slapping against her forehead. "Your birthday. Of course, September twenty-seventh. I'll talk to your teacher tomorrow morning, and if she says it's okay, we'll bring cupcakes for everybody."

That settles it, Julia thought as she got out of the car. *I have enough to think about. This poor kid. Mama. The store.*

The Girl called MoonPie, who never even had the nerve to tell her mother to quit putting cakes in her lunch, who never had been able to say no to anybody, will tell Cameron that she can't do any more for him.

By EIGHT O'CLOCK, Julia had finished her chores. Katie was bathed, sweet-smelling and satisfied with the outfit they'd chosen for her first day as a Glen Springs chipmunk. Cora had put the dinner dishes away. The theme from *Jeopardy!* played softly from the console TV.

"I have to run back up to Cameron's," Julia said when she entered the living room after putting a load of clothes in the washer.

Cora looked up from her newspaper. "Now? It's dark."

Julia pulled back the curtain from the front window and looked out. "I do have headlights on the Toyota."

"I don't like you driving up this road at night."

"I'll be back before too long. I just have to check on my patient and talk to him for a few minutes."

Cora slipped her reading glasses to the tip of her nose. "What about?"

Since she'd made up her mind, Julia didn't have a reason not to tell her mother the purpose of this visit, so she said, "Nothing important. He asked me to help him with a writing project he's working on."

"Is it something you want to do?"

Yes. Maybe. "No. I have enough to think about around here."

Cora folded the newspaper into a neat square and placed it on her lap. "You don't have to hang around here all the time, Julia. Katie's going to school and I have Rosalie. It's enough that I know you're nearby when I need you. If there's something you want to do…"

"No, Mama. I'm going to tell him no."

Cora reached for the remote, turned off the television. "Fine. I was just saying that it would be okay with me."

Julia took her jacket from the hall stand. "I appreciate that, but I've decided."

"Well, hurry up then and get going. It's growing darker by the minute."

Julia stopped at the front door and took a long look at her mother. Suddenly filled with compassion for this woman who was trying, despite her grief, to give her daughter the freedom to live her own life, she said, "You know, Mama, you're still a very nice-looking woman."

Cora's brows came together in a doubtful scowl. "For heaven's sakes, Julia, what made you say that?"

"Nothing in particular. I just thought that you and I should stop at Pope's Drugstore tomorrow after we drop off Katie."

"What for? You have to get Cam's medicine?"

"Yes, but I was thinking you and I could shop, too."

Katie looked up from the book she was reading, made a sound almost like a giggle. An impish grin brightened her face. In that moment, she looked more like a normal happy girl than the somber child she'd been since coming to Whisper Mountain. She looked first at Julia, then Cora. "Watch out, Grandma. I think you're going to get some bubble bath."

JULIA GREW more nervous with each twist and turn up the mountain. The road seemed narrower, the night darker than she'd imagined. She needed her headlights just to pick out Josiah's cabin in the midst of its fortress of trees. But she was cheered by the soft light coming from the front room when she pulled up to the porch.

She got out of the car, went to the entrance and knocked. "Cameron?"

He appeared in the doorway, and her heart slammed against her ribs. "Look at you."

He held the screen door open for her. "Appearance-wise, I had nowhere to go but up," he said.

Dressed in a Whisper Mountain Falls T-shirt and a pair of loose-fitting athletic shorts, he looked relaxed, handsome, strong—if she didn't take into account the apparatus on his right arm. And clean. The abrasions he suffered in the accident had faded slightly to a yellowish purple. And Julia realized when she couldn't take her eyes off him that he'd become a pleasantly matured version of the professor from Riverton College who'd made her fall in love with...words.

The man before her now no longer had the bright, expectant glow of a recent graduate who must have considered the future his personal playing field. This Cameron Birch had lived life, with its triumphs and pitfalls, and his brushes with experience had left him leaner and seasoned, with lines of understanding and acceptance etched around his full mouth and confident, intelligent eyes.

Unfortunately the change in him had not lessened his effect on Julia, and she forced her gaze to the floor as she crossed in front of him to enter the room. Cameron still caused her pulse to race, and this fact only increased her resolve to resist whatever pull she'd felt toward this man in the past. She went to the fireplace and warmed her hands over the crackling logs. Pure pretense, since her palms were damp with perspiration and as flushed as she was certain her face was.

When she'd managed to quell a momentary panic, she turned toward him. "How did you take a shower?" she asked with feigned clinical curiosity.

"There were some plastic bags under the sink. I was able to tape one around my arm and keep the gauze dry."

"And how do you feel?"

"Pretty good. I took the next dose of painkillers as directed. I guess I'm going to need them for a while." He pointed to the seating area consisting of a pair of overstuffed easy chairs opposite a rustic plaid sofa. "Sit down, Julia. Do you want coffee?"

"No, I'm fine. I won't be staying." Despite that announcement, she walked to one of the chairs and sat. "I just came to check on you…and to give you my answer about working on your project."

He sat in the chair next to hers. A small end table separated them, and he fixed his eyes on her. "Don't keep me in suspense."

She swallowed. "I've thought about this long and hard, Cameron. With my circumstances what they are…you know, with Mama's grief and Katie's adjustment to a new environment…"

His eyes darkened, the only indication that he anticipated her answer. Well, if he was disappointed, that was too bad. She'd made up her mind. "And, of course, I'll be returning to Manhattan as soon as possible. I have my job to think of."

He nodded, remaining silent. He was going to accept her decision without arguing. Just as well.

"So…" She stared at him, waited for a sign, anything. A furrowing of his brow, a tightening of his lips. Nothing. Just a shadow over those brown-gold eyes. "So I'm afraid I must tell you…"

He leaned slightly forward. His left hand reached out, hovering inches from hers but failing to connect. And she felt somehow disconnected, herself, as if she was losing something vital to her existence.

"I must tell you…" the next words that came from her mouth were those of a stranger "…that I can only promise to try this arrangement for a while to see how it works." The hands of the stranger fluttered, pointed to him then back at herself in a gesture of reconnecting. "How we work together."

His grin seemed to light up the room. "Wonderful,

Julia! For a minute, I thought you were going to turn me down."

She averted her gaze and shook her head, lying to herself in silence.

"This is going to be great," he said. "I have no doubt we'll work together like two gears in the same machine."

She laughed self-consciously, still reeling from her sudden one-eighty. "That's perhaps a bit optimistic," she said.

"I don't think so." He patted her hand, a casual gesture that could have sealed a deal between two good buddies. And yet she felt his touch in a tingling pulse that ran all the way to her elbow. She pulled her hand away and stood. "Do you need anything else tonight?"

"No. I'm good. Better than good. I'm ready to get to work in the morning."

"Okay. I'll be here after I take Katie to school and stop for your prescription."

"And we can go over my notes."

She pointed to his wrist. "After we change the bandages."

"Right. After that."

"And then we have the weekend coming up. I'll have to help in the store some and be with Katie. The first day of school could be a challenge for her."

He smiled. "She's a Sommerville. She's strong," he said, and she didn't contradict him. "It'll all work out. You'll see."

She hesitated before walking to the door. Why, she didn't know. She wasn't going to take back her words, as unexpected as they'd been. She was committed now to trying this arrangement, and she'd just have to rationalize her temporary insanity with her tiredness or an atypical impulsive behavior or…whatever. Anything but the truth, because it scared her to think that she didn't rush out to her car simply because she didn't want to go. Finally, she went to the door and opened it. "I'll see you tomorrow, Cam."

He laughed. "I imagine I'll be here."

She got in her car and sat for a moment before inserting the key. "Now you've done it, Julia," she said. "I hope you're not risking more than you did by climbing down that gully. That was just physical."

KATIE'S TEACHER was a middle-aged fifteen-year veteran of the Glen Springs school district. She was heavyset, wore practical, creased tan slacks and a sky-blue blouse with a bow at the neck. Other ornamentation consisted of a wedding ring, a simple gold necklace with an apple charm and a leather-strap watch with large hands. She had a sweet, natural smile and a soft, kind voice. Julia was delighted with her and extremely relieved.

Mrs. Lunsford bent down to Katie's height when she came in the room. "We are so happy to have you join us," she said. "Some day you'll have to tell us all about that wonderful store on Whisper Mountain and that beautiful waterfall."

Wow. Julia grinned. This woman had done her homework. Julia slipped her a folded piece of paper. "My cell number," she mouthed.

Mrs. Lunsford stuck it in her pocket. "Very good, dear, but I think we'll be fine," she said. "But if it makes you feel better, I'll call you this afternoon."

"Yes, I would appreciate that." Wondering where this fairy-godmother teacher had been when she was in school, Julia said, "I'd like to know if it would be all right to bring cupcakes next Wednesday."

Mrs. Lunsford smiled at Katie. "That's right. Someone has a birthday coming up."

Katie looked up at Julia. The panic Julia had expected to see in her eyes wasn't there. But there was no enthusiasm, either. And no confidence. But an absence of panic was a good start. Bless you, Mrs. Lunsford. Julia gave Katie a hug, hoping that wasn't a public breach of peer acceptance and said, "I'll be on the sidewalk when school is over. I'll be so excited to hear about your day."

Katie allowed herself to be led to a desk near the teacher. She sat woodenly and watched Julia leave.

Cora was standing beside the Toyota when Julia reached the parking lot. "How d-did she do?"

They'd decided that only one of them would walk Katie into the building. If the separation proved to be difficult, it was easier to deal with one crisis than two. "She's okay," Julia said, giving her mother's arm a squeeze. "I think she'll be fine."

Cora wrung her hands anxiously and then opened the car door and got in. "Good. Let's do our errands."

They'd just left the school parking area when Cora said, "I suppose I should tell you. Wayne called last night while you were at Cam's."

Julia jammed her foot on the brake pedal, pulled off the road into a convenience store lot and put the car in Park. "What? You didn't tell me."

Cora loosened the seat belt, which had activated at Julia's sudden stop. "I know how you react to Wayne, and I thought I'd wait for a better time."

"Like when I'm driving a car?" When Cora didn't

respond, she said, "Sorry, Mama. What did Mr. Sensitive want?"

"He said he was staying in the cottage a while, and that he was still looking for a job. But he didn't know where he'd eventually end up."

"Very interesting, but did he say anything of any real importance? Did he ask about Katie?"

"Yes. He talked to her a minute."

Julia watched a mother and child leaving the store with a couple of Slurpees. "Swell."

"He said his finances were a little iffy at the moment."

"Iffy? He said *iffy?*"

"He didn't know when he'd be able to send money for Katie's care."

Julia gave her mother a deliberate stare. "We don't want or need his money!"

"Why would you say that, Julia? It's not like I'm made of money. You know I love Katie, but I wouldn't turn up my nose at a few extra dollars from the man who should be supporting her."

"Mama, if you need money, I'll give it to you. I don't want that creep to think he can buy his way back into Katie's life with a paltry contribution every now and then." Julia drummed her fingers on the steering wheel. Big talk from a woman who barely made ends meet.

"He's her father, Julia. He has a right…"

"You can't convince me he has any rights." *Not after how Tina died.* She was thankful she hadn't blurted out the reference to her sister. Then an even more distressing thought occurred to her. "He didn't say he wanted to see Katie, did he?"

Cora shook her head.

"Good. If he calls again, please tell him we're managing just fine."

"Okay, whatever you think is best."

POPE'S DRUGSTORE opened at nine, an hour before Cora's General Store. Being a few minutes early, Julia angle-parked at Glen Springs Circle, a pleasant, grassy area in the center of town where she and Cora could wait on a bench and watch citizens come and go from coffee shops and local businesses. By the time Linus Pope raised the blinds on his front entrance, Julia had let the cooling breeze from off the mountain take away the last of her resentment at Wayne. She took Cora's arm and they walked across the street.

"Good morning, ladies," Mr. Pope said when they came in. "You're up bright and early. I have that prescription for Cameron Birch you dropped off, Julia."

She stopped halfway down an aisle. "Thanks. I'll pick it up in a minute." She scanned labels on boxes, her finger tapping her bottom lip.

"What are you looking at hair color for?" Cora asked her. "I thought you paid a beautician to give you those streaks."

Julia raked her fingers through her hair. Cora had always thought her professionally applied blond highlights were a waste of money. "I'm not looking for me, Mama," she said.

"Well, then, who…"

Julia's grin tipped her off and Cora backed up a step. "Oh, no. Not me. I'm not going to get started with that nonsense. Have to spend money and time to color it every few weeks. No way. Besides, I don't have anybody interested in my looks these days."

Julia raised her eyebrows. "Oh, no?"

"Of course not. The only living souls I ever see are tourists and raccoons."

"And Oscar."

Cora's fists landed on her hips, and her voice raised an octave. "Oscar? The deliveryman Oscar? He doesn't pay me any mind."

"Yes, he does, Mama. He pays you lots of mind." She took a box from the shelf and pointed at the words on the front. "And he'd pay you even more mind if you covered those strands of gray with a *soft champagne blond.* You might even get him to say what's been sitting on the tip of his tongue."

"The only thing sitting on that man's tongue is icing from a Sunny Vale cupcake."

Julia cleared her throat to prepare for her best Italian accent. She touched her thumb against her index finger. "And the words, 'Ah, bella Cora, come with me to Vincenzo's where I can gaze across the table at linguini with clam sauce and your beautiful blue eyes.'"

Cora giggled. The sound was rusty and a bit muffled, but definitely a giggle.

Julia palmed the box of Miss Clairol and headed for the prescription counter. "And this is my treat. The beauty shop appointment I made for you on Wednesday is your responsibility."

Cora followed, her sensible Keds pounding softly on the linoleum. "You didn't!"

"I did. Now, come on. We've got to open the store, and I've got to get to Cam's place."

Cora chattered all the way to the counter. "Oscar delivers snacks to this drugstore, Julia. He could walk in here any minute. You get a sack and put that—that *package* in it right away. I don't want him seeing it and thinking…"

Julia shot her a grin over her shoulder. "Mama, it's not birth control. It's hair color."

"Julia Sommerville! I can't believe you just said that."

Julia set the box in front of Mr. Pope and gave her mom a wide smile. "Well, Mama, you're the one who raised me."

CHAPTER EIGHT

JULIA AND CORA opened the store at 9:45 a.m., and Rosalie showed up at 10:00 a.m. Julia waited a few minutes while the ladies counted the cash in the register, set hot dogs on the rotary grill and fired up the coffee machines. When she announced that she was leaving to go to Cameron's, neither lady seemed to hear her. Cora was going on about the silly purchase Julia had made that morning, and how she supposed she'd have to let her fiddle around with her hair, because "you know how persistent Julia can be."

"I'm going now," Julia repeated as she went out the door.

Cora looked up from arranging Whisper Mountain souvenir spoons on a velvet tray. "Tell Cameron I hope he's feeling better today."

"Will do." As Julia drove up the mountain, she wondered how she would react to her first attempt at dressing Cam's surgical wounds. She'd never been particularly squeamish. Living in the Appalachians, where a black bear population of more than two thousand meant less fortunate animals often ended up as roadside carcasses, didn't allow one to indulge every stomach twinge. Still, she was worried. Even though the nurse had described the incision points, Julia hadn't actually seen them. She had the nurse's phone number in the pocket of her jeans, and she patted the soft denim now to reassure herself that help was only a phone call away.

Cameron was sitting on the front porch when she pulled up to the cabin. He stood and waited for her to get out of the car. "Nice morning, isn't it?" he said.

Actually considering her answer, she walked toward the house and lifted her face to a crisp, clean breeze ruffling her hair. She paused at the steps, turned, and peered through a gap in the trees. Below her, a sweeping valley dipped in the morning sun and rose to meet the peaks of other mountains every bit as grand as the one she used to call home.

"It is," she said and looked at him. "And too chilly for you to be out here in shorts and a T-shirt."

"Never," he said, "unless it's snowing." He inhaled deeply. "This is a refreshing change from the stifling humidity of Raleigh. It must be twenty degrees cooler here than in the city." He frowned at his arm. "Besides, this sling is hot."

She opened the door. "You can take it off now so I can dress your arm. I just hope my nursing skills don't leave you wishing you could keep it on full time."

He grinned. "Let's do it."

He followed her inside where she accepted his offer of a mug of coffee. She took a few sips, hoping the warm brew would steady her nerves before gathering the medical supplies she needed. She washed her hands at the kitchen sink and realized the coffee might have been a mistake. She was jittery.

Cam sat at the table and rested his arm on top. Smiling at her, he said, "You're not nervous about doing this, are you?" He removed the sling, revealing yards of gauze wrapped around the rods and pins in his arm. "It's just a few holes, or so they told me."

She tried to laugh off the question. "Nervous? Me? I watched my father skin rabbits when I was five years old."

His eyes widened. "Gene skinned rabbits?"

She chuckled as she tore the tape from the end of the gauze strip. "No. Tina and I would have had a fit." When her fingertips brushed the skin on the back of his hand, she was keenly aware that her anxiety had less to do with coffee and the medical precision required and more with the personal nature of the task.

She removed the gauze from his palm first, slowly unraveling the end and gathering the surplus into a bunch, which she let accumulate on the table. Cameron watched her with an amused look on his face. "So far so good," he said when his hand was free of the wrapping and she began to unwind the strip from the first set of pins.

"Don't distract me," she said. "I have to pay attention to how the nurse wrapped these things."

"It's not rocket science, Julia, relax."

She nearly gasped aloud when she stared down at the first pair of entry points. Two rods, which had been inserted into his bones, protruded from half-inch slits in the skin on the back of his hand. The flesh around the slits was slightly puckered and pink. Julia had been told to expect this, but the sight still startled her. "Wow," she breathed. "I can't believe this doesn't hurt."

He kept his hand a few inches above the table, his fingers spread. "It doesn't." Then he smiled at her. "Not yet, anyway."

She kept unwinding the gauze until the next fixators at the side of his wrist were revealed and finally the last ones on his lower forearm. Six steel pins in total had been drilled into his bones during the surgery, each sticking up with a flexible rubber covering at the tip. When his wrist and hand were completely exposed, Cameron lifted his arm and studied the incisions. "Interesting," he said with detached curiosity.

She considered his observation an understatement. "Can you move your wrist at all?"

"No. But I think that's the point."

She took a deep breath. "Are you okay?"

"Sure. Why wouldn't I be?"

I don't know, but my heart is racing like mad. "No reason. But the hardest part is yet to come."

"You're doing fine," he encouraged. "And I'm kind of enjoying this." He let his hand fall into her palm and kept it there. "In fact, I was thinking of asking you for a manicure when you're done."

She smiled. "Not in my job description, Professor. You've got me doing enough around here."

"Okay. No manicure."

She opened a bottle of peroxide and a few extra long cotton swabs. Tightening her fingers around his hand to provide stability, she dipped the first swab into the bottle and swiped the fizzing liquid over the skin surrounding a surgical cut. She tried to be gentle but winced when he squeezed her hand. She stopped, looked up. "Did that hurt?"

"No." He straightened his fingers. "I don't know why I did that. Reflex, I guess."

She looked at the points where his fingertips had touched her skin, almost expecting to see a mark, a physical explanation for the current of energy he'd sent up her arm. There was only his hand, lying in hers, the undersides of his knuckles slightly rough and calloused, pleasantly abrasive against her own soft fingers. A couple of days ago, she would have thought it odd for an intellectual like Cameron to have hands almost like a workingman's, but she'd learned there was much more to this university professor than his scholarly environment suggested.

She forced her thoughts back to the procedure, tossed the first swab into the wastebasket and reached for another. "No problem. At least that proves you can still move your fingers."

"Yeah. That's a good thing." He paused, smiled at her again. "It's all good, Julia. You're a fine nurse."

"Right." She finished cleaning the rest of the incisions, applied antibiotic ointment provided by the hospital and wrapped fresh gauze in a pattern resembling that of the one established by the medical staff yesterday. "I think that about does it. How does it feel?"

"Just like when the professional did it yesterday."

She checked his blood pressure with a cuff on his left wrist and began packing up the supplies. "Okay, then, we're done."

"We haven't even started," he said, helping her clear the table. "Follow me." He went into the living room and walked to the table where Katie had been painting the day before and where his computer sat now. Tapping his index finger on the touch pad, he brought the hibernating machine to life. "I thought we might start with ballads," he said. "There's a lady over in Killdeer Hollow. I read about her in an obscure volume in the university library. She's the unofficial folklorist for southern Appalachian songwriters."

He navigated through several computer prompts

until a photo appeared on the screen. "I thought we might try to see her in the next few days, whenever you have time."

Julia stared at the faded black-and-white image of a woman who appeared to be in her mid to late thirties. She stood next to a rhododendron bush, which were plentiful in the Blue Ridge Mountains. She wore what looked to be a simple cotton blouse tucked into sensible twill trousers. Her hair was pulled severely away from her face, but a subtle smile softened her otherwise sober demeanor. Her name, Maude Doolittle, appeared next to the old photo, followed by a brief bio of her accomplishments.

"How long ago was this photo taken?" Julia asked.

"I'm not sure. I'd say at least forty years ago, maybe longer."

Julia read part of the paragraph aloud. "A native of Vickers County, North Carolina, Miss Doolittle earned her master's degree at Duke University. She worked for the Peace Corps as a linguist for six years before accepting a teaching position at her alma mater, where she pursued her doctorate degree."

She glanced up at Cameron who stood behind her looking over her shoulder. "This woman has her doctorate," she said. "Are you saying she lives in Killdeer Hollow now?"

"That's right. About an hour's drive from here."

Julia frowned. "Sure, if it's not raining or snowing. If it is, it doesn't matter how much time you have. There's no way into the hollow from the main roads."

He conceded with a shrug. "Let's hope the weather's good when we go."

Julia spoke softly, asking a question to herself as much as to Cam. "Why would a Duke professor be living in Killdeer Hollow? It's a little remote for academic pursuits."

"Maude is from there. Grew up in the Hollow."

"And she came back when she retired from teaching?"

He glanced away before giving an evasive answer. "Sort of."

"Sort of?"

"I've heard it's a long story. I don't know the details."

Julia studied the photo again. Something about Miss Doolittle was both fascinating and troubling. Her smile, which had appeared pleasant at first, suddenly seemed secretive, as if she knew things the rest of the world did not. "Have you contacted her? Does she know you want to talk to her?"

Cameron pulled a chair from the table and sat. "I tried to. No luck. I don't think she has a phone."

"No cell phone, even?"

"Don't know about that. Or if it would work in the Hollow if she did."

"So you're thinking that we'll just go there, into Killdeer, uninvited?"

"Julia, I don't think too many invitations are issued from the Hollow." He smiled at her, a knowing look in his eyes. "Hey, you're not worried about going there, are you?"

"Me? No." *Well, yes, a little.*

"It's not like the old days. There aren't any continuing feuds that I know of. No moonshiners or bootleggers. And *Deliverance* was filmed in an entirely different location."

She narrowed her eyes at him, once again trying to reconcile this overtly practical and adventurous side of Cameron Birch with the serious academic she used to know. This Cameron had rolled his Jeep in the Rockies and risked Whisper Mountain in the middle of a storm. Why should she be surprised now that he was willing to trek into Killdeer Hollow without a care. She almost hated to burst his bubble with an irrefutable fact that would keep them from venturing into the wild. But he had to face reality. She leaned toward him, spoke in her most sensible voice. "There's one thing you haven't considered," she said.

"Oh, I doubt it."

Smart-ass. "I'm your driver and I have a four-cylinder compact car that takes to these mountains like a turtle to a NASCAR track. We'll get as far as the first shallow creek bed and have to call a tow truck."

He responded with a nod. "You're probably right. *If* we took the Toyota."

"Thank you…I think."

"What time is it?" he asked.

Dumbfounded at the change in conversational direction, she checked her watch. "11:30 a.m."

"Let's start thinking of questions to ask Professor Doolittle. We might not have much time. I'm expecting a delivery." He stopped, leaned toward the open screen door. "Do you hear that?"

She heard the faint hum of an engine. "Yes. What is it?"

He stood. "Come with me."

She followed him out the front door just as a pair of vehicles came up the path. One was a shiny pickup truck with the name of a rental car agency emblazoned on the door. The other was a bright yellow utility vehicle. The SUV coasted to a stop by the front porch and purred with the self-satisfied ease of a powerful engine that hadn't even gotten its second wind yet.

Julia stared at Cameron. "What's this?"

"A Nissan Xterra," he said.

"You rented it?"

"Yep. Complete with all 265 horses, six cylinders, rack and pinion steering and double stabilizer bars. Not to mention off-road performance shocks and dual-tread, steel-belted radial tires." He beamed at Julia. "This vehicle is almost as trustworthy as my Jeep... almost."

The driver of the Xterra got out. A stack of paperwork caught the breeze and fluttered in his hand. "Are you Cameron Birch?" he asked.

Cameron placed his good hand on the small of Julia's back and took her with him down the porch steps. "That's me."

"Long way up here."

"Yes, it is. That's why I was glad to see you have delivery service."

The man approached, giving Cameron's arm a serious once-over. "Are you going to drive the Xterra? Because I have to tell you, our insurance..."

"No, not me," Cameron said. He slung his left arm over Julia's shoulder. "She's the driver, an expert at navigating any road in the mountains."

"Okay, then." The agency rep gave the paperwork and a pen to Cameron. "Can you sign?"

"Left-handed, but it'll have to do."

Next the rep asked to see Julia's driver's license.

She headed toward the house for her purse, trying to ignore a rush of excitement. In some deep, previously unrecognized part of her, there existed a woman who secretly longed to get behind the wheel of a spunky off-road vehicle.

"SO HOW'D YOU do it?" Julia asked when she and Cameron had finished lunch and established priorities for their interview with Maude Doolittle.

"Do what?"

"You don't have your cell phone. How'd you contact the car rental agency?"

"Nothing to it." He stood up from the kitchen table, walked to a large cupboard and opened the doors. "My grandfather lost phone service in a storm a few months after my grandmother died. That was twenty some years ago. He never had a landline reconnected."

He stepped back and revealed an elaborate electrical box, with a microphone sitting in front. "This is all he ever used until he got a cell phone."

Julia came close, examined the dials and settings on the box. Guessing its function, she said, "That's a ham radio?"

"Yes, it is. Gramps bought it a few years after the war."

She stared at Cameron's satisfied expression. "And you know how to use it?"

"Sure. He made me learn when I was kid so I'd be able to get help if we ever needed it."

"And you ordered a rental car with it?"

He laughed. "Well, no. Marcus called and ordered it for me after he got home last night. He has a ham also. He and Gramps used to radio back and forth when Marcus was searching for missing people." Cameron patted the top of the box. "They never had any problems with these trusty radios. They pick up signals anywhere in the mountains and they work fine on backup generators. With a radio like this, you can contact anyone in the world if you're patient enough."

"So you radioed Marcus and gave him the specifics of the automobile you wanted."

"Right. And using his regular phone, he called and arranged for the delivery."

"Clever. But you still need a phone. There aren't many ham operators anymore."

"True, although there are still a few in the Appalachians. More than you would think." He closed the cupboard doors. "But don't worry—I asked Marcus to order me a cell phone, too. It's supposed to be delivered by five o'clock today."

This man was nothing if not resourceful. "Then you won't need the ham radio anymore."

"Oh, I have a use for it. I'll try to find a contact in the Hollow to see if Maude still lives there and if she'd welcome company on Monday, if that works for you. It's the best way to reach someone like Maude who doesn't have a listing."

Julia washed the lunch dishes and put them in the drainer. "Something tells me Monday is going to be an adventure."

He grinned at her. "Something tells *me* you're going to love it."

She looked at her watch. "I have to go. School will be out soon."

"When will you be back?"

"Tomorrow. As soon as I can get here. I'll probably bring Katie with me."

"Sounds good. Tell her I want to see that finished picture."

Julia picked up her keys, headed for the front door but stopped before going out. "One more thing, Cameron."

"Yeah?"

"Call me tonight with your new phone number."

He returned a teasing look. "That's a challenge, isn't it? You don't think I'll have one."

"Oh, no. I'm sure you will." *I'm starting to think there isn't much you can't do.* "You know, I'm wondering what you'd be like with two healthy hands."

He followed her to the door. "I'm good, Julia. Hopefully you'll stick around long enough to let me prove it to you."

She blushed, hating herself for reacting to what was no doubt an innocent statement.

If he noticed her discomfort, he didn't let on. "But even if I had two good hands now," he said, "I'd still want you working with me, so don't worry. Your job is safe."

As she headed back toward Whisper Mountain Falls, Julia decided it wasn't her job she was concerned about. Her heart was beating a warning of its own.

KATIE WAS AMONG the first dozen children who appeared on the sidewalk after the dismissal bell. She spotted Julia right away and hurried to meet her.

They walked together to the car. Julia waited until Katie had removed her backpack and set it in the rear seat. "So how'd it go today?" she asked when they were both buckled in.

"Okay."

"Did you meet any kids?"

Katie stared out the front window. "No."

"Did you like your lunch?"

"Yes."

"Was the work hard?"

"No."

"Do you have any homework?"

"A little."

Julia glanced at her niece, waited for her to return the look. "Are you going back on Monday?"

Katie chewed on her bottom lip. "I guess I could give it another day."

Whew! Julia realized she'd lucked out with Katie's answer to a question that left an eight-year-old too many options.

Katie took an envelope from her jeans pocket. "The principal wanted me to give this note to you."

Since they were at a red light, Julia opened the envelope. Inside was a brief note from Mr. Dickson confirming that he'd talked to the school psychologist, as well as a more elaborate memo from the therapist herself, whose name was Marilyn Marshall. Miss Marshall explained that she'd spoken to Katie today and had made a preliminary evaluation of her situation. She indicated she found nothing overtly alarming in Katie's demeanor, but she would continue to meet with her and notify Julia if findings suggested more analysis was required.

While relieved that the school had taken measures to meet Katie's needs, Julia hoped the psychologist would follow up with more sessions as she promised.

"What does the note say?" Katie asked.

"Only that a lady talked to you today. Was that all right with you?"

Katie shrugged. "She was nice. Why did she want to see me?"

Julia thought a moment and opted to tell the truth. "She talks to kids who are sad because something bad has happened in their lives."

"Like their mommy dying?"

"Yes, like that." The light changed, and Julia had to look at the road. "You and I haven't talked much about that, and I think it would help you to meet with someone who could understand your feelings. Would you talk to her again?"

A huge sigh preceded Katie's answer. "I suppose. But only because I can't talk to you."

Julia blinked, replayed her niece's words in her mind. When had she given Katie the impression that she wouldn't listen to anything she had to say about her mother? "You can talk to me, honey. About anything, anytime."

"Not about this," Katie said. "Because I know you must be sad, too, and so is Grandma. I don't want to make you sadder."

Julia regretted having turned onto Whisper Mountain Road because she had to pay extra attention to her driving. Right now, all she wanted to do was wrap her niece in a protective hug. She cast a quick glance at Katie, saw her shoulders hunched in a sort of determined acceptance. "Oh, honey, I am sad, but you won't make me any sadder. You can talk to this lady at school. I think it's a good idea. But, please know that you can also talk to me whenever you need to."

She reached over and patted Katie's arm. "That's why I'm here. So you can talk to me or cry with me or even yell at me if you want to. Sometimes things happen to us in life that just aren't fair and it's not good to keep your anger and sadness locked up inside." She smiled. "Understand, Katie? You're a brave girl, and I'm proud of you. But you have to know that if you need me, my shoulders are strong enough for both of us."

Katie didn't say anything, but nodded once.

And Julia realized that she'd just spoken the truth and that her shoulders *were* able to bear a little more weight than they had just a week ago. And surprisingly, some of that strength had come from this child.

CHAPTER NINE

SATURDAY BROUGHT another picture-perfect morning. The sky was crystalline blue, the breeze from the top of Whisper Mountain fresh and sweet with the scent of the last of the summer wildflowers. Julia waited until Rosalie came to the store before announcing that she and Katie were heading up to Cameron's.

Cora glanced over from the revolving rack of postcards she was rearranging. "How long will you be?"

"We might stay through lunch if you think you can spare us," Julia said.

"It takes that long to dress Cam's wounds?"

"Well, no…" Julia paused, acutely aware she hadn't told her mother that she'd changed her mind about helping Cameron with his project. "I have some things to discuss with Cameron," she finally said, sensing the gleam in her mother's eyes had nothing to do with the scenic pictures on postcards she'd sold for years.

Cora stepped away from the rack. "You're helping him with his work, aren't you?"

In the past, Cora's woman's intuition had functioned in spurts, most effective when Julia was trying to hide something and practically nonexistent when Tina was. True to form, she'd honed in on Julia's thoughts. "Yes. I told him I would."

Cora smiled. "Good. Maybe you'll forget all this makeover nonsense you've got going on with me and put your creative juices into Cam's activities."

Julia laughed. "Not on your life, Mama. Don't make any plans for tonight. It's going to be Miss Clairol time." She picked up Katie's schoolbooks and drawing pad, took her hand and headed for the door. Setting foot onto the porch, she heard Rosalie's enthusiastic chatter as she pursued the makeover topic. As expected, Cora feigned irritation. But there was no mistaking the edge of excitement in her voice while she pretended to criticize her daughter's extravagance.

In the parking lot, Julia took her cell phone from her pocket and programmed Cam's number into her list of contacts. She started her car and pressed the key that now automatically dialed his number. He answered on the second ring. "You on your way?"

"Yep. I've got Katie with me."

"Great. Tell her I've got something to show her."

"Okay. She's got homework to do."

"This won't take long."

When they reached the cabin, Katie set up her work on the coffee table and Julia listened to Cameron's explanations of the native ballads he'd collected from the Internet over the past couple of months. "Of course, these are well-publicized ballads from this region that everyone knows," he said. "But I believe Maude Doolittle has dozens of truly rare ones."

"I wonder why she never had them published," Julia said.

"I don't know, but I'm hoping to change her mind about that. We need to convince her to agree to a collaboration."

Julia snickered. "Sure, no problem. I'm an entertainment critic for a major Manhattan glitz magazine. Why wouldn't she trust me with her private collection of mountain lore?"

Cameron smiled, obviously recognizing her sarcasm but refusing to let it bother him. He cupped her chin in his hand and tipped her face up. "Exactly. But even if she is a little reluctant to put faith in your credentials, all she has to do is look into these soul-searching eyes and she'll willingly unlock the mysteries of the Blue Ridge in a heartbeat."

Julia sat perfectly still until Cameron withdrew his hand, leaving her with a strange sense of longing. She gave her head a shake. "Right. And since I'm so trustworthy, let's get busy with cleaning those pins and changing your bandages."

They went into the kitchen, where he'd already set up the supplies. Julia applied peroxide to the pin points and redressed the wrist, shaving at least a minute off yesterday's time. "You're getting good at this already," he said when he slipped his arm through the sling again.

"Yeah, I can see a whole new career for myself. As long as enough people break their wrists by driving off the edge of a mountain, I'll be a success."

He packed up the supplies. "There must be a few of us out there."

Julia walked toward the living room. "I'll start looking over those ballads now. Maybe I can find some common themes so we can sort them into categories."

"Great idea. In the meantime, can you send Katie out here?"

"Okay." Julia brought Katie into the room.

"How would you like to do a little exploring this morning, Katie?" Cameron asked her.

"It'd be okay, I suppose," she answered, her voice typically flat and uninspired.

"I thought we might look for wildflowers while they're still blooming."

Katie scratched at a spot on her arm. "Okay." She looked at Julia. "Are you coming, too?"

Julia declined, not wanting to intrude on an opportunity for Katie to bond with someone else. "I've got a lot to do here. But you go ahead."

Cameron held out his hand, and Katie took a tentative step toward him. "How far will we go?" she asked.

He smiled, opened the back door and pointed through the screened porch. "Not far. Just to the edge of that stand of maple trees. Your aunt will be able to see us out the window the whole time."

Katie approached, placed her small hand in his. "What kind of flowers will we see?"

"All different kinds, but today I thought we'd look especially for the shy ones."

Her eyes widened. "Shy flowers?"

"Absolutely. They're scared to show themselves to anyone. That's why they bloom upside down."

Katie walked outside. Julia sighed with relief and went to the door. Another baby step for Katie.

"How do they do that?" Katie asked, her face lifted toward Cameron's.

"Their blossoms are underneath the leaves. Have you ever heard of a shrinking violet?"

Katie nodded.

"That's kind of what these are. Quiet but exceptionally brilliant."

Cameron and Katie stepped off the porch. He picked up an old basket from the ground and looped it over the pins on his hand. His voice, strong and confident, faded in the whisper of the mountain breeze. "We're going to find Wood Sorrels and May-apples and maybe even a Little Brown Jug or two. But we have to look very carefully or we'll miss them."

Katie nodded with new understanding. "Right. Because they're shy."

A half hour later, Julia returned to the kitchen and looked out the window. They were still there at the edge of the forest, Cameron bent over, holding a small bit of greenery. And Katie, her hand outstretched toward his, reaching to take it. Julia drew a trembling breath. She was suddenly filled with gratitude for the man who had once tantalized her senses with the beauty of the written word and who now shared his love for the mountains with a sad little girl who seemed equally spellbound by his unique way of looking at the world. And yet, despite the warmth seeping through every inch of her, Julia felt an indistinct longing once again, as if perhaps she had missed something very special by staying in the cabin to read ballads.

LATE SATURDAY AFTERNOON, Cameron sat on the front porch of his grandfather's house. The mountains rolled ahead of him, crowned with venerable trees whose leaves rustled in a soft Appalachian breeze. Perhaps it was this sense of timelessness and endurance that drew him back here after so many years. Perhaps it was the sense of calm that came over him whenever he contemplated a sky that stretched beyond hills and valleys so green they appeared as a carpet undulating hundreds of feet below. Certainly it was the sense of mystery held deep in the mountains, mysteries he longed to uncover and record for posterity.

He took a sip from the glass of iced tea Julia had made for him before she left with the little girl. When he'd suggested the trip to the herb porch for a natural sweetener, she'd agreed to add a sprig of his grandfather's peppermint to the mix. The drink tasted smooth, a little tangy, a little spicy on his tongue.

The day had been fruitful, as well. Julia's enthusiasm for the ballads of the hill people reinforced that he was right to ask her to help him. She was still a bright, willing woman eager for knowledge. Only this Julia revealed dimensions of her personality he'd never have discovered if he hadn't met her again. Now her zest for reading and writing was tempered with maturity, clarity and the beginning of a passion that might someday rival his own.

Cameron set his glass on the rustic pine table beside the rocking chair, leaned his head back and let an image of Julia as she'd looked this afternoon fill his mind. He'd come in with Katie after collecting flowers and walked into the living room where Julia sat poring over the ballads he'd saved to his computer. Her long hair had been fastened with a tortoise shell clip, leaving strands of it curling against her temples and framing her rimless reading glasses. Silver earrings with tiny green stones twinkled in the light from the living-room window.

He'd felt the intensity of her thought from across the room. When she'd looked up, the spell of concentration was broken, but Cameron hadn't regretted the loss because her smile had filled the void.

What was it about Julia that made him so comfortable in her presence? She was quieter than the women he'd been drawn to in the past. Her very seriousness, so much like his own, should have made him wary of being alone with her. He'd always chosen outgoing, vibrant women who'd bridged the gaps in his personality.

It wasn't that he was a loner exactly, except for those occasions, and perhaps there had been too many of them in his thirty-five years, when he chose to be by himself. Cameron was at ease alone, sleeping in his tent in the mountains, camped on the stark landscape of a Midwest plain, behind the wheel of his twenty-eight-foot sloop on a mirror-smooth lake. These times were golden, and he'd only ever had his grandfather to share them with. Yet he'd experienced a pleasant anticipation when he'd thought of Julia's arrival today. And even a satisfaction in spending time with her distraught, suffering niece.

Katie. A sweet, withdrawn, but obviously bright child. Cameron didn't know much about children. Mostly he just had a gut-level desire to have one or two…or three of his own. And being with Katie today only reinforced that desire, though the child was nothing like her mother.

Tina Sommerville had been a burst of sunlight in his otherwise staid, academic existence. He thought about her now and might have continued to relive those few months in his mind, but his cell phone rang. The image of Julia's golden-haired, laughing sister faded as he reached for the phone, expecting to see Julia's number on the digital screen. *She's probably had another idea,* he thought. *Another way of approaching Maude Doolittle on Monday.*

But it wasn't Julia's number he saw. It was his parents'. He hit the Connect button. "Hey."

"Son, it's Dad."

"How are you?"

"Fine, but this call isn't about me. How are *you?*"

Cameron had phoned his parents the night before when he'd received his new phone. His mother had gotten on the kitchen extension, and he'd told them about the accident, his surgery and expected recuperation time. They'd reacted as he'd thought they would. His father had asked the sensible questions. Do you have everything you need? Did you get the best medical care? Do you want us to send money?

His mother had cried and ordered him to come home. And Cameron had reminded her that he was thirty-five years old.

"I'm fine, Dad," he said now. "I have all the help I need."

"I'm calling while your mother's at her bridge club," Michael Birch said. "She gets upset thinking about you being all alone in that cabin."

Cameron sighed. "I'm not all alone. I told you yesterday that a very nice young woman is seeing to my medical care. She's working out beautifully."

A derisive snort was his father's initial reaction. "I'll bet. She's probably boiling up potions and applying native poultices...."

Cameron reined in his impatience. His father was basically a caring, practical man, but he had never been able to reconcile his own fast-paced lifestyle with the one his father, Josiah, had chosen. Michael Birch was not a man of the mountains. "No, she's not," he said, masking his irritation as well as he could. "She's following the doctor's orders."

"I still don't know why you wanted to go up to that godforsaken cabin in the first place. We would have picked you up, brought you back here to Raleigh where you would have gotten the best care."

"I'm getting the best care, Dad. I've got a broken wrist. It's not complicated. It's been pinned back together and will require a few months of healing time. That wouldn't change if I were sitting at home."

"I know your mother will want me to ask you one more time…are you sure you don't want us to come there? I could take a few days away from the office."

"No. There's nothing you can do for me that isn't already being done. And besides, I need this time to work on my research project."

"And to forget about Louisa, you mean?"

There was no point denying what his family knew to be true. "Yes, that, too."

"By the way, her candidacy is in full swing. I can't believe she's going to be elected to the State House of Representatives. But her posters are everywhere. She's got an aggressive television campaign."

Cameron stood. He walked to the porch rail to better view the mountains and restore the sense of peace he'd felt just minutes before. "Good for her. She'll have what she wants then."

"She won't get our votes. It's all I can do not to tell everyone on the street what she did."

"Don't do it, Dad," Cameron warned.

"That was your baby, too, and she had no right to abort…" His voice hitched.

Cameron tried to ignore the all-too-familiar ache in his chest. "We've been over this. You've got to let it go."

"She lied to her own husband. She'll deceive her constituents, too."

"She won't. She has principles where her political

career is concerned." *Ones she didn't extend to me.* "She wants to get ahead and will do what she has to."

After an uncomfortable silence, Michael said, "She called here the other day."

Not long ago, this announcement would have caused a reaction in Cam. Sadness, regret, anger. Now he felt nothing. "What did she want?"

"She heard you'd taken a sabbatical. Wanted to know where you were."

"I hope you told her. If she knows I'm at Whisper Mountain, she won't even consider tracking me down. She hates this place and it isn't in her voting district."

Michael chuckled. "I guess there is one advantage to your being in the wilds, son."

If you only knew, Dad. "Tell Mom I'm fine, okay? Because I am. I really am." After disconnecting, he returned to the rocker and set it pitching at a slow, even rhythm.

Louisa was a political-science instructor at NC State. Slightly older than Cameron, she'd fired his admiration from the moment he met her at a faculty dinner. She was learned, powerful, ambitious.

Tina. A flash of pure brilliance, like a firefly in a meadow, fleeting, always out of reach. Free, wild, fickle. The two women who'd most affected his life, neither of them anything like him. Yet they'd made him the cynical man he was today, determined to leave the voice of romance to poets and songwriters. Twice burned, he thought. Never again.

He got up and went into the cabin among the familiar things he'd come to reconnect with on Whisper Mountain. He sat down in front of the computer, the one link to Raleigh that he couldn't leave behind, and put his mind to work. That's why he was here—to work his mind.

BY NINE O'CLOCK Monday morning, the sparkling Xterra was blazing down the four-lane highway that ran through the center of Vickers County to country roads that wound deep into the forests. Both windows were down and the voice of Emmylou Harris blasted from the car speakers.

Cameron pulled his arm from the sling and rested his elbow on the door frame. He smiled at Julia. "Did I forget to mention the Fosgate audio package that came with this SUV?"

She stopped humming along to "Beneath Still Waters." "Yes, you did, and it's the feature I like best about it."

"Have to admit, this sound system puts the one in the Jeep to shame. Good thing the Jeep has so much cool going for it in other areas."

She laughed. "Yeah. It looked really cool stuck in the mud of the ravine."

"Hey, that truck will be back, better than ever, you'll see." He reached down to the floor and picked up a plastic CD case. "Don't forget, on the way back we listen to my pick."

"I remember. A deal's a deal, though I never figured you for a Bruce Springsteen fan."

"There's a lot you don't know about me," he said.

She'd been thinking that very thing for days now, all the while finding herself much too fascinated with the things she'd learned. "I hope one of your hidden talents is getting along with folks in the Hollow," she said.

"No problem." He pointed to a sign a few hundred yards up the highway. "County Road 312. This is it, Julia."

At the end of the off-ramp, she turned right onto a paved two-lane road as he instructed. "How far?"

"About another twenty miles. But only eight on this road. After the next turn, I imagine the going will get rough." He moved his index finger over an inch of the map in his lap. "The road we take after this is nothing more than a faint black line that hardly shows on the map."

"Great."

He was silent for a few minutes and then said, "Do you know how Killdeer Hollow got its name?"

"I know there's a bird called killdeer."

"Right. And it's the nature of that bird that made the locals apply it to the Hollow."

"What is the nature of a killdeer?"

"Sneaky. My grandfather pointed one out to me once. It was just sitting by the side of the road, not moving. Looked like one of its wings was broken. I felt bad for the poor creature and thought I'd rescue it. I went closer, and it flopped around and tried to fly but couldn't."

"That's not sneaky," Julia said. "It's sad."

He grinned at her. "Right. That's what you're supposed to think. It's all part of the killdeer's plan. When I got close enough to almost reach out and grab the bird, its wing suddenly healed and it took off into the air, with a screech that mimics its name. That's what these birds do. If they sense someone is too near their babies, they pretend to be sick and draw the culprit away from the nest."

Julia laughed. "That's one smart and very protective bird."

"The old-timers used to say the Hollow is like the killdeer. It pulls you in until you think you know your way around. But then the light and the shadows and the sounds from the underbrush play tricks on you and you follow the wrong path and end up wandering without direction. The moral is, the next time a trespasser considers going into the Hollow without an invitation, he'll think twice."

Julia shot a quick glance at him. "It's just a tall tale if you ask me," she said.

"Maybe so, but I saw that look on your face. It was the look of a woman determined to research the killdeer so she'd recognize one if she saw it and never be taken in by its antics." He tapped the CD case against his leg. "Even tall tales have a lesson," he said after a moment. "People tend to exaggerate for a reason."

Julia thought of the clever killdeer and decided Cameron was right. But the moral of the story wasn't to sharpen one's wits to avoid being the victim of a cunning scam. No. The point of the story was that parents will go to any length to protect their young. Maybe Tina had sacrificed herself to save Katie. Julia fought another stab of guilt. If only someone had been there to save Tina.

JULIA SENSED Cameron's excitement mounting with each bounce and shock absorption of the intrepid SUV. They'd just made their third and last turn onto a narrow rutted road that wound through dense trees, natural vegetation and dry creek beds. More primitive, private lanes ran off in different directions, their destinations the decades-old homes of the folks of the Hollow. Here, on the hillsides sloping up from the bottomland, people still lived in the original cabins of their ancestors, some as simple as the day they were built, others modernized with room additions, electricity and satellite dishes.

An excellent navigator, Cameron consulted the directions he'd gotten from a ham operator who'd confirmed that Maude Doolittle did indeed live in Killdeer Hollow. As to whether the lady would welcome company, Cam's contact couldn't say, but he provided directions to her cabin, which included passing the community-school bus stop and general store, counting mailboxes and marking the distance from a tin-roofed covered bridge.

"Slow down," Cameron said when they approached an old pickup fender now serving as a planter for geraniums. "That's our marker. We're here." The name *Maude* had been spray-painted across the front of the bumper. And straight ahead about a hundred yards away sat a simple log house with bright red shutters next to its windows and oak buckets full of flowers on the front porch.

Julia pulled close to the house and parked. She and Cameron got out and walked to the steps leading to the small porch. They hadn't climbed the first one when a strong voice came from behind them. "If you're looking for Maude Doolittle, she isn't in there."

They both turned and saw a tall, willowy woman whose advanced age could only be estimated by the crude wooden walking stick in her hand and a mass of pure white hair reaching halfway down her back. She wasn't alone. A large heavily furred dog stood by her side. While the animal made no sound or outward show of aggression, the hackles on its back bristled, indicating alertness and a readiness to defend its master.

Cameron took one step forward. So did the dog. Cameron moved in front of Julia and stretched out his left arm, a subtle warning to the animal. The woman placed her hand on the dog's powerful neck. Recognizing a signal, it sat back, waiting. "Professor Doolittle?" Cameron said.

"I am. You must be the one who radioed Tucker Deeds to inquire about my whereabouts."

"Yes. I'm Cameron Birch." He stepped back and indicated Julia. "This is a friend, Julia Sommerville."

Julia attempted a smile, but gave up when it was met with a deliberate frown.

Undaunted, Cameron continued. "I would have contacted you directly but I couldn't find a phone listing or address for you."

Her sharp gaze honed in on his face. "There's a reason for that."

"I'm sure there is. And I don't intend to intrude on your privacy for very long."

She squinted, leaned forward. "You're a tourist. I don't talk to tourists."

"No, I'm not. What made you think that?"

"You're wearing one of those cheap T-shirts produced by poor Chinese laborers."

Julia sucked in a deep breath and held her tongue. Sensing her indignation, Cameron raised his hand in a placating way.

She croaked in his ear. "They're not cheap. They're made in the U.S.A. and Mama pays the manufacturer in Charlotte almost five dollars a piece for them."

"Okay," he mumbled, "but let's not make an issue…" He stopped, thought a moment and said, "I paid $17.99 for this shirt."

Julia looked straight ahead. "You're right. Let's not make an issue of it."

He looked at Maude. "Believe me, Professor Doolittle, we're not tourists." He glanced down at the shirt.

"I'm only wearing this because all my clothes were ruined the other day. I had to purchase these at the store on Whisper Mountain Road."

She appeared to weigh the veracity of his claim. "I don't take to tourists coming into the Hollow in their fancy little off-roaders to stare at us backwoods hillbillies. We don't like our privacy invaded with video cameras and nosy hikers in their outfitters gear."

"No, I'm sure you don't. Julia and I aren't like that. We're here for a specific reason."

"Then state it and be on your way."

This woman was not just unsociable. She was rude. And Julia was in favor of sacrificing an attempt to interview her. Obviously she was not willing to cooperate. She studied Cameron's face, looking for a sign of a similar reaction. Unlike her, he appeared unruffled by Professor Doolittle's demeanor.

"I'd be happy to," he said. "I just want to ask you a few questions about a collection of folklore ballads I understand you've kept through the years. I'm from the university…"

Maude Doolittle strode forward and jabbed her walking stick in the air aligned with Cameron's chest. Her dog bared its teeth and matched her step for step. "The university?" she said. "That settles it. Get in your car and leave Killdeer immediately."

CHAPTER TEN

JULIA CLENCHED her fists at her sides and counted to ten. She didn't know if she wanted to bolt for the car or march up to Maude Doolittle and show her she wasn't the only one who could be rude. Neither option being conducive to their purpose in coming here today, she instead gave Cameron a warning look strongly suggesting that he defuse the situation.

He glanced at Maude, his wounded arm and then followed with a self-deprecating grin. "Look, Professor Doolittle, we don't mean any harm. I couldn't cause any even if I did. I just want to talk to you."

She lowered her cane but only to pound it into the dirt with each word. "I don't talk to people from that university."

"But that's…" He paused, scratched the back of his neck and said, "Do you mean Duke University, where you used to teach?"

"Of course that's what I mean. I don't associate with anyone from that bastion of right-wing do-gooders."

He rolled his eyes at Julia. "I'm not from Duke. I'm part of the faculty at North Carolina State in Raleigh. I teach literature courses there."

She squinted suspiciously at him. "For all I know it's just as bad there."

"I don't think so, but anyway, I'm not *there* now. Won't be for a year. I'm on sabbatical. That's why I've come to see you."

Maude pointed the cane again, this time at Julia. "And her?"

"She's from Whisper Mountain. Went to school at Riverton, an hour's drive from here."

"I know Riverton," Maude said. Her voice mellowed a notch, suggesting that she thought Riverton wasn't quite as bad as Duke. "Good school," she added. "Basically good folks at Riverton. I taught a couple of classes there in the late seventies."

"I taught there, too," Cameron said, cashing in on the common thread. "Can we sit down and talk, Professor Doolittle? Wherever you want. Inside or right here on your porch if you're more comfortable."

She considered his proposal for a good twenty seconds before pointing the walking stick toward her front steps. "Go on. I guess you're all right." She headed for the porch. "But when I say we're done talking, we're done."

"Absolutely." The dog shadowed her every step. Cameron shifted out of the way as the animal got closer.

Maude chuckled at him as she walked past. "Don't mind Sugar Beet. She won't bite you unless I tell her to."

Julia didn't take her eyes off the menacing Sugar Beet. "That's what I'm afraid of," she whispered to Cameron.

Maude opened her screen door and went inside with the dog. Julia and Cameron followed. The interior of Maude Doolittle's house smelled like autumn, an inviting blend of hickory kindling and natural spices from an incense stick on her mantel. Sandalwood and cinnamon wafted through the air, intermingling with the unmistakable scent of well-preserved old books.

All four walls of Maude's cabin were lined with shelves, every one of them stuffed with reading material. Cameron's rapt expression said more than words could that he ached to scan every title. Julia, nearly as dumbstruck with the sheer magnitude of Professor Doolittle's library, stood in the center of the room, stared at the walls of knowledge and said to Maude, "Have you read all of these?"

The old woman had gone to a small cooking area in an alcove off the main room. She threw logs into a wood-burning stove and lit them. "I've read most. Have a few more to go before I die." She gave Julia a challenging look over her shoulder. "But I'll make it."

"I have no doubt that you will," Julia said.

When Maude ordered, "Seat yourselves," Julia and Cameron sat at a crude plank-top table. Maude took a tin plate from an open hutch next to her stove. "I don't have much to offer in the way of company food."

"Please, don't go to any trouble," Julia said. "We had breakfast before we got here."

"I invited you in. It's only right to offer you something."

Julia started to protest again, but Cameron held up his hand. A moment later, Maude brought an assortment of Oreos and Fig Newtons to the table. She stood with her hands on her hips and said, "Tea?"

Julia hesitated, wondering what homegrown herbal concoction might be considered "company tea" by Maude Doolittle. But emboldened by the normalcy of store-bought cookies, she said, "Yes, thank you. That would be lovely."

Maude set three mugs on the table, each with a familiar Lipton tag hanging over the edge. She poured steaming water from an old galvanized kettle into the mugs and sat down. "Okay, young man, where do you want to start?"

Cameron smiled. "Do you mind a personal question, Professor Doolittle?"

"Not if you don't mind not getting a personal answer."

"Fair enough." He settled against the stiff spines of a ladderback chair and said, "Why did you elect to leave Duke University?"

She gave him a curiously amused look and said, "I didn't *elect* anything. I was more or less asked to leave."

"Oh?"

"You're wanting to know why, aren't you?"

Cameron shrugged. "Well…"

"The Vietnam War was going on. It divided this country right down the middle. A few of us on the faculty were accused of being too vocal with our opinions about that war and a few other political issues, as well. Our stand wasn't favorably looked upon by the Board of Trustees, those know-it-alls."

"How were you too vocal?" Cameron asked.

Maude smiled. "Apparently in a few too many open demonstrations."

Cameron nodded. "Sit-ins? Rallies? Peace movements?"

"That was some of what I did." She chuckled. "I might have managed to stay on at the university if I hadn't somehow ended up on the White House lawn." She paused, then added, "With two ounces of an odd-looking weed in my satchel." She took a sip of her tea. "As I recall that was the beginning of my macular degeneration. I used some unconventional herbal remedies."

Cameron laughed out loud. "And despite an early and exceedingly rare diagnosis of a disease that afflicts older people, you don't show any signs of it now, some forty years later."

"I've been lucky." She smiled. "And I continued to self-medicate…when the mood struck me."

Julia grinned down into her tea. She pictured a young, zealous Maude Doolittle standing before an agitated crowd, raising her fist in defiance of principles she believed were unjust, perhaps even burning her bra as a pioneer for women's liberation. And suddenly Julia wanted to know everything about this woman who lived her life in the backwoods of the Blue Ridge in a little cabin decorated with dozens of bright red geraniums. "How have you managed, Professor Doolittle?" she asked.

Maude stared across the table at her. "You mean money?"

"Well, yes. And help, companionship."

"I've always had companions, of one sort or another. Now I've got Sugar Beet. I don't need help yet. And I've got plenty of money." She stared out a window at the mountains rising in the distance. "My granddaddy owned one thousand acres of mountain land when the government came in and bought it all up to establish the national park. He ran a sawmill at the time which was outside the boundaries of the park, so he took the money, kept working and never spent a dime of it. It's not a fortune, but I have most of it still in the bank. It'll see me to the end."

Julia sensed that the history of Maude Doolittle was as rich as the legends of the mountains.

Cameron cleared his throat, flipped open his computer and angled it toward Julia so she could make notes. "Let's get started," he said. "Professor Doolittle,

I want to see your collection of ballads. Not the ones everyone else knows. The other ones."

"You heard about those, did you?"

"Yes, ma'am."

She stood, went to a closed cabinet nestled under a roof eave and opened the doors. Reaching inside, she pulled out a wooden box and brought it to the table. She stared at Cameron with such intensity, Julia thought she might snatch the box back after tempting him with it. "If I show you what's in here," Maude said, "how will you treat it?"

"With the utmost respect, Professor Doolittle."

"I've never published them, not because they don't matter, but because they do." Her gaze held a steely purpose. "I won't have anyone minimize the importance of these words or poke any kind of fun at them."

"I understand," Cameron said. "And I promise you the original intent will be preserved and respected. But I won't keep the ballads to myself. That's not my purpose in coming here today. It's time to let people appreciate this part of mountain history."

She studied him, thinking, perhaps evaluating his worth as someone to whom she could entrust her lore. "We'll see," she finally said. She lifted the lid, removed several tablets of yellowed paper and spread them on the table. "These are the written ones." Next she returned to the cupboard for an ancient reel-to-reel tape recorder. When she sat down again, she said, "On these tapes you'll find ballads sung by the folks who wrote them. My dad recorded their voices in the fifties right here in this cabin."

Cameron took a miniature recorder from his computer bag. His hand shook when he placed the modern machine on the table next to its ungainly predecessor. "Do you mind if I copy them?"

Maude gave her permission with a barely perceptible nod.

THREE HOURS LATER, Julia drove out of the Hollow. She and Cameron had read only a part of the writings Maude Doolittle had accumulated over the years. At the end of the interview, and with Maude's blessing, Cameron had returned the ballads to the box and carried it to the Xterra for transport to his cabin. During their time at Maude's table, Julia had taken copious notes, typing as fast as the old lady talked. She now had a wealth of material on the families who had settled the Blue Ridge, especially Killdeer Hollow, including specifics about those who had contributed to the culture and legends of the area.

Leaving the Hollow behind, Julia turned onto the two-lane road that led to the highway. Cameron had been almost completely silent since they'd left, but she looked over at him now. From the intensity of his expression, she knew he wasn't seeing the landscape flying by. He was reliving the last powerful hours.

Julia spoke softly, breaking the silence. "She's an amazing woman."

His body jerked slightly, bringing him back to the present. "I know. She could live anywhere she wants, but she chooses to live at the most elemental level. And what she hasn't personally witnessed growing up in the mountains, she's chronicled from the stories she'd heard."

"And the most interesting thing to me," Julia added, "was that the original songwriters never intended to put their words to music. Everything was sung a capella. No notes were ever written down."

"That's because ballad-singing was a private matter," Cameron said. "The songs were performed for families. No one envisioned selling their words until somewhere around the middle of the last century when instruments like the dulcimer and the banjo became popular."

"The recordings Maude gave us must be extremely rare."

"And the only way we'll ever know how the words were meant to sound."

"Most of the songs were about either love or tragedy," Julia said. "Even the ones about love were more about love gone bad and broken hearts. And there were so many tragic events in their lives. Train wrecks, mine accidents, people dying before their time."

"Tragedy is a part of everyone's life," Cameron said. He gave her a look of sincere sympathy. "Look at what you've endured in the past year. First losing your dad, and then Tina."

She noticed the strong set of his jaw and drew a conclusion about Cameron's recent past. "How about you, Cam? Any tragedy in your life?"

He waved off her question with a flick of his good wrist. "Not to compare with yours."

Sensing he wouldn't elaborate with details, she said, "I think the saddest songs are about children dying."

"Losing a child is horrible." He paused a few seconds. "But I admire the way the mountain people handled their grief—expressing themselves in ballads as a way of letting it go."

Julia thought about what he said. She was a writer, but she recognized her limitations. She wished she had the talent and the willingness to express her emotions as freely as the mountain people did. Maybe then Tina's death wouldn't haunt her day and night.

But at this point, Julia longed to bury her grief and her guilt, not put it into words. She knew she wasn't nearly as brave as the folks she'd learned about today. They released the most basic of human feelings in a way that combined their belief in tradition with a cleansing process that allowed them to accept life's tragedies. And Julia, who wondered if her pain would ever go away, envied them.

"That's our turn," Cameron said.

She squinted at the highway sign.

"You okay?" he asked. "You seemed a million miles away."

She looked over at him, grateful for his presence. "I'm fine. Just thinking."

He reached over, covered her knee with his hand. "I'm really glad you were with me today, Julia. It wasn't easy hearing all that raw emotion."

Her breath caught in her lungs. For one clarifying moment, she felt that his hand on her knee tied her not only to him but to all those people from the past. She said a silent prayer that he wouldn't pull away.

"And you know the best part?" he said.

"What's that?"

He smiled. "You get it. More than anybody I've ever known, you understand. You see the value in what we're doing."

She turned onto the four-lane highway. The breeze from the open window lifted her hair from her neck and cooled her skin. And she sighed with a sense of fullness over what she'd witnessed today. He squeezed her knee before taking his hand away. And she suddenly understood that much of the completion she felt at this moment was because the man she'd once idolized for perhaps the most shallow of reasons now filled her senses to the brim for all the right ones.

AFTER STOPPING for cheeseburgers and fries, Julia and Cameron returned to Glen Springs with only fifteen minutes to spare before school let out. "Do you mind if we pick Katie up first and then I'll take you home?" she asked Cam.

"Of course not."

They parked in front of the school and waited. This time, although Katie came out the door soon after the dismissal bell, she wasn't alone. She walked with another girl to where the sidewalk divided, sending some students to school buses and others to waiting cars.

Cameron got out of the Xterra as Katie approached. "Hey, Pussy toes," he called to her. "We're over here."

Pussy toes?

Katie ran to him. "Hi, Cameron. You've got the cool car today."

"Only the best for you," he said. "Besides, it's good for getting around the mountains."

She climbed in the backseat. "You're not going to wreck this one, are you?"

He laughed. "I hope not. But just to avoid that possibility, I'm letting your aunt drive it." He shut her door and got in the front.

"Are we going to look for more flowers today?" Katie asked.

"I don't know. We have to leave those decisions up to your Aunt Julia. But I imagine she wants to hear all about your day."

Katie leaned over Julia's seat. "Can we go to Cameron's?"

"I don't think so. Grandma is waiting at the store. She wants to see you."

"Oh, okay." She turned to Cameron. "Sorry, I guess we can't."

"Hey, you're not as sorry as I am."

Julia started the car. "So, what's with this new name, Pussy toes?"

Katie explained, obviously repeating Cameron's words. "It's a flower we saw the other day. It's very rare and we were lucky to find one in September." Looking at Cameron again for confirmation, she said, "Right?"

"Absolutely," he said.

Julia reminded Katie to put on her seat belt. "Now tell me more about this flower."

"It hardly looks like a flower at all," Katie said. "But when you get real close you can tell that the top of it is actually bunches of little blossoms."

"Kind of reminds me of some people," Cam said. "It's hard to tell just how beautiful they are because they keep their best qualities hidden. It takes an expert flower hunter to spot these enchanting little guys."

Julia broke through the school traffic and headed for Whisper Mountain Road. "I'll be sure to keep a look out then," she said. "I wouldn't want to miss any pussy toes that come into my life."

She dropped Katie at the store and continued up the mountain. "Can you come in?" Cam asked when they'd parked in front of the cabin and both gotten out of the Xterra.

"No, sorry. I've got to help Mama and see that Katie does her homework."

He joked, "I'm striking out with all the Sommerville women today. How about tomorrow? I've got to be here all day because someone from the phone company is coming to see about getting a line in here. I have to have an Internet hookup. But I'm going to start sorting through the ballads and I'd sure like your help."

She headed toward the Toyota. "I'll be here in the morning to change the bandages, but I can't stay. I have to go shopping."

"Oh? Where are you going?"

"Into Asheville. Wednesday is Katie's birthday, so I want to get her something really special." She opened the car door. "Do you need anything? Groceries? I'll be glad to pick them up for you."

"Thanks, but I've set aside tomorrow as delivery day. My things from Raleigh are arriving from UPS. And I found a guy in Glen Springs who'll bring food up here, so I'm all set."

She got in the car. "Okay, see you in the morning," she called through the open window.

"Thanks again for everything you did today, Julia. I'm glad you found it at least a little inspiring."

She waited before starting the ignition. I found it more than *a little inspiring,* she thought, and I don't have any idea what to do about it.

"Are you still mad at me?"

Julia clutched the steering wheel when her sister's voice suddenly invaded her thoughts. As she started down the road to Whisper Mountain Falls, she recalled everything about that October morning, ten years ago. Tina had come into the living room, a mug of coffee in her hand. Julia had been sitting among storage boxes, sorting the family's Halloween decorations.

"What makes you think I'm mad at you?" she asked without looking up from her task.

"Oh, come on, Julia. I'm not stupid. You're mad at me because I've been going out with your precious professor."

Julia looked up at her, a ridiculous strand of orange garland hanging from her hand. "All right. If you know so much, why bring it up?"

"Because I want you to know I did you a favor."

Julia hadn't been able to contain a burst of cynical laughter. "Right. And how do you, in any way, interpret what you've done as an act of kindness?"

"He's not interested in you, so I saved you the heartache of rejection. But mostly I saved you from boredom. Maybe you won't believe me, but your Mr. Birch is incredibly dull. And certainly not the kind of man who would put a spark in your own uneventful life."

Julia yanked a bundle of Indian corn from a crate. "How do you know what kind of man I want or need?"

"Because I know you, and if you were with Cameron, you'd both die from boredom the first week." She got up from a chair and walked to the front window. "But Happy Halloween. You can have him now if you want. I'm breaking up with him. A girl can only take so many walks. She can only look at so many trees, hear so many stories before she zones out." She looked back at Julia, flashed her impish grin and added, "No matter how sexy he is. And I'll say that much for the professor. He's pretty damn good in that department."

Well, Tina, Julia thought. I've been with Cameron for a week now. I've cared for him, helped him, touched him, and you're wrong. The last emotion I've felt with him is boredom.

CHAPTER ELEVEN

JUST BEFORE NOON on Wednesday morning Cora parked her old Ford next to her daughter's rented Toyota in the store lot. She got out of her car and checked her reflection in the driver's window even though she'd admired her new hairdo in at least a half dozen mirrors since she'd been to the beauty shop. Combing her fingers through the short, layered style, she smiled. She didn't look like Cora Sommerville exactly, but she looked pretty good.

When Cora entered the store, Julia looked up from a carton she was unpacking on the counter. Whisper Mountain ball caps and visors sat waiting for price stickers. Julia's grin was immediate and enthusiastic. "Mama, you look wonderful!"

Cora gave her a little wave, an offhand gesture to indicate she wasn't all that impressed with her appearance. "It's not so much of a change," she said.

"Yes, it is. It's fantastic. The color. The style. You look years younger."

Cora busied herself with checking the supply of hotdog buns, but since she'd just counted them at closing the night before, she knew darned well how many were there. "You would say that just because this was all your idea."

"I would say it because it's true," Julia said. "What did Ella think of it?"

Cora thought about the beautician's reaction, as well as the positive comments from the other women in the shop. "All in a day's work for her," she said. "Truthfully, Julia, I was too occupied with getting candles in all those cupcakes this morning to give this silly hairdo much thought."

Julia smiled. "You delivered them to the school?"

"Of course." She laughed. "Those kids' eyes were big as saucers when I brought in that giant box."

"I'm sure Katie will enjoy the special attention today."

Cora walked over to the baked goods area and was relieved when she noticed that no new items had been added. "I guess the bakery delivery hasn't arrived yet," she said.

Julia kept applying price stickers. "No. I thought Oscar came on Thursdays."

"I asked him to come a day early," Cora explained. "I told him we were running low on certain items."

Julia kept clicking the pricing machine over cap bills, but her low chuckle indicated she was aware of Cora's lie. "We're not," she said smartly. "I just checked before you came in."

Cora grabbed the box just emptied of hats and marched to the bakery shelf. She scooped prewrapped cookies and muffins into her arms and dropped the whole bundle into the carton. When she carried the box back to Julia, she said, "Then start eating, because when I say we're out, we're out."

Julia split open a pack of chocolate chip cookies and nibbled on one. "Yes, Mama, I'll do my best."

"And wipe that smile off your face."

"Yes, Mama," she said, the smile growing wider.

The sound of a diesel engine sent both women to the front door. When she saw the Sunny Vale truck in the lot, Cora flattened her hand over her chest and tried to draw a deep, calming breath. "H-here he comes," she said, hating the speech impediment that always appeared at the worst possible times.

Julia raced for a glass of water and handed it to Cora. "Drink this."

Cora took a sip, leaned against the door frame, and said, "I'm okay. Don't fuss over me, Julia." She reached up and did the hair-ruffling thing again. "How do I look?"

Julia took the glass and wrapped her free hand over Cora's shoulder. "You look great, Mama. Bowl-him-over great."

Whistling a cheerful tune, Oscar mounted the porch steps, pushing his hand truck in front of him. When he reached the door, both women stepped back to let him enter.

"Hello, ladies," he said, letting the screen door close behind him and standing the hand truck upright. "A beautiful day, isn't..." He stopped, stared at Cora for several tortuous seconds before a huge mustachioed grin spread over his face. "What have you done to yourself, Cora?"

She fluttered a nervous hand at her throat. "What do you mean?" But since coyness had never been one of her strongest traits, she plopped both hands on her hips and said, "I changed my hairstyle. Lightened the color, got it cut. Julia likes it, but I don't have a man's perspective." She turned slowly in a circle, caught Julia's shocked, amused expression as she spun, and added, "Being that you're a man, Oscar, tell me. What do you think?"

Oscar pursed his lips with utter seriousness and gave Cora a thorough once-over. When the skin at the roots of her bouncy blond hair began to heat with mortification, he smiled. "You are right—I am a man, and, Cora Sommerville, you are a vision."

"Well, good," she said. "That's two for, none against."

Oscar leaned forward, bringing his face within inches of hers. "Make that three to zero. I like it so much my vote counts twice."

Cora came to a sudden conclusion that this flirting business could actually be kind of fun, if a girl had a willing participant. She had more to say to Oscar, but she decided to play it cool for a while. "Do you have my order?" she asked. "We're out of everything here." She sent Julia a look over her shoulder, letting her know she should get rid of the evidence to the contrary. Julia hurried back to the counter and slipped the box out of sight.

"I've got it all," Oscar said.

"Good. What time will you be finished with your deliveries tonight?"

He grinned. "I can be done most any time, I expect."

Oscar agreed to come back that evening for Katie's birthday dinner of sloppy joes and homemade macaroni and cheese. Cora then decided that it was time for another of the Sommerville women to arrange for her own date. After Oscar left, she walked over to Julia. "What's Cameron doing tonight?" she asked.

"I don't know. Probably working on his research."

"Invite him here for Katie's party."

Julia hung the last visor on a display rack and waited a moment before responding. "I'd have to pick him up," she finally said.

"So? What else have you got to do? I'm taking care of the cooking."

"Katie would like him to be here, I suppose," Julia said.

"Yes, *Katie* would. She talks about him nonstop."

"All right. I'll call him now."

She picked up the store phone and dialed his number. Cora couldn't hear her daughter's muffled voice as she extended the invitation, but she could definitely read Cameron's answer in Julia's face. She set the phone back in its cradle and valiantly tried to hide a crestfallen expression behind a forced smile. "I offered to go get him," she said. "But he said he didn't have time now. He was wrapped up in something really important."

Cora tried to make sense of Cameron's response. "What could be more important than our Katie's birthday?"

"I don't know. Apparently something." Julia grabbed a wet cloth, strode over to the snack area and scrubbed the tops of the already clean booths. "It doesn't matter," Julia said. "We'll have a wonderful party without him."

"You bet we will," Cora said, but she knew that somehow the sparkle of the festivities had been tarnished.

JULIA STUCK the ninth large candle into a frothy confection of thick, sweet chocolate and stood back to examine the effect. From outside the closed kitchen door, Katie called, "Can I see the cake? Please, can I see it?"

"No, you cannot. No one in the Sommerville family ever sees their cake until the candles are lit."

"But everybody's here. Oscar and Rosalie, you and Grandma. So it's okay to bring it out now."

Julia remained firm. "Not till after we eat supper and you open your presents. Then you can see the cake."

"Can't you let me call Cameron?" she pleaded again.

Julia had lost count of the number of times Katie had asked. "No, sweetie. I told you that Cameron wanted to come, but he couldn't."

"But I want him here. He'll come if I call him."

Darn you, Cameron. How could you do this? Julia walked to the window and looked over the meadow behind the cottage. "I'm sure he would be here if he could," she said. "But he just can't, and you'll have to accept that. It's going to be a great party, anyway."

"I know, but…"

Katie's voice was lost in the patter of her footsteps on the wood floor of the living room. A moment later she called out, "Aunt Julia, he's here! Cameron's here!"

Julia hurried from the kitchen. She opened the front door just as the Xterra hummed to a stop. Cameron, his right arm encased in the sling, got out on the driver's side. Katie raced down the steps to meet him.

"Hey, Pussy toes," he said. "I heard that somebody around here is having a birthday."

She jumped from one foot to the other. "It's me. I am."

"Oh. Then I'm just in time." He reached into the backseat and brought out an oddly-shaped package wrapped in a piece of colorful cloth and tied at the top with a length of twine. "This must be for you," he said.

Katie grabbed the package and brought it into the house. And Julia stormed down the steps and headed straight for him. "What do you think you're doing?"

Cameron gave her an innocent smile. "I was invited to a birthday party and I'm here."

"You turned down that invitation as I recall."

"No, I didn't. I turned down the ride to get here."

Julia blew out a breath strong enough to lift the hair off her forehead. "Then you're even crazier than I thought. You can't be driving on this road with the condition you're in."

"I know, but I made it. I passed only two cars on my way here, and I pulled over to the side and waited till they went by so I wouldn't endanger any other mountain citizens."

"Why didn't you just let me pick you up when I said I would?"

"Because I wasn't ready to go then. I still had things to do. And the paint had to dry."

"What?"

He took her elbow and turned her toward the house. "Why don't you just enjoy the party, Julia?" Leaning close to her ear, he whispered, "I'm not trying to usurp your driving responsibilities, but this was a special case. I promise I'll make it home safely tonight and leave the rest of the driving to you."

She angled her head to look into his eyes. A pleasant shimmer of energy flowed to her knees and she almost stumbled. "I don't know whether to throttle you, or…" She gulped back the words that she'd nearly blurted from her subconscious.

"Or what?" he asked, a grin lifting a corner of his mouth.

"…or bury your car keys in the backyard."

He laughed. "At least you didn't say bury the car. I've already had that happen once."

BY NINE O'CLOCK, the party had come to an end because the guest of honor was too sleepy to hold her head up. But she insisted on taking every one of her gifts to her bedroom. "This is the most birthday presents I ever got," she said when Julia helped her get ready for bed.

"I'm very glad you had a good time," Julia said. "Which of your new tops do you want to wear to school tomorrow?"

"I think the one Oscar got me. The one with Johnny Depp as Captain Jack."

"Arghh," Julia growled while pretending to curl a moustache at her upper lip. "Fine choice, matey."

"And I want to take the lunch bag you got me because it has all the pretty flowers on it. And the new pencil box."

Julia pulled back the covers and Katie slid into bed. "You are going to be the envy of all the other chipmunks tomorrow, my dear. Enjoy the notoriety while it lasts."

Katie grinned. "Thanks for the party, Aunt Julia."

Julia bent down and kissed Katie's temple. "You are very welcome." She reached for the light switch on the lamp by the bed, but Katie's small voice stopped her. "Aunt Julia?"

"Yes, honey?"

"Do you think Mommy saw my party from heaven?"

A spiritual person, but not necessarily a religious one, Julia realized she had no idea what Katie had been told about life after death. All of Tina's life, at least the part of it that included Julia, she had lived for the present, taking pleasure any way she could and damning the consequences. Julia couldn't remember Tina ever contemplating existence beyond this one on Earth. Invincible and irrepressible—that was Tina. And immortal, as well, if her lifestyle was any indication of her beliefs. But that was before...

Julia took Katie's hand. "Did your mommy ever talk to you about heaven?" she asked, hoping Tina had provided some explanation to the child when their father died a year ago. Surely Katie had asked questions then.

"Mommy said heaven was beautiful and had flowers growing everywhere and castles and colored lights on all the streets like at Christmas. And nobody worried about anything because they had everything they wanted."

Julia smiled. "My, it sounds like a wonderful place."

"Is that what you think heaven is, Aunt Julia? Do you think my mommy has everything she wants?"

Julia took a deep breath. She had no idea what her sister wanted or needed at the end of her life on Earth. "I think she's happy in heaven, honey, but I don't think she has everything she wants." She smoothed wispy strands of hair from Katie's brow. "I think she misses you."

Katie nodded. "Yeah, she prob'ly does."

"Is it okay if I turn out the light now?"

"It's okay, but Aunt Julia?"

"Yes?"

"Would you bring me the basket Cameron got me? I want it beside my bed."

"Sure." Julia went to the dresser and picked up the hickory basket. Katie had been delighted when she'd untied the twine and revealed the homemade gift, which Cameron had filled with all sorts of goodies he'd found in the forest. There was a rock that looked like an old man's face, a pinecone with the tips painted silver, a small canvas bag filled with fragrant herbs, a doll made of corn silk with blue painted eyes and a cherry-red mouth.

Julia had been amazed that Cameron had been able to gather and decorate all the things with only one hand. He'd told her he'd begun his search for the items the day she drove him home from Maude's after she'd mentioned Katie's birthday.

Her thoughts were interrupted by a knock on Katie's door. "Can I bother you girls a minute?"

Katie's face shone at the sound of Cameron's voice. "Yes," she said. "Come in."

He opened the door, stuck his head inside but stayed in the hallway. "Would the two of you like to go to the library in Little Creek on Saturday? It's a very small place, but I'm told they have an interesting collection of Jack tales."

Katie's eyes rounded. "What are Jack tales?"

"Some people call them tall tales, but they're really more than that. They're stories of magical powers and strange occurrences. They were made up and passed down by folks here in the mountains years ago and one man donated his whole collection to the Little Creek Library."

Katie clasped her hands under her chin. "Can we go, Aunt Julia?"

"Yes, honey, we can go."

Cameron nodded once. "Great." He wiggled his fingers at Katie. "Good night, Pussy toes, and happy birthday."

Julia pulled the covers around Katie's shoulders and switched off the bedside light. After closing the bedroom door, she backed into the dark hallway and released a tiny squawk of surprise when she collided with Cameron's arm. "Sorry. I thought you would have returned to the party."

His features were indistinguishable in the meager light from the living room, but his eyes drew her gaze and held it. She sensed, rather than saw, his smile. "I was waiting for you," he said.

"Oh." Julia wrung her hands, dropped them to her sides and finally used them to brush the hair off her forehead, all in an attempt to keep some part of her body occupied since her brain didn't seem to be functioning.

"You're doing a wonderful job with her, Julia."

"Thanks. I hope I am. She's a good kid and doesn't deserve all this sadness in her life."

"Yeah." He glanced at the closed door. "It's hard to explain, but there's something unique about her. She's sweet, of course. And appreciative. But there's a depth to her that I can't imagine finding in most children her age. She sees beauty in the simplest things, and she seems to possess this natural urge to know everything."

"I can't take credit for that. I was absent for most of her life."

"You're the one she depends on now, though. You're the one getting her through this awful time." He reached out, touched Julia's hand. "Whatever you're doing, it seems to be working. She's a special little girl."

She's Tina's girl, Cameron, Julia thought, an old, unwanted bitterness rising up inside her. *She's special to you because she's Tina's. It's the memory of her mother that connects you to Katie.*

While she believed her assumption to be true, Julia couldn't fault Cameron for his affection for Katie. The fact that his warm feelings for the child were tied to a relationship that Julia had not been able to forget or forgive was her problem, not Cam's. And certainly not Katie's.

"Saturday could be a memorable day," Cameron said, looping his good arm around Julia's shoulders and heading toward the living room.

His touch was so natural, so familial, Julia had to choke back a sob of emotion. Like a brother's, like a former professor's. But not the least like a lover's. "What do you mean?" she asked.

"I'm one lucky guy to be squired about the county in the company of Pussy toes and MoonPie."

She playfully jabbed his chest even as she allowed

herself the momentary comfort of his casual embrace, gave herself up to the extravagance of imagining what this simple walk down a hallway from a child's room could have meant if circumstances had been different. "Wait till we come up with a name for you," she said. But she couldn't think of one. What whimsical, silly name could she give a man whose special gift seemed to be reaching out to the heart of a child?

JULIA HAD A PROBLEM and she knew it. Unexpected and certainly uninvited, Cameron Birch was back in her life with the force of the mountain storm that had brought him to her door. She'd lived just fine for ten years without him. Well, maybe not fine exactly, but well-enough—if she didn't stop to consider her recent dependence on antidepressants. Now she couldn't go ten minutes without thinking about him.

She supposed there was only one thing she could do about her renewed fascination with the man. Avoid him as much as she could without having to explain her un-usual behavior. Unfortunately, avoiding him was exactly what she didn't want to do.

Thursday morning, she went to Cam's cabin and changed his dressings. She stayed a while, helping him sort through and store the personal items that had been delivered from his home in Raleigh. She worked on the material they'd gathered from Maude and Marcus and discussed what he hoped to accomplish at the Little Creek Library on Saturday.

Keeping busy, she almost wasn't aware of him every second that he sat across from her at the kitchen table. She could almost convince herself that her heart didn't quicken every time he walked behind her, tugged on her hair or lightly brushed her shoulder. And she could almost believe that it was her inner strength and not the renewed passion in her life that made her see the Sommerville family doctor in Glen Springs that afternoon and begin being weaned off her pills.

On Friday she took Cam to the office of the surgeon who had performed his wrist operation. X-rays showed that the bones were knitting nicely. The doctor examined the pin insertion points and complimented Julia on keeping the wounds clean and properly bandaged. And he announced that her visits to her patient could be reduced to every other day. On the way back to the cabin, Julia commented on the encouraging news. "You won't have to put up with me every day now," she said.

He lifted his arm from where it lay against his chest in the sling. "Are you kidding? *This* is the least important reason I like seeing you so often. We're making real progress on the compilations and I still need you to take me where I have to go."

"You're moving your fingers better now," she said. "Maybe the doctor will give you clearance to drive pretty soon."

"I doubt it. You heard him today. A few more weeks of these pins and then I'll need an immobilizer of some sort." He frowned. "I could probably handle highway driving at that point, but Whisper Mountain Road could still be a challenge. I learned that the other night when I drove to Katie's party."

As if a troubling thought suddenly occurred to him, he swivelled in the seat and stared at her. "Julia?"

She glanced his way, noticed the furrowing of his brows. "What?"

"You're not getting sick of me, are you? I know I'm not the most exciting guy that ever lived."

She laughed. "You're plenty exciting enough for me. That's what *I* learned from you driving to Katie's party."

"Okay, good. Are you growing tired of the project? Once I sink my teeth into something, I can be awfully tunnel-visioned. I put all my effort into my work without stopping to think that everyone else isn't as excited as I am."

"No, I like the work." That was the truth. Julia had grown up in the Blue Ridge but had never appreciated the area as much as she did now. She'd spent her years at Riverton trying to educate herself *out* of the mountains. Now she found herself being educated *by* them.

He settled back in his seat and stared out the front window. "So you're not trying to avoid me?"

"Of course not." *Though I should be. I already know what it's like to be on a one-way street in a relationship with you.* "But after our trip tomorrow, I've decided to visit only every other day to change your bandages. I need to spend more time with Mama in the store. I'm supposed to go back to Manhattan soon, and I want to make sure Mama and Katie are adjusted to their living arrangement and have a comfortable routine."

She stole a look at his profile. If her announcement had affected him, he didn't show it.

"That makes sense," he said.

Neither spoke the rest of the way up the mountain. When she pulled in front of the house, Cameron got out of the car right away. "Are you coming in?"

"No. I'll see you in the morning, though."

"It's supposed to be rainy and chilly."

"I'll make sure Katie and I have our jackets."

As she drove back down the mountain, Julia couldn't ignore a stab of regret. By limiting her time with Cam, she was only protecting herself. But still, she was sad to think that the last conversation she'd had with Cameron today was about the weather.

CHAPTER TWELVE

RAIN PATTERED against the windshield as Julia navigated the narrow road to Little Creek, a small, picturesque town situated in a deep valley between two towering Appalachian peaks. She and Cameron each had coffee in their cup holders. In the backseat, Katie sipped a hot chocolate. She'd been chattering the whole way about Jack tales.

"So is Jack the hero of every story?" she asked.

"He was originally," Cameron explained. "Our mountaineer Jack is based on the old story of *Jack and the Beanstalk.* That fella, because he battled with a giant, is probably the best known Jack of all. When the mountain folks started making up their own Jack tales, they made the star of their stories a teenaged boy who came from the Appalachians and used his strength and cunning to better conditions for his family."

"What kinds of things did our Jack do?" Katie asked.

"Oh, he fought with grizzlies and tamed mountain lions and brought bald eagles into bed with him to keep them warm."

"Weren't there any girl Jacks?"

"Sure. Lots of the folktales are about girls every bit as clever as the boy Jack. Hopefully today I'll find you a book about Penelope Brine, the strongest girl in the Smokies."

Katie gasped. "What did she do?"

"We'll find out together, but I remember one story where she arm-wrestled a black bear and another where she talked the mountains into swallowing an evil lumberjack and he was never seen again."

"Go faster, Aunt Julia. I can't wait till we get there."

Julia laughed. "I'm going as fast the law allows, honey." She turned to Cameron. "Is this the only library that has a self-published copy of Henry Babcock's book?"

"The only one I know of. Henry died thirty years ago at the age of ninety-two. He had a few copies of his original Jack tales bound by a printer in Asheville. Most of the copies are lost now, but this one remains at the Little Creek Library. They keep it in a Plexiglas case to preserve it."

"You can't check the book out, can you?"

"No." He tapped his shirt pocket. "But I have a letter from Babcock's granddaughter stating that I can handle the book and make copies of the pages. Once I evaluate Henry's work, I'll contact the granddaughter again and get permission to include the stories in my research."

"Will she agree to that?"

"She should. Especially when I convince her of the value of her grandfather's contribution to the culture… and offer her a fair percentage of any royalties I may see from the book I'm going to write."

Once at the library, Cameron divided his time between finding stories for Katie and copying pages from Henry Babcock's book. Julia researched other local storytellers, both deceased and still living, and found out about a local group called the Jack Tales Club, which met every other month to swap stories. She knew this was something Cameron would like to do. She would be back in Manhattan the next time the group met, but Cam might feel more comfortable driving by then.

They left the library at one o'clock, stopped for lunch and continued back to Whisper Mountain. Julia dropped Katie at the store and drove Cameron home.

"You have to come in today," he said when she parked the Xterra. "We have tons of notes to go over."

Julia didn't even consider saying no. She was as excited about their findings as Cameron was. "Sure. I can stay awhile."

They went into the cabin and Cameron started a fire. A steady rain was still falling, pinging on the tin roof and sending wind-driven leaves against the windowpanes. "Are you cold?" he asked Julia.

"A little." Clouds had blanketed the sky in the last few minutes and the temperature had dropped by ten degrees.

"I'll make hot chocolate."

"Sounds good." While he went into the kitchen, Julia removed her raincoat and settled on the sofa, curling her legs underneath her.

Cam returned a few minutes later with two steaming mugs of chocolate. He handed one to Julia. "Should have included marshmallows on my grocery order."

She took a sip. "This is fine."

She expected him to sit in one of the easy chairs across from her, but he spread his notes on the coffee table and sat beside her on the sofa. She gave herself a moment to look at him before starting to work. His clothing had arrived from Raleigh, and it appeared that his love of the mountains extended to his wardrobe in the city. He wore a dark blue-and-tan flannel shirt with narrow-cut blue jeans. His light brown hair curled over the shirt collar and lay neatly brushed over the tops of his ears. Drops of rain still glistened on the ends. He seemed content to leave them there.

His voice broke through her thoughts. "Everything okay?"

"Sure. Why do you ask?"

"You sighed. I didn't know if something was bothering you."

She smiled. "It had to be a sigh of contentment, from being here, in front of the fire with—" she caught herself in time "—hot chocolate. What more could a girl want?"

He laughed. "Probably not to go over these notes." He leaned forward, setting his mug on the table. "Here's what I've been thinking. We can approach this part of the book as a study of folktales as an art form. Perhaps have a chapter on the significance of realism versus the obvious exaggeration in the tales. Talk about exaggeration as an instrument of humor. Point out what traits are common to tall tales and, last, tackle the subject of morals." He stopped, studied her. "That would be a good project for you—determining what themes or morals are common to the tall tale and formulating them into lessons for living."

It was her turn to laugh, but not with amusement. "Are you kidding? Your ideas are great, but they're out of my league. Much too scholarly for an entertainment reporter."

He sat back, gave her a serious look that trapped the laughter in her throat. "Don't do that, Julia."

"Do what?"

"You seem to put yourself down whenever I suggest that you become a major contributor to the book. You shouldn't underestimate your abilities. You're a bright young woman..."

He stared at her in almost a fatherly way, as if evaluating her capabilities with the eye of a seasoned professional, a mentor. And something inside her snapped. "That's enough, Cameron."

His eyes rounded with shock and he pulled away from her. "What did I do?"

The old bitterness churned inside her, and the only outlet for it, the only way to still protect her secrets, seemed to be anger. She stood up and glared down at him. "Stop treating me as if we were still in a classroom. As if you were the teacher and I the student."

"I'm not doing that. I only meant…"

"I know what you meant and, yes, you are doing it. I'm not your apprentice, or your protégée, or even your 'bright young woman'!"

He rose from the sofa and stood a few feet from her, his gaze intent on her face. "Where is this coming from?"

To answer that question would have been to bare her soul, her heart, and she wasn't about to risk that. So she evaded, a skill she'd learned years ago. "How old are you, Cam?"

He shook his head, released a bark of baffled amusement. "Thirty-five. Why?"

"I'm thirty. Maybe those five years meant something ten years ago when we faced each other across a podium in a Riverton classroom. But they don't mean anything today. The relationship we had then doesn't mean anything, either. We're different people now. We've grown…" She stopped, bit her lip. Where was she going with this? To an admission? To the truth, that she had loved him then and loved him now? This certainly wasn't the time or the place. He wasn't ready to hear it. Nor was she anywhere near ready to tell it.

She walked around the coffee table, putting more distance between them. "Never mind. I have to go. You get back to work."

He exhaled a breath of disbelief. "We haven't even started working, Julia. And I don't care about the project right now. I care if I've hurt or offended you."

"You haven't hurt me." *Lie, lie, Julia. It's safer than the truth.*

"Then at the very least I've insulted you. You must think I've been patronizing you, and I haven't meant to. I swear. You've become…"

His inability or reluctance to finish his sentence only fueled her frustration "What, Cameron? I've become a super student after all these years, still willing to soak up your knowledge and generous encouragement?" She clenched her hands until her nails bit into her palms and tried to restore herself to some semblance of calm. But her sarcasm only sounded irrational, and if she tried to explain she would only convince him she truly was the fool she appeared to be at this moment.

He came toward her, reaching out his hand. "Please, sit down, Julia."

"No." She slapped at the air, accidentally knocking his hand away. "I'm sorry."

"It's okay."

"I need to get out of here." She hurried to retrieve her jacket. Slinging it over her arm, she scrambled in the pocket for her keys as she ran out the front door and across the porch. A second later, racing through the rain toward her car, she found keys in the other pocket. She heard Cam call her name, asking her to come back. She fumbled through the ring. Only then did she realize she was holding the set to the Xterra. And Cameron was just a few feet away.

She stopped searching and collapsed against the side of her car. He halted in front of her. Rain dripped from his hair into his eyes. His sling was already discolored from exposure to the weather. "Go back," she said. "Your bandages are getting soaked."

"I don't think of you that way," he said.

SHE FLICKED a soaked strand of hair from her forehead and glared at him. "What?" Her eyes, damp and luminous, nearly toppled his resolve to maintain a distance from her. A trickle of rain ran down her cheek. His finger itched to brush it away.

"I said I don't think of you that way."

He'd been relieved to see her standing there, staring at the wrong keys. The mistake had bought him some time. Otherwise she would have been headed down the mountain by now while he'd waited in the house, grappling with indecision.

He hadn't wanted her to go, and when he stepped onto the porch and saw her next to her car, searching the pocket of her raincoat, he'd realized that he truly didn't think of her that way. Maybe he had once, that first night when she appeared in the ambulance, all humble about what she'd done. Maybe he'd seen her then as he remembered her from before—cute, attentive, bright. And then she'd come to him at the hospital and his impression changed. He saw her then as brave, strong-willed, determined. And then she started coming to his house, filling in the gaps of his life, making him better physically and spiritually.

And he saw her now as…what? His mind seemed as

misted as the sky over Whisper Mountain. He, a literature professor, a lover of words, a self-proclaimed chronicler of the past was unable to phrase exactly how he thought of Julia now. He only knew that he wanted her to stay. "Come back inside," he said.

"No. I have to go." She glanced at the keys in her hand. "I need mine." She gave him a look of such utter confusion and desolation, his gut twisted into a knot.

He drew closer to her, sensed the tension building in her body. Her eyes rounded. "Julia, I don't think of you as a student. I don't think of you as anyone who needs to learn anything from me. I don't know that I have any bit of knowledge to impart to you. The truth is, I simply care about the person you are. Very much."

"You don't have to say that. What I blurted out in there was the result of some spontaneous…"

He touched her forehead, trailed his finger over a strand of dripping hair. "You made your point." He smiled. "Maybe not as eloquently as you'd hoped, but even a man as dense as I am got it." He leaned closer, smelled the fresh scent of rain on her skin, felt the subtle heat building inside her. "Now I'm going to make mine."

As he lowered his lips to hers, he glanced down at his arm. "I hope these pins don't stick you, but whether they do or not, this is going to happen."

She swallowed. "Maybe it shouldn't. It will change things."

He smiled at her. "Exactly."

Her response was no more than a whisper. "I suppose we could try."

He pressed his lips to hers, gently at first, savoring the softness of her mouth, the slight tremble that might have suggested resistance, but he didn't think so. He deepened the kiss, running his tongue along the line of her lips. Rain sluiced down his neck, between their lips. He licked the drops from her mouth and a sound like the whimper of a child came from her throat.

He threaded his fingers into the damp hair at her nape. The rain jacket fell from her arm and she reached around him. He held her as tightly as he could and silently cursed his injury. He wanted her next to him, pressed against his chest, supple and yielding to every confounding, exhilarating emotion he needed to express.

When he drew back, she lay her forehead against his shirtfront. He set his chin on top of her head. "Are you glad we tried this out?"

She chuckled. "I'm not sure. I can't decide if we should never let it happen again, or if we should make plans to do it on a regular basis."

He tilted her face up to his. "It was an astounding kiss, Julia. Nothing like one a professor might give his prize student."

"I—I really have to go."

"I know you do." He pulled her keys, which he'd found on the fireplace mantel, from his pocket and exchanged them for his.

"You had these all along."

He shrugged. "A guy's got to have some secrets."

She reached down, scooped up her slicker and threw it into the backseat. "I really don't know how I feel about this," she said.

"It's okay. I have to be honest with you. I didn't come to the mountains thinking I'd meet someone. In fact…" He stopped, dangerously close to revealing more of himself than he wanted to. He shook his head. "I never included any of this in my sabbatical presentation."

She laughed softly. "I can imagine."

"The truth is, I came here to escape."

She touched his face, smiled and opened the car door. "It's okay, Cameron," she said as she got behind the wheel. "We can pretend it never happened."

"I doubt that. But we should each think about where we want this to go from here."

He stood in the opening of her door, knowing the rain was going in, yet reluctant to close it. "Will you come tomorrow?"

"Yes. I have to dress your wounds. And like you said, I made my point. Now, go inside. You can wrap dry gauze around your wrist and toss the sling into the dryer."

"Yeah, I can do that." He stepped back from her car, then watched her drive down the lane and had the strangest recollection of the recent past. For the first time, he remembered Julia's arms around him at the bottom of the ravine. And, of course, he clearly remembered his around her just now. Would he ever again experience a rainy mountain day and not think of Julia? Would he get through this night and not think of Julia?

He shook his head and walked to the house. "You didn't come here for this," he said again, this time to convince himself. "You came to bury feelings, not ignite new ones." Cam knew Whisper Mountain was magic. A special place in time. *But,* he reminded himself, *you have a life away from here, and so does she.*

CORA SCOLDED Julia the instant she came into the store. "Look at you. You're soaked!" She gave Rosalie one of those withering mother looks. "That's my daughter. Doesn't have the sense to come in out of the rain."

Julia conceded her mother's hasty analysis with a

nod. "Right now I don't feel like I've got the sense for anything."

Katie ran to her but put up her hand before accepting Julia's kiss on her cheek. "What happened to you?"

The edge of panic in her niece's voice brought Julia back from the last troubling, exciting minutes with Cameron. "Nothing. I got caught in the rain at Cam's. Silly of me. But I'm fine."

Katie stared uncertainly.

"I'll go change into dry clothes, and then I'll expect you to give me a big hug and we'll plan what we're having for dinner. Maybe later you can read me one of the stories you got at the library today."

"Okay."

Julia walked to the back of the store but was stopped by Cora at the door. One look at her mother's face convinced her something was wrong. "What's happened, Mama?"

"We g-got a package from Wayne today."

Julia tensed, experiencing the flare-up of recurrent anger in her stomach. "What was in it?"

"I don't know. I d-didn't open it."

Julia took Cora's hand. "After Katie goes to bed, we'll open it together."

"I won't be here. I'm going to dinner with Oscar."

Despite hearing the news that Wayne had contacted them again, Julia was happy for Cora. "That's great. Then don't even think about the package for now. I'll wait until you get home and we'll look then. Or tomorrow. Whenever you want."

Cora squeezed Julia's hand. "That's just it, Julia. I don't want to open it at all. You do it while I'm gone and tell me if there's anything I need to see. You can always go get Cameron if you need moral support. After all, he knew Tina. He would understand."

"No, I don't think so. There's no need to involve Cam…"

"Aunt Julia!"

Both women turned at the sound of Katie's voice. "Over here, honey."

Katie came through the storeroom entrance and walked up to them. "Can we go to Cameron's tomorrow?" she asked. "I want to show him one of these stories."

Julia released Cora's hand. "Probably. I've got to go in the morning and you can come with me."

"Great." She went back into the store.

Cora sighed. "Thank goodness for Cam. Katie is taken with him, and he's been so good to her."

Julia considered her response to her mother's comment and decided to be honest. "Yes, he has, but I wonder if they're becoming too close."

"Why would you say that?"

"Katie's counselor says she's doing well, and I believe her, but we have to remember that I'll be going back to New York." Julia tried to ignore Cora's disapproving frown. "I doubt Cameron's attention to Katie will continue with such regularity after that. He'll be busy with his project and he'll return to Raleigh eventually. I worry that both of us leaving Katie's life will set her back."

"You both don't have to leave, Julia."

She sensed what was coming next. The same old discussion. "Mama, don't…"

"You can stay here with us."

"No, I can't, and you know why. I have responsibilities in New York. I make my living there. This store can hardly support you and Katie without adding another mouth to feed."

"But Cam is paying you."

"Yes, but that's only temporary."

"Then we'll make changes. We'll expand, maybe have entertainment on the front porch during the summer tourist season. You know about that kind of thing."

"Mama, be realistic. You can't take on any more. And I can't stay."

Cora's facial muscles tightened. "We'll talk about it later. Right now we have to decide what to do about that package from Wayne."

"I have decided," Julia said. "After Katie's asleep, I'll open it. Don't worry, Mama. You just have a nice time tonight." She gave her mother a smile of encouragement. "Everything will be all right."

Julia walked across the yard to their house. She'd said the words she'd needed to say for her mother's benefit, but she couldn't help suspecting they might not be true.

CHAPTER THIRTEEN

CORA CAME INTO THE living room where Katie and Julia were watching a video. She stepped between them and the TV, cleared her throat and said, "Well, what do you think?"

Katie grinned. "Wow, Grandma. You look pretty."

Julia paused the movie. "I'll second that." She appraised her mother's brown velvet skirt and tan knit top with gold threads running through it. "That's a really nice outfit."

"I got it last September for the Harvest Potluck at your father's lodge." She stood in front of a wall mirror and dabbed the lipstick at the corner of her mouth. "I wore it only that one time."

Julia walked over to her. "Are you okay with wearing it tonight? If not, I can help you pick out something else."

"Nonsense. This looks good on me. At least, I feel like it does." She squared her shoulders. "Gene liked it, so I'm hoping Oscar will, too."

Julia put her arm around Cora's shoulders and gave her a squeeze. "Daddy always did have good taste. And he'd want you to have fun."

Cora turned toward the window when headlights shone into the room. "I think you're right, Julia. He would." She picked up her pocketbook from a table.

"Should I wait for Oscar to knock, or should I go out? I'm a bit rusty on dating rules."

Julia smiled. "There aren't many rules anymore, Mama. This is your night, so do whatever feels right."

She exhaled a deep breath. "Okay. Then I'm off." She blew an air kiss at Katie and headed for the door. "Don't wait up."

Two hours later, Julia carried an empty popcorn bowl and two soda cans into the kitchen. When she came back, Katie was yawning and trying to cover it by hiding her face behind a throw pillow. "Too late," Julia said. "You're busted. It's bedtime. We've had a full day."

Katie gave in without argument and thirty minutes later, sweet-smelling from her grandmother's lavender soap, she was sound asleep.

Julia went straight to the hall storage closet, where she knew her mother would have hidden the package. She moved a wicker basket of cotton swatches Cora intended to use in a quilt "someday" and a tin box that rattled with Cora's mad money, even though there had never been a reason to hide it from anyone.

Julia spied the object of her search in the corner, a box about the size that would hold a hundred manilla folders. The label was made out to Cora Sommerville with a return address in Tennessee.

Julia took the carton into the living room, put it on the coffee table and went to the kitchen for scissors. She cut the tape with slow, precise movements, almost as if she were sneaking a peek at something she had no right to see. Silly, of course. Cora wanted her to look at the contents. Still, not knowing what the box contained made Julia uneasy.

She lifted the lid and took out the item on top—a note

from Wayne. It consisted of a few hastily scrawled lines. *These are some of Tina's things, the ones I thought you might want. Wayne.*

Julia turned the paper over, thinking she might have missed something. Nope. That was Wayne, concise and to the point, if he could ever figure out what the point was.

Next was a photo of Tina and Katie. Julia judged it to be about three years old. Both were smiling. Tina had her arm around Katie. Underneath was a square cardboard jewelry box. Inside, among costume pieces, there was a sterling locket. Julia opened it, saw Katie's baby picture in one frame and the other empty. Didn't Tina have anyone other than Katie in her life who she believed worthy of the locket?

The rest of the box contained various papers. Tina's passport. Julia remembered her sister going to Mexico a few years back. A life insurance policy whose meager value had been cashed in soon after Katie's birth. Julia decided the inclusion of this worthless document was Wayne's way of saying that she and Cora shouldn't expect any money from Tina's death. "Like we're waiting on a windfall," Julia said, setting all the items aside.

The document at the bottom of the box interested her the moment she saw in Tina's handwriting the inscription on the outside of the white envelope. *Katie's birth certificate.* She ran her hand over the large rounded letters and pictured her sister writing the words. "At least this is important," she said. Julia had promised the officials at Glen Springs Elementary a copy of this document if she ever located it. Katie would need her proof of birth later in life, as well.

Julia took the envelope from the box and walked across the room to the mahogany desk where her parents had kept copies of all their important papers. She would put Katie's certificate in the drawer until Cora could make a copy and put the original in the safe-deposit box at the Glen Springs Bank. She opened the drawer and started to slide the envelope inside, but curiosity made her pause. If she read the certificate, at least she could find out where Wayne had been born and where he might run off to now, not that she'd ever want to contact him. But Katie might want to someday.

She sat in the desk chair and removed two sheets of paper from the envelope. The first one contained details of Katie's birth. *Katherine Eugenia Sommerville.* It was a nice name. Tina had used the feminine version of their father's name for Katie's middle. Under that was Katie's exact birthday, Sept. 27, nine years ago. Julia read the mother's name. *Christina Rae Sommerville.* Under that, Father: *Cameron Birch.*

Julia's hand shook. She dropped the certificate to the floor. Struggling to draw a breath, she bent to retrieve the document. She'd misread, that's all, she told herself. She'd been with Cameron so much, perhaps she was even subconsciously thinking of him now. She closed her eyes while she smoothed the paper over the surface of the desktop. Then she forced herself to focus on what had most assuredly been a mistake.

Father: Cameron Birch.

It couldn't be. Julia's mind flashed back ten years to that morning in October when Tina had come into the living room and told Julia that she could have "her precious professor," that she had broken up with him. Tina never saw Cameron after that. She left Whisper Mountain with Wayne before Christmas. Simple mathematics proved that what the certificate said was wrong.

A baby takes nine months to grow. Katie had been a couple of weeks premature, but she'd been nearly six pounds and healthy. That meant she had to have been conceived no earlier than January. Definitely not October, when Tina had last dated Cameron.

Julia stared at the certificate as if the words would somehow mutate before her eyes and the name Cameron Birch would suddenly become Wayne Devereaux. She resisted the urge to crumple the document in her hand. Instead she clenched her empty fist, pounded it into her lap and glared at the photo of her sister she'd just placed on the coffee table. "You would lie about even this, Tina?" she said. "How could you? What did you hope to gain?"

But suddenly Julia knew because she knew Tina, at least the irrational, self-centered woman her sister had been then. Tina intended to use this fake document some day if it suited her purpose. She realized Cameron would be a better father to Katie than Wayne ever would be. Cameron was her "father in the wings." Julia swallowed, scowling at the photo. Tina had never stopped conniving.

But even that scenario, while it explained Tina's motives, didn't make sense. Tina had to have known that Cameron was too smart to fall for such a deliberate attempt to alter the truth. Katie knew her birthday, and now, so did Cameron, and he certainly comprehended the simple mathematics of childbirth. And even if he considered the dates had been falsified, he would demand certain tests and the facts would come out. So then, again, why did Tina lie?

Aware that Cora could come home any minute, Julia got up from the chair and, with hands that wouldn't stop shaking, stuffed the certificate in the envelope. Only then did she see the note scrawled on the back in Wayne's block printed style. *I guess you know not to expect any child support from me after reading this. Tina was a real piece of work.*

Julia picked up the second sheet of paper, which she'd left on the desk. It was a clinical lab report. The details cleared up Julia's assumptions about Katie's paternity. Tina hadn't lied about Wayne not being Katie's father. The facts were indisputably revealed in a blood test analysis. Tina's blood type was listed as *O*. Somehow she'd gotten Wayne's blood type, which was *AB*. Katie's blood type matched her mother's.

Even knowing what further research would prove, Julia hurried to her room, where her laptop computer sat on her desk. She keyed in the words "blood type paternity" into a search engine and pulled up a medical site that charted hereditary blood samples. Scanning the chart, Julia came to the one that mattered. Mother: *O*, Father: *AB*, offspring: *A* or *B*.

Katie was *O*. Wayne was not her father.

And Julia knew in her heart, perhaps the most reliable indicator of all, that Katie was Cameron's daughter.

A car pulled up in front of the house, and Julia panicked. Tossing back her bedclothes, she lifted the mattress and slid the documents underneath. Then she frantically smoothed the linens into order. Cora couldn't see the contents of this envelope. Not now. Not until Julia had a chance to dissect this information and understand the ramifications for all of them.

Cora's voice came from the hallway, muted yet charged with an energy Julia hadn't heard in a long time. "Julia, I see your light on. You still awake?"

Julia rechecked her bed and hurried to the door. When she went into the hallway, Cora was there, waiting. "Hi, Mama. Did you have a good time?"

"It was such fun, dear. Oscar is very gallant."

Julia took Cora's elbow and steered her down the hallway. "I'm so glad. Let's have a cup of tea. I want to hear all about it."

They stepped into the living room where the items on the coffee table seemed to fill the small area with a threatening presence. Cora stopped, looked at Julia. "You opened the package."

"Yes, and there's nothing to worry about." Her voice hitched.

Cora walked slowly to the table, picked up the photograph. "I remember this. It was taken at Cumberland Gap. We all went there one time when your father and I drove up for a visit. I asked Tina for a copy, but she never got around to making one." Her smile was sad. "I guess I've got one now."

"It's a nice picture, Mama. And that's really about all that's here." She opened the white box. "A bit of jewelry. A few papers, none of much significance." She held up a document she hadn't noticed before. "Here's Tina's high-school diploma."

Cora held it in the palms of her hands. "I remember the day she graduated. Your father and I considered it quite a triumph. There were a few times we thought she'd never make it."

Julia scooped the items off the table and returned them to the shipping box. "Tina always seemed to surprise us, didn't she?" *Never more so than now.*

Cora chuckled. "Never a dull moment with that one."

They went into the kitchen and Julia filled the tea-kettle and put it on the stove. "There's one thing I've always wondered about," she said.

"What's that?"

"Why Tina stayed with Wayne. She'd had so many boyfriends before she left Whisper Mountain with him. And we always suspected there were troubles in their relationship. And yet she stayed."

Cora took two mugs from the cupboard and carried them to the table. "Oh, she left Wayne on at least a half dozen occasions."

"She did?"

"I just never told you about it. She didn't want you to know. She saw it as a failure, I guess."

Julia filled the mugs. "Did she come home during those times?"

"Often, not always." Cora added sugar to her tea. "The first time was just a couple of months after she left with him."

Julia had pulled out her chair, but she stopped, gripping the top rung so tightly her hand ached. "But I was living here then. I don't remember that."

"She knew you were here and couldn't face you. So she stayed with a girlfriend. It was only a week or so before Wayne came and got her." Cora sighed. "She went back with him. She always did."

"I never knew," Julia said, releasing her grip on the chair. She sat down. "When was that, Mama? Do you remember?"

Cora continued stirring her already mixed tea. "Let me see. It must have been January. I know Christmas was over, and we hadn't seen her during the holidays. Christmas was a sad time that year. But when Tina came back, I'd hoped she'd stay." She finally set her spoon on the table and took a sip of tea. "As I recall, she had even started up with Cameron again for a time."

Julia flinched. "She did? Cameron took her back?"

"No, I don't think so. Tina tried. She saw him, but Cameron didn't fall for her antics."

Julia closed her eyes and pictured Katie asleep in her bed. *You're wrong about that, Mama. I think he did, at least once that January.*

ON SUNDAY MORNING, Katie came into Julia's bedroom and roused her from the semisleep she'd eventually fallen into after spending a restless night. When her niece softly touched her cheek, Julia snapped alert and sat up. "What's wrong?"

Katie giggled. "Nothing. You said we were going to Cameron's this morning. I just came in to tell you I'm ready."

She looked adorable in blue jeans and her official Glen Springs chipmunk T-shirt. Julia glanced at the clock by her bed. "It's only 7:30 a.m. There's a good possibility Cam isn't up yet."

"That's okay. I'll fix breakfast for you and me and we'll go after."

Julia sighed, leaning back against the headboard. "Great idea. I'll be out in a couple minutes."

Breakfast consisted of a bowl of Froot Loops and the last of the birthday cake. Unfortunately, even that sugar fix didn't leave Julia eager to start her day or to face Cameron. During the ride up the mountain, she questioned her motives and resolve. *How am I going to do this? How can I watch these two people together— Katie with the man she's come to idolize almost as much as I did ten years ago? And Cam with the child he's just*

*told me was "special" because of her quest for knowl-
edge and enthusiasm for everything she learns. The
child so much like him?*

Cam was waiting for them on the front porch. He
stepped down and opened Julia's car door. Katie ran toward the cabin. He smiled down at Julia and reached for
her hand to help her out of the car. She reacted instantly
to his touch with a twinge of both pleasure and pain.
"How are you girls this morning?" he asked.

She quickly pulled her hand from his and walked
briskly to the porch. "Katie was so excited to get here,"
she said over her shoulder, "she was up with the sun."

He laughed. "And, let me guess. You wanted to sleep
in?"

"It might have been nice." She went into the house,
where Katie was already poring over the papers on the
coffee table.

"Whoa, kid," Cam said. "Don't you even want to
know what I've planned for you today?"

"Sure. But first I want to read more of the Jack
tales. The ones about Penelope. Will you find them
for me, Cam?"

"Give us a moment," Julia said, her tone harsher than
she'd intended. "I have to take care of Cameron's
wounds. Then we'll talk about Jack tales."

Cam raised his eyebrows at Katie and grinned.
"Guess we'd better do as we're told," he teased.

In the kitchen, when Julia was halfway through the
procedure that had become routine, Cameron covered
her hand with his. "I got some great news after you left
yesterday," he said.

Forgetting her task, she lifted her gaze to his face.
"What?"

"They've started to work on the Jeep. It'll take a while and I'll need new carpeting and seats, but hopefully she'll be good as new."

Julia concentrated on his wrist. "Oh, that's nice." She knew her response was less than enthusiastic and hoped he hadn't noticed.

He had. He covered his reaction with a chuckle. "Obviously you're not as excited as I am about the resurrection of a vehicle running on its second hundred thousand miles."

"I suppose not. But I'm happy if you are."

He remained silent a moment and then said, "So what will it take to get a smile out of you today? Something going on?"

"No. I'm fine. Why wouldn't I be?"

He shrugged. "No reason. Other than the marked change in the direction our relationship took yesterday."

Having cleaned his surgical wounds, she began unwinding a roll of gauze. "I don't think we should draw any conclusions about what happened," she said.

"I didn't think I was."

She wrapped his wrist, keeping her focus on the job. "Nothing has to change," she said. "I've promised to see to your medical needs while I'm here on the mountain, and I'm doing that."

His eyes narrowed. "Yes, and you're also helping me with the project."

"But I probably should keep my participation to the things you can't do, like driving, keyboarding information onto the computer, taking notes. Secretarial chores, mostly."

"Why? You've proven you can do so much more. And I've seen your enthusiasm for the project in everything you've done." He sat back, appraising her with an intense gaze. "You're much more than a secretary, Julia. You're part of this. You have been from the start."

"I've enjoyed it, yes, but I've let other responsibilities slide to be with you. I'm going to have to start dividing my time more fairly." She taped the end of the gauze, stood up and moved away from the table. "I'm leaving soon, remember."

He positioned the sling over his arm. "I know. But I was talking about what happened yesterday. Reading between the lines, it seems to me you're saying that because of the kiss, you won't be coming here as often."

This conversation was going badly. She'd meant to put space between them without setting off alarm bells that anything significant had changed—even though everything had now. "I'll still come, but only when you need me to take you places. I won't be as involved with the project."

She headed for the door, using the excuse that she had to check on Katie.

He grabbed her arm. "She's fine. She's twenty feet away in the next room."

Julia fixed her gaze on the floor.

"What's really going on here, Julia? Is it the kiss? Are you sorry it happened?"

"No. It probably wasn't the wisest thing we could have done, but how can I be sorry when I know we weren't behaving rationally?" When his facial expression gave her no indication of his thoughts, she blurted out the only excuse she could think of to explain her sudden aloofness. "I think it's best that we maintain some distance because of Katie."

He dropped her arm. "Katie? You've decided to stop coming here as often because of Katie? Julia, I adore her."

His words were a direct hit to her heart and conscience. "That's just it, Cameron. Katie is infatuated with you. She's already suffered one abandonment. I don't want to subject her to another."

"But I'm not leaving the mountain for nearly a year. What about you? You're returning to Manhattan in a couple of weeks."

"Yes, and I'm concerned about how my leaving will affect her. But I *have* to go."

"Right. And so do I, but not for a long time. I'll be here to help Katie and provide stability for her after you've gone."

"It's not the same."

"No. I'm not family, but she and I have grown close. I can act as a buffer when you go."

Julia stared out the window to avoid looking into Cam's eyes. "But your presence is still only temporary," she said. "When you leave her after all that time, the loss could be devastating."

He remained silent for a moment, then said, "I think you're making a mistake. Unless I'm totally misreading the situation, I believe I've helped Katie already. I believe I can continue to help her."

She faced him, unable to deny the truth of his statement. "But that doesn't change the fact that your attention and your help, won't continue into the future."

He leaned forward to rest his arm on the table. "I don't know what the future holds, Julia. You may find this hard to believe, but what happened yesterday between us violated every goal I'd established for myself in coming back to Whisper Mountain. I came here for the inspiration, yes. But for the isolation, as well. If I hadn't broken my wrist, I would be here at the top of this mountain by myself, every day, the way I'd planned."

"You wanted to be alone. I understand that. All the more reason…"

"I *needed* to be alone," he corrected. "At least, I thought I did. My divorce was unpleasant. I came here hoping the mountain would heal old wounds."

"I'm sorry about your divorce," she said. "It's hard to lose someone you love."

"I lost more than my wife, Julia. I lost a child."

He'd lost a child? She swallowed, sank into the nearest chair and said simply, "How?"

"Louisa always told me she wanted children. We talked about it before we married. We planned for it. I started a savings account for future college educations. I imagined bringing my children here to Whisper Mountain, teaching them the secrets of the hills just as my grandfather did for me."

"And you had a baby?"

His eyes clouded with regret. "No. Louisa became pregnant, but she didn't tell me. The pregnancy happened at an inopportune time in her career. She'd just decided to run for public office. A baby would have forced her to change her plans. She had an abortion, quietly, without consulting me."

Julia knew the answer before she asked her next question. "You would have tried to stop her?"

"God, yes. I would have done anything. Let her go to pursue her dreams, kept the child on my own." He threaded his hands on top of the table. "Unfortunately Louisa knew me too well. She knew that was exactly what I'd do. And she couldn't risk the damage to her reputation if it became known that her maternal instincts were lacking. She chose the easiest way out…for her, and hoped I wouldn't find out."

"How did you?"

"She taught political science at the university. We often crossed the campus to meet for lunch. I went into her office to wait for her one day. A letter lay opened on her desk, one I obviously wasn't meant to see. Since it appeared to be a statement from a clinic in Raleigh, I was curious. Louisa and I didn't keep secrets."

He released a bark of cynical laughter. "I thought she might be ill and was not telling me. I was right about the letter. It was a statement from a medical billing office, and it clearly outlined the procedure my wife had had."

Julia put her hand on his shoulder. "Cam, I'm so sorry."

"I packed my things and left. That was just over a year ago. I finished out the terms for which I was responsible in my contract with the university and applied for this sabbatical." His voice hitched, but he kept control of his emotions. "I never even knew what sex it was," he said. "She told me she hadn't asked. It didn't matter."

Julia tried not to think of the awful truth she'd discovered the night before, but the words on the birth certificate rang in her head struggling to find their way to her lips. *But you have a child, Cameron. A child you adore.* By sheer force of will, she stopped herself from saying them aloud.

"You'll stay a while today, won't you?" he asked. "I had something planned for Katie I think she'll like."

"We'll stay. And you'll see her again. I'll bring her when I can. But I have to think of her welfare…" Her concern for Katie, while foremost in her mind, suddenly seemed groundless because, deep down, she realized the false nobility of her offer. How dare she presume, as she sat here face-to-face with the child's father, to know what was in Katie's best interest?

He nodded. "You'll do the right thing. You're her aunt."

Julia picked up the medical supplies and carried them to the cupboard as she'd done many times in the past days. But she felt as hollow as her words, as if all the blood had been drained from her body. And worse, as if she were soulless. Yet how could she tell him the truth? She hadn't sorted out its significance for herself. And she had her mother to think of. Cora loved Katie. The three Sommerville women were working through their grief together. It was a delicate balancing act, one that Cameron couldn't understand.

She closed the cupboard door and turned around. Cameron had left the room, though she hadn't heard him go. She leaned heavily against the door and closed her eyes. And she knew at that moment why she hadn't told him. She loved Katie with a fierceness she'd never known she was capable of. She didn't know how she would leave her when the time came. And she certainly didn't know how she could ever give her away.

CHAPTER FOURTEEN

THE NEXT WEEK passed in a haze of guilt and indecision. Julia kept her visits to Cameron to a minimum, only going up the mountain when his wounds needed to be dressed or when he had to be driven to appointments. Their relationship was strained and uncomfortable, which was understandable since Julia was now guarding every word she spoke, fearful she would say something to alert him to the awful, weighty secret she was keeping inside. He was distant, polite and, most of all, respectful of her time—as if they had become associates, not friends, and certainly not a man and a woman who had kissed in the rain one fall afternoon.

Cam responded to her just as she'd asked him to the day they'd argued—with the utmost consideration, requesting little and appearing to expect even less. Now when she touched him in the course of her medical duties, she reminded herself that it was a job, a pledge she had made and would keep. But each time she left him, she felt more alone with her guilt and more unsure that she would ever learn to live with the burden of hiding the truth. And all because she'd begun to care deeply for him all over again.

The first Saturday morning of October dawned with an artist's palette of jeweled earth tones. Here at the higher elevations, the treetops appeared like cotton balls in shades of deep scarlet and honeyed gold. Looking out the kitchen window of her family home, Julia appreciated the splendor of the phenomenon she'd always taken for granted while, at the same time, she mechanically rotated a small plastic medicine vial in her hands.

"This isn't working, Julia," she said to herself. "You tried weaning off the pills before you were ready." She stared at the bottle in her hand, unscrewed the cap and dropped one tiny pill into her palm. And then her cell phone rang. She returned the pill to the vial and read the caller ID. "Hi, Ed," she said to the editor of *Night Lights Magazine*."

"Julia, how's everything going there?"

"Pretty well," she lied.

"Your mother? How is she?"

"Better."

"Glad to hear it. I figured you would have called by now to give me an update of your plans."

He sounded impatient. She couldn't blame him. She'd promised to keep her employer informed of her status, and she hadn't called him in more than three weeks. "Sorry, Ed. Things have been kind of hectic around here."

"You know, Julia, come Friday you'll have been gone a month. Are you still keeping to the original schedule? I have it on my calendar that you'll be back a week from Monday."

"I told you that?" Of course she did, believing a month would be enough time. That left her only nine days. But with one day or nine, Julia didn't know how the problems in her life would ever be solved. She heard herself speak words that had no basis in reality. "Everything should be fine here, Ed. I'll be back when I promised."

"So, I can count on you being at your desk in a week? I've been holding off on assigning some dynamite projects. There's an exhibit by Swiss sculptors coming to the Baker Gallery, several hot new movie releases."

"Sounds good. I look forward to getting back to work next Monday." Lie after lie. "I'll see you then."

She disconnected, stuffed her cell phone into her pocket and looked at the prescription bottle on the counter. She picked it up and returned it to the cupboard. She wouldn't take the pill. She would find relief in the fact that a plan had just been laid out for her. She knew what her near future held, and while it wasn't what she wanted now, and maybe never had been, it was hers to live. Maybe Ed's call had provided her with an answer and, with a little luck, maybe even her salvation. She could start thinking about getting back to the person she'd been and there was some comfort in that.

She went into the living room. Katie glanced up from a book. "Are you ready to go to Cameron's?" Julia asked her.

"Yes."

Julia got their jackets from the hall stand. "Just 'yes'? Usually you'd have your coat on and your backpack stuffed with things you wanted to show him by now."

"I don't have anything to show him today," she said.

"Oh. Well, that's all right. I'm sure he'll have something fun planned for you. I'm going to leave you at Cam's while I go into town and run errands. That's okay with you, isn't it?"

"Sure."

"Let's go then."

Katie set the book on the coffee table and walked

to the foyer. And Julia noticed that the book had been upside down on her lap.

CAMERON WENT to the front door when he heard Julia's car pull up. He watched her give her niece a quick hug before Katie got out of the car. Julia looked at Cam through the windshield. She smiled, a tentative uplifting of her lips and leaned out the window. "I have errands," she called to him. "Is it okay if I leave Katie with you?"

He stepped outside, put his arm around Katie when she mounted the steps. "Sure."

"I'll be back in a couple of hours. I'll change your bandages then."

"Okay. No hurry."

"Thanks. I appreciate this."

Polite but detached, as usual. A week had passed since the afternoon rainstorm. This strange and strained relationship that had started to evolve between him and Julia that day should be feeling normal by now. It wasn't. Cam's mind wandered once again to last Saturday, the day the rain fell. She'd warned him that if they allowed the kiss to happen, things would change between them. He'd thought things would change for the better.

Katie squirmed against him. He looked down into her luminous eyes—Tina's eyes—and he was filled with regret all over again. The man who'd come to Whisper Mountain determined to find the solitude to give his wounds time to heal was right back where he didn't want to be, wondering how things had gone so wrong. And how he'd let another Sommerville woman into his life and his heart.

He turned Katie around and gave her a gentle push

toward the door. "What are we going to do today?" she asked him.

"*That* is a very good question, to which I have a most interesting answer. Today, I need your help. I thought we'd go through the Jack tales we've read over the last week and see which ones are especially interesting to girls. I've decided to include a children's perspective in my research. And since you're the only child I know on the mountain, I'm counting on your expertise."

She kept walking, even released a great sigh of exaggerated disinterest. "Okay, we'll do that."

Confounded, Cameron switched gears. "We don't have to. I gathered a bucket of pinecones yesterday with the thought of painting them black and orange for Halloween. Would you like that better?"

She shrugged her shoulder, a gesture of indifference he hadn't seen in a long time. With what he assumed was typical preadolescent boredom, she said, "Whatever."

And so they did both. After spending an hour selecting Jack tales, they moved outside to a table Cameron had set up in the clearing before the trees and covered with an oilcloth. The sun was growing warm, though the morning temperature was still crisp. Cameron opened two cans of paint and handed Katie a brush. He showed her how to paint the tips of the pinecones. After forty-five minutes, he heard Julia's car.

"Your aunt's back," he said. "We should probably quit now."

"That's okay. Just call me when she's ready to go." She glanced at Cam's arm. "She still has to do that, right?"

"Yes. I'd almost forgotten. I'll go inside. It should only take a few minutes."

Another shrug. Another dip of her brush into the orange paint.

Cameron shook his head as he walked back to the house. Something wasn't right. Was his own recent moodiness affecting Katie? He hoped not. He'd tried to hide his feelings behind a mask of cheerfulness. But Katie was smart. He'd figured that out over the past couple weeks.

He went into the kitchen. Julia had opened the cupboard and was starting to take out the medical supplies. He walked up behind her and closed the cabinet door. "Never mind that now," he said.

She spun around, her blue eyes wide, her hair loose to her shoulders and shimmering in the sun coming through the window. She looked so utterly and enchantingly feminine that she took his breath away, and he didn't want her to.

Uncertainty veiled her eyes. "We have to do this, Cam."

He took her hand, led her to the table. "No. We have to talk."

"I don't think…"

He pulled out a chair. "Please, Julia." She sat.

He positioned a chair next to hers. "About Katie," he said.

She started to rise, her attention on the window.

He placed his left hand over her arm, holding her still. "She's fine. She's painting in the meadow."

"Then what's wrong?"

He tried to relax, thinking to relieve the tension in the room. "Maybe nothing, but have you noticed that she's extraordinarily quiet today?"

Julia sat back. "Oh, that. Yes, maybe a little. I wouldn't worry too much if I were you. The counselor said she'd have good days and bad. I know the warning signs if something should be seriously wrong."

He didn't say anything, opting to watch for more reaction from Julia. She held his gaze for a moment before staring down into her lap.

"What about you, Julia?" he finally said. "Do you know the warning signs for yourself?"

She looked up. "What? I don't know what you mean."

"I think you do. A week ago I kissed you, and if I'm not mistaken, you kissed me back."

She remained silent, neither denying nor confirming, her eyes fixed on a spot across the room.

He plunged ahead. "Since then, you've been agonizingly polite. You've been different toward me and, God knows, we've been uncomfortable in each other's presence. If these aren't warning signs of something going on, I don't know what is." He leaned closer to her hoping she'd focus on him. She didn't. "I thought the kiss was pretty spectacular. I thought we connected. But if you didn't feel it, just tell me."

Her gaze met his. "It was just a kiss."

"Really? I've kissed a few women, and I'd take that description up a notch. Instead of 'just a kiss,' I'd call it quite a kiss."

"It only seemed that way because we'd been arguing."

Not following her line of reasoning, he frowned at her. "Yes, but we'd stopped, rather suddenly."

"I know, but it can be difficult to distinguish the passion of one moment from the passion of the next. Both incidents were highly charged with emotion."

"I think I know the difference between verbal warfare and intense sexual attraction." She stood up, walked to the window. He spoke to her back. "And I think you do, too."

He waited a moment and then followed her. He wrapped his hand around her upper arm, leaned so close he could smell the citrus scent of her hair, feel the heat from her flushed face. "What are you afraid of, Julia?"

She faced him. "I'm not afraid. I'm being sensible for the first time in my life."

"And being sensible means ignoring your emotions, refusing to admit that you were affected by that kiss?"

"Yes, it does."

She stared at him, unblinking, hiding her emotions as she'd been doing for a week. But he didn't buy it. "There's more, Julia. I know there is."

Her hands fisted at her sides in a show of determination that might have worked if he hadn't noticed her bottom lip quiver. "Tell me what's going on," he insisted.

"I'm leaving, Cameron. I'm going back to New York."

"Not yet. We have time…"

Her eyes shone with a glimmer of moisture. "And you're leaving. We have our own lives. I have responsibilities and so do you. I was just getting back on track with my life and then Tina did this awful thing."

His grip on her arm tightened. "What awful thing? She died. It's tragic, yes, but…"

"She killed herself, Cameron!"

He shook his head, awestruck.

"She left her house in the middle of the night and walked into the lake. All on her own. Without telling anyone goodbye. And I—none of us—did anything to stop her."

Her body shuddered and she bit her bottom lip. Cameron pulled her close, wrapped his arm around her. "Oh, God, Julia. I'm so sorry."

She lay her forehead against his chest and cried. He

smoothed his hand down her hair, over her shoulder, felt the rigidity of her spine as the awful tension of guilt spread to every part of her. Everything suddenly became clear to him. This woman who had climbed down a ravine to save his life was, at this moment, as fragile as china. "It's going to be okay," he murmured in her ear. "It's not your fault."

"I didn't even know her at the end," she sobbed. "I had stopped trying."

He crooned soothing sounds, pressed his lips against her temple. "She was a complicated woman," he said. "I don't think she wanted anyone to know her, to sense her unhappiness. She dealt with it the only way she knew how." Again he said the words he hoped she would believe. "It's not your fault, baby. It's no one's fault."

Her sobs subsided, but he continued to hold her because she continued to let him. He looked over her shoulder out the window and watched Katie. And then a shock of awareness made him draw away. "Does Katie know?" he asked.

She nodded. "It's been so hard for her. Wayne didn't even try to mask the truth."

Cameron's jaw clenched. "And where has he been through all of this? What kind of a father is he?"

Her body stiffened. She grabbed a fistful of Cam's shirt. "He's gone, for good I hope. Katie is better off without him."

He sensed her resentment in the fierceness of her voice. When a horrifying thought occurred to him, he lifted Julia's face to see into her eyes. "Is this what's changed in Katie?" he asked. "Has she heard from her father? Has he hurt her in some other way?"

Julia closed her eyes. Her wet lashes lay against her

cheekbone. Her voice quivered when she answered. "No. He's called only one time and then he spoke to Katie for less than a minute. That's the way I want it."

"You know if there's anything I can do to help, I will. I hate seeing both of you going through this."

He almost expected her to deny needing help, to staunchly declare her independence. But she stared up at him, her eyes a shimmering blue, her lips full and trembling. She placed her hands on each side of his face and spoke so softly he barely heard the words. "Cameron, I'm so sorry."

"You have nothing to apologize for. I'm the one who's sorry. I didn't know. Here I am, demanding some response from you about what happened last week…"

She traced his bottom lip with her index finger and smiled. "The kiss?"

"The kiss."

Rising up on her toes, she pressed her lips to his and lingered there, moist, gentle and giving without restraint. He moved his mouth over hers, coaxed his tongue inside and sought the most warm, sensitive places. She bent against him and moaned, leaving no doubt in his mind that she shared his passion equally. When she drew away, the smile returned. "Last Saturday…"

"Yes?"

"That was quite possibly the best kiss I've ever had. Until now." She pressed her hand against his chest. "If things were different…" She stepped away from him. "I'm sorry, Cam. So very sorry."

There it was again. That apology spoken as if her heart were breaking. She'd done more than put physical space between them. She'd broken the emotional bond of a moment before, and he didn't have a clue how to get it, or her, back. He reached for her, but she moved farther away. "I have to get Katie. I have to go." Then as if suddenly remembering her purpose for being there, she glanced at the cupboard and said, "Your bandages."

He looked out the window, finding solace in watching Katie. "I can manage on my own if you have to go."

She went to the door. "Maybe it's better if you do."

He allowed his gaze to linger on her as she walked across the meadow and took Katie's hand. They didn't return to the cabin, instead heading around the side to Julia's car. Cameron knew they'd left when he heard the car start down the mountain.

THE ROAD blurred before Julia's eyes. She pulled a tissue from a box between the seats and wiped her eyes.

"Is something wrong?" Katie asked.

"Allergies, I think. Sometimes the wildflowers affect me this way."

"Oh." Katie stared straight ahead.

"Did you have fun this morning?" Julia asked her.

"It was okay."

Julia rolled down her window, grateful for the blast of cool air that bathed her face. "Has something happened?" she asked. "Do you want to talk to me about it?"

"No. Nothing happened."

"Cameron thought you might be upset. You're not angry at him are you?"

Katie darted a narrowed gaze across the space between them. "At Cameron? No."

"At me?"

"No." This time the denial was less emphatic.

Despite the torrent of emotions still raging inside her, Julia kept her voice even. "You can tell me if you are."

"I'm not."

"Okay, then."

They rounded the last bend before the store, and Julia slowed for the turn. The parking lot was full of tourists' vehicles, everything from four-wheel drives to shiny motorcycles. A crowd of falls watchers had gathered on the opposite side of the road. Cora and Rosalie would be grateful she was back to help. She was relieved she had something to do that might help her forget the last several moments.

They got out of the car and stepped onto the porch, where a group of tourists sat sipping apple cider. They exchanged friendly greetings. It was a typically beautiful autumn mountain day. And Julia had no idea how she was going to get through it. Her thoughts were at the top of mountain, not here. In her mind, she was still wrapped in the embrace of the man she'd once adored and now simply loved.

Katie ran inside the store. Needing a few minutes, Julia leaned over the porch railing and listened to the chorus of the waterfall, a sound she usually found soothing, but which only increased her anxiety now. How could she not tell Cameron he had a daughter? She knew of his past heartache at losing a child, and she felt his pain as certainly as if it were her own. But if he gained a child, she would lose one. They both loved Katie, but right now, only Julia and Cora had a claim to her. Cameron didn't know the truth, that his rights were much stronger than theirs, and Julia was the one person who could guarantee that he never would. The proof was buried under her mattress, keeping Katie close.

She rubbed away a tear that slid down her cheek. Today she'd done nothing. And that was easier than facing the decisions that would have to be made in the next nine days—decisions that could change all their lives.

JULIA FINISHED putting away the few supper dishes she'd used to prepare hamburgers for her and Katie. She wiped her hands and went into the living room. "Where are you going tonight, Mama?"

Cora patted her hair in front of the mirror. "Oscar's taking me to a restaurant in Asheville." She gave Julia a wink over her shoulder. "They have dancing, too. I don't know how late we'll be."

"Don't worry about it. Katie and I are tired, anyway." She smiled. "Just behave yourself…or not."

Cora seemed to float toward the front door when Oscar drove up. She paused with her hand on the knob. "I can't help myself, honey. I'm having the time of my life. I thought I would feel guilty, but I don't. I never imagined I'd have so much fun again."

"You deserve it, Mama," Julia said. "Enjoy yourself. There's been enough guilt in this family to last a lifetime."

She smiled at Katie. "Thanks. You girls keep warm. On the news, they said it could get down to the thirties on the mountain tonight."

Once Cora left, Julia piled logs on the hearth and made a fire. "What do you want to do?" she asked Katie when the fire had bathed the room in toasty warmth.

"I don't know."

"Do you want to watch a movie? I got a couple at the video store this morning knowing Grandma would be out and we'd be curled up on the sofa."

"Okay."

They watched *The Princess Diaries* and shared a bowl of popcorn. When the movie ended, Julia suggested they play a game of Double Trouble, one of Katie's favorites.

"I think I'll just go to bed," Katie said. "If that's okay with you."

The mantel clock said nearly ten o'clock. Julia yawned. "That's a good idea. I'm right behind you." She walked Katie to her room and helped her into bed. "See you in the morning, sweetie."

Within a few minutes, Katie was asleep. Julia set the screen before the dying fire and turned the thermostat to a comfortable sixty-five degrees. She tried to read but found her mind wandering to Cameron, as it almost always did. She turned out her light and lay still, picturing him in front of Josiah's rugged fieldstone fireplace, a mug of coffee at his side, his head bent over his work.

He'd been right to insist that he stay on the mountain after his accident. He did belong here, at least for now. He was as connected to this mountain as she was, maybe more because his ties were stronger than family. He was connected by his soul. At the top of Whisper Mountain, Cameron was where he wanted to be, and tonight, that was where Julia longed to be, as well.

An hour passed before Julia gave up trying to sleep. She got up, put on her old flannel robe and slid her feet into warm slippers. She padded into the kitchen thinking maybe she'd try the old warm-milk sedative. She felt a chill the instant she went into the room. Without turning on the light, she looked out the window. Like limbs of a skeleton in the rays of a full moon, the branches of the tallest trees whipped up a frenzy at the rear of the yard. Cora's manicured shrubs rustled against the windowpanes. Julia opened the back door and stepped onto the service porch. A cold wind swept down the mountain and stung her cheeks.

"Wow, Mama was right," she said. She went into the living room to adjust the thermostat and decided to check on Katie. Thinking she might need an extra blanket, Julia pulled a quilt from the linen closet. She opened the door to Katie's room and blinked, letting her eyes adjust to the darkness. Believing her mind was playing tricks on her, she leaned over and ran her hand across the mattress.

And a chill far worse than the one descending on Whisper Mountain gripped her. Katie's bed was empty.

CHAPTER FIFTEEN

"THERE'S AN EXPLANATION. There has to be." Her own words of encouragement did nothing to stop the pounding of Julia's heart. *Of course there's always an explanation,* she thought. *But lately I've learned that often it's not one we like.*

She raced across Katie's room to the switch by the door and turned on the overhead light. She searched everywhere. In the closet, under the bed, beside the dresser, even though it wasn't like Katie to play hide-and-seek games.

"Katie, where are you?" Julia hollered as she went into the hallway. My room, of course. She woke up, was cold and went to be with me. Julia hurried down the hallway and flipped on the light in her room. No Katie. She performed the same manic search routine.

She checked Cora's room, the bathroom, the kitchen and living room. Katie was not in the house. By the time Julia opened the back door to the porch, she was imagwining the worst, which involved the dark night and some very cold temperatures. "Katie!" She went outside and tore across the yard in her slippers. The chill penetrated her soft soles.

She circled the meadow at the tree line and climbed partway up the slope that bordered the cabin's rear boundary. "Katie!" The night was filled with sounds of creatures seeking warm shelter, the wind moaning through the tallest trees. Leaves, buffeted by the breeze, fell around her, hitting her shoulders and face before swirling to the ground.

She ran through the house again thinking she might have missed something obvious, the one place she hadn't thought to look. After another fruitless search, she stood in the middle of the living room, her hand pressed to her mouth, her lips trembling. "My, God, what's happened to her?"

She went to the front door and discovered the dead bolt had been turned. Numb with shock, Julia verbalized the obvious conclusion. "Why? The road…" She stepped outside among the wildly rocking chairs caught in the first fury of a cold front. Hanging plants battered the eaves, their delicate petals raining down to the porch floor.

She stopped at the steps, looked left and right on the road and was reminded of a similar night a few weeks ago when Cameron had plunged over the ravine. "That storm was worse," she told herself as she went down the steps. "It's not raining tonight. It's just windy and cold." She darted across the road, her breath catching in her lungs, her throat constricting from panic and the biting chill. *It's freezing,* she thought. *A little girl can't last long out here.*

And then she saw her. On the other side of the newly mended guardrail, Katie stood at the edge of the gully. So still. Like a statue, her white nightgown billowing around her legs, her hair whipping against her cheeks. An instantaneous analysis of that particular stretch of road nearly caused Julia to drop to her knees with panic. Katie was perched like a delicate bird on a rocky border perhaps no wider than a foot or two. One false step…

She started to scream Katie's name, but reason and logic stopped her. The last thing she wanted to do was startle her. What if she were sleepwalking? Any sudden noise could waken her to the unfamiliar environment and cause an instinctive movement to protect herself that could instead send her over the side.

Julia thought her heart would burst the walls of her chest as she crept silently along the road, each footfall taking her closer. The falls thundered beside her, wild and threatening. Spray hit her face. She knew Katie must be getting soaked. She kept her eyes on the child, never once looking down even when she stepped over the railing. She had no idea where her own feet were landing on the rocky outcropping. Then, fearful she'd make a misstep, send a loose bit of gravel skidding down the ravine or break a twig, she stopped about fifteen feet from Katie. She knelt to keep her profile nonthreatening. Swallowing, she drew a breath of icy air into her lungs.

"Katie?" No reaction. She tried again, louder this time. "Sweetheart? Can you hear me? It's Aunt Julia."

Katie's head turned. She stared across the space separating her from her aunt. In the moonglow, Julia could see tracks of tears on Katie's face. She must be terrified. Julia rose, held out her hand. "Stay right there, sweetie. I'm coming to get you."

"No. Go back."

Julia dropped her arm to her side. "Katie, you're frightened. But I can reach you. Just stay still."

"I don't want you to get me," she said. "Go back. I want to be here."

This wasn't making any sense. Katie was obviously awake and aware, but perhaps living through some bizarre nightmare from which she hadn't fully awakened. To keep her niece talking, Julia said, "But why are you out here, honey?"

Katie inhaled a deep, trembling breath. "I'm going to be with my mommy."

She lowered her gaze and, for a moment, Julia thought her heart had stopped beating. "No, Katie, don't look down. Look at me, sweetie. Your mommy's not down there."

"But she went in the water, and I'm going in, too. I'm going to be with her."

Julia shivered, not from the cold but because she was caught in the worst indecision of her lifetime. Should she go forward or stay back? She clasped her hands until they hurt, using the pain to stay rational. "Your mommy wouldn't want you to do this, honey. She would want you to stay right there and let me come to you."

Katie's small chest heaved. She ran a finger under her nose. "You don't care about me."

"What? Of course I do. I love you."

"You're going away."

"Not for a while."

"You're going soon. I heard you on the phone this morning. You told someone you were leaving here."

Oh, God, what have I done? Julia replayed in her mind her phone conversation with Ed. Katie had been in the next room only pretending to read. She'd heard everything. That's why she'd been sullen and unresponsive for most of the day. Guilt slammed into Julia with a force as great as if she'd plunged headfirst into the ravine.

She sank back on the rocks and clung to the guardrail. "We'll work something out, baby, I promise."

Katie shook her head. "No. I'm going with Mommy."

"You don't have to do that. I'll take care of you." Her next words came from a deep well of love more powerful than she'd known she could feel. "You'll come to New York with me."

Katie's head swivelled. She stared at Julia. Her lips moved. And then headlights veered into the parking lot and tires ground on the gravel. Katie shifted her attention to the waterfall again. A moment later, Cora was running toward them. "Katie, what are you doing? My God, Katie!"

Julia pulled herself up and spoke in a harsh whisper. "Mama, stay back." She held her hand up toward Katie. "Don't move, sweetie."

"Julia, what's going on?"

"Mama, don't come any closer."

"But she's at the edge. She'll fall."

Julia lowered her voice even more. "No, Mama, she'll jump. Please stay back."

"But why? What's happened?" Oscar came up behind her. "What do you want me to do?" Cora asked.

Julia instantly knew the answer. "Call Cameron," she said. "Tell him to come."

Cora ran to the store. Oscar followed.

"It's going to be okay, Katie," Julia said. "I know you must be scared, but Cam's coming. He'll help you. Just don't move, baby. I won't come near you if that's what you want. But stay very still. Please, sweetheart. Promise me."

When she saw the girl's head bow with what she hoped was acceptance, Julia felt the tears flow down her cheeks. She sank to her knees and concentrated on the seconds passing. Cameron should be able to reach them in ten minutes. "Please be careful," she whispered as if he could hear her. Driving on the mountain at night was dangerous enough, but with one hand…

As time crawled, she talked. About the movie they'd seen that night, about school, about the wildflowers and the beauty of the leaves. And about the cold and the night sky, brilliant with stars. She didn't stop talking until she saw the Xterra pull to the side of the road and Cameron get out.

He spoke briefly to Cora and crossed the road. When he bent down to Julia, the last of her strength ebbed from her limbs. Words came from her mouth in choking sobs. "I've done this," she said. "I sent her to this ledge. She's going to jump, Cam. I can't stop her."

He lifted her up, made her step over the railing. "No, no, sweetheart, you didn't do this." He motioned to Cora. "Bring blankets. Stay with Julia."

Julia clutched his sweatshirt. "You've got to save her."

"I will. You wait for your mother. It's going to be all right."

He edged away from her, slowly approaching Katie. "Hey, Pussy toes," he said, his voice unbelievably calm. "You want to tell me what's going on?"

Katie wrapped her arms around her middle. "I'm going in the water like my mommy did. She wants me to be with her. She misses me."

"Sure she does. But she doesn't want you to do this. She wants you to have a happy life. That's why she sent you here to Whisper Mountain, the best place on Earth."

"Stop, Cameron," Katie said, her small voice steely with determination.

He stopped, though every instinct urged him to cover the few remaining feet and grab her. But a mistake in timing wasn't an option. "Okay, but can I talk to you from here?"

"I guess."

"As I see it, Pussy toes, we have two choices."

He waited for a reaction. She glanced at him, held his gaze for a moment, long enough to let him know he'd at least reached her.

"You remember that man I told you about? The guy named Marcus who has the hound dogs?"

"The man who finds people?"

"Yep. If you go over the side of this ravine, I'll have to call him so he can look for you because that's what he does and he's good at it. But I don't know if he'll find you or not. It's dark. And it's cold and he's an old man. And those old hounds will have to go down in the gully with him, and I don't know if they can do that anymore. But that's what'll happen if you go through with this. So I was kind of hoping you'd change your mind and keep an old man and his dogs warm tonight."

She sucked on her bottom lip, considering.

Cam kept talking. "And what'll also happen if you do this is I'll have to ask a favor of that old gal in the Hollow."

Katie swept strands of hair from her face, the first sign he'd seen that she was aware of the bitter wind. "You mean Maude?"

"I do. If you disappear into the gully, she'll have to find a ballad for you, and it'll be a sad one. No one likes to hear a ballad about a smart little girl who ended up making a decision like this one. A lot of people will be sad to hear it." He pointed over his shoulder to where Cora, Oscar and Julia waited. "Those who love you and even those who don't even know you yet."

She nodded her head ever so slightly, and he smiled.

"Now, I know you pretty well, kiddo, and I know you're not the sort to make people sad."

She whispered, "No." At least he thought she did.

"But here's our other option. It's the one I like."

She sniffed. "What is it?"

"I want you to let me come over there and pick you up and bring you back to your grandma's house so I can start writing the greatest Jack tale this region has ever read. I want everyone who lives on the Blue Ridge to know about Katie, the mountain girl who spit in the jaws of Whisper Mountain Falls and didn't let the water take her down, because she's the bravest gal I've ever known."

Katie rubbed her eyes, and Cameron waited for a glimpse of her face, a sign that she'd heard him. When she dropped her hands to her sides, it was as if the moon broke through the panic and lit his soul. She was smiling.

"So what'll it be, Pussy toes? Option number two?"

She nodded. He reached her in about three seconds and pulled her over the guardrail where he held her so close he could feel her tiny heartbeat, strong and sure. He was trembling as he handed her over to Julia and watched Cora wrap them both in a blanket. Oscar hugged Cora and the four of them plopped right down on the rough edge of the road and held on to each other. Cameron couldn't tell who was crying and who was laughing, but he suspected they were all doing a bit of both.

Julia stood, walked away from the others and cupped his face in her hands. "Thank you, Cameron."

He squeezed her hand.

A moment later, Katie tugged on his sweatshirt. He'd forgotten to grab his coat. "Will you really write that Jack tale?" she asked.

"You bet I will. Promises are made to be kept."

And when he looked back at Julia, he saw a sober determination in her eyes.

WITH OSCAR BY her side, Cora took command of the situation and mothered to perfection. She immediately put Katie into a clean, warm nightie. Then, in between gentle scolding and words of love, she sat her down at the kitchen table, where she fed her soup, hot chocolate and a Sunny Vale Bakery cupcake. Only when Katie promised never to go near the ravine again did Cora allow her to leave her watchful eyes and return to bed.

"It's okay, Grandma," Katie said as she went through the living room, her eyes drooping and her hand covering a yawn. "You don't have to worry about me."

Julia glanced at Cameron beside her on the sofa. The looks they exchanged said they both understood that only careful watchfulness and constant reinforcement would make her statements true.

"Oscar's leaving and I'm going to bed," Cora said when she'd put Katie down.

Too exhausted to move, Julia smiled up from the sofa. "Thanks for everything, Oscar."

"It's no problem, Julia. I only hope the precious little one will never scare us like that again."

Julia noticed how easily he'd slipped the word *us* into the conversation. He was beginning to feel like part of the family, and after what they'd all been through tonight, he had a permanent place at the dinner table as far as she was concerned.

Cora walked him out, returned immediately and headed for her room. "Brr. Don't forget to put the fire out, Julia," she said. "And Cameron, if you're determined to be fool enough to drive back up the mountain, be careful."

"He's not going anywhere but this sofa for the rest of the night," Julia said. "I won't risk another emergency befalling the Sommerville women."

"Now you're talking sense." Cora patted Cam's shoulder. "Thanks for what you did tonight. It doesn't seem like enough to say, but you know I mean it more than words can tell."

"I know you do, Cora. I'm glad I was here. Your granddaughter has found a place in my heart almost as much as she has yours and Julia's."

Julia flinched at his words, spoken so honestly, so innocently.

Cam pulled a quilt tighter around Julia's shoulders. "You cold?"

"A little."

With Cora gone and Katie sound asleep, the room was quiet, cozy in a way Julia had never appreciated before. The entire world seemed secure within these four walls, a protective barrier keeping her family safe. The crackling fire provided enough warmth, yet Julia shivered. The real world was still out there and had nearly swallowed up her niece tonight. And the problems in their lives still existed.

Cameron slipped his arm around her and pulled her close. "Let's see if I can take away the chill. You mind?"

She shook her head, hating herself for so desperately craving his comfort and support, while she kept secrets that would change his life. He stroked her arm through the T-shirt she'd put on when she came inside. His touch was soft and constant and seemed to reach to her core.

"You're not still blaming yourself, are you?" he said.

About this, about you, about everything. "I can't

help it. If Katie hadn't heard my phone conversation this morning…"

"She would have heard the news another way," he reasoned. "And maybe when she reacted then, you wouldn't have been here to help her."

He settled his chin on top of her head. "You saved her tonight, Julia. You didn't hurt her."

"I wish I could believe that." She shifted, lay her head against his solid chest near where his sling crossed his rib cage. Then, mindful of his injuries, she said, "Am I hurting you?"

He reached up, smoothed her hair off her forehead. "My bruises and cuts have healed. If it weren't for this damn wrist, I'd be good as new." He chuckled. "Physically, at least."

"I'm so sorry, Cameron." She pulled her bottom lip between her teeth and squeezed her eyes shut. She'd been saying that every day, it seemed.

"What for now?" he teased. "It certainly isn't your fault I banged up my arm."

"I know."

"So why do you keep apologizing?"

"Do I?"

"Yes."

She needed to answer him, to come up with a logical reason she was so desperately sorry. "I'm taking Katie back to New York with me," she said. "I promised her while we were at the edge of the ravine. I think, at least for that moment, the idea calmed her."

His hand stilled, resting on the top of her head. He didn't speak for several moments until finally he murmured, "You're her aunt. You would know best."

Defending her decision, she said, "Yes, I would. I

can't abandon her. You saw what she did after hearing me on the phone. And this is a way I can repay Tina, perhaps make up to her for the past."

"I thought we'd covered this ground, Julia. You don't owe Tina." When she didn't respond, he said, "Have you told Cora about this plan?"

"No. And I don't look forward to telling her."

"She's become very attached to Katie. Their relationship has helped her through the tough times."

"I know. But I have to think of Katie."

Cameron tucked a strand of hair behind her ear. "It's not my place to say this, Julia, but I think the mountain has been good for Katie."

Julia clenched her hands in her lap. *You have been good for Katie.*

"She's done well here," Cameron said. "She seems happy."

"She'll be happy in New York," Julia said. "I'll get a bigger apartment, enroll her in school." *Sell my car and try to convince my boss I'm worth twice my salary.*

He turned toward her and cupped her chin in his hand. Raising her face, he said, "You'll do what's best for her. I know that."

Julia nodded. "I'll try. I won't let her down." *And I need her. I can't let her go.* And with that thought came the undeniable, undiluted truth that Julia had resisted putting into words. She needed Katie more than Cameron did. He didn't know she was his flesh and blood. He would miss her, but he would forget. If Julia told him about his connection to Katie and then left the mountain without her, her heart would break more with every passing day.

Once she began this pathway of rationalization, she

couldn't stop. How did she know Cameron would even be a good father? What if now that he was a bachelor he didn't want the responsibility of a child? What then? Would he take Katie in just to do the right thing? He was that kind of man. But would that be best for Katie? She'd already had one part-time father.

But Julia knew the answers to all those questions. Cameron Birch did not *try* to do the right thing. He simply did it. He cared, and if she kept this secret as she knew she must for her own sake, that thought would haunt her the rest of her days.

He smiled at her as if forgiving her for the horrible sin she'd convinced herself to commit. His hand still holding her face he said, "You and I got a lot more than we expected when we came back to this mountain, didn't we?"

"What do you mean?"

"You know." He bent his head. She moistened her lips in preparation for his kiss. His mouth covered hers and he kissed her deeply, hungrily. When he ended the kiss, he held her against him. His voice, low and husky, vibrated in her ear. "Neither one of us came to Whisper Mountain for this," he said. "And frankly, Julia, I don't know what to do about these feelings I have for you."

She touched his cheek. "You'll go on with your life as you've planned it," she said. "You know what you came to the mountain for. None of that has changed."

"You're wrong," he said. "You've changed it. You deny it, but it's true. I expected a year of introspection, of study, a chance to pursue a lifelong interest. And then you were there, at the bottom of the ravine, telling me that everything would be okay." He kissed her again.

"God, Julia, when you go, I'm not sure anything will ever be okay again."

How long had she wanted to hear such words from Cameron? And now she couldn't let herself believe them. She couldn't let herself trust that they could have a future. Letting herself trust in Cameron meant she could lose Katie. But for now, this one night…

She reached behind him and pulled him down to her. Their mouths blended in a desperate need to satisfy an unquenchable emotional thirst, to find solutions that simply weren't there. But the need was real. She kissed him with a passion that rocked her with its intensity. His hand tunneled under her shirt and found her naked breast. She responded immediately and completely with a low, needy groan. Her body longed for this man. It always had.

His touch was gentle yet firm, his fingertips calloused from the simple chores of living on the mountain. Her nipples puckered, ached. Her yearning spiraled into mindless hunger for what they'd too long denied.

And then, as if they both knew that this was not the time or the place to fulfill their desires, they parted. He drew a deep breath and she snuggled close to him, unable to break the contact entirely. "This isn't the end, Julia," he said. "I'll be here for a full year. You'll come back often to bring Katie. We'll find out where this is going."

She nodded, the words to respond to him simply not there. He reached down beside the sofa and picked up a pillow. Settling it on his lap, he drew her down. "It's okay, baby. Just sleep."

With his fingers tracing lazy circles on her arm, she tried to do what he told her. But her mind wouldn't let her rest. *Please, Cameron, don't be nice to me. It's the one thing I don't think I can bear.*

CHAPTER SIXTEEN

BY THE TIME Julia had dropped Katie off at school Monday morning and had had her third cup of coffee, she'd managed to convince herself once more that taking Katie to New York was best for everyone. She ignored the persistent nagging voice in her head that kept repeating, *Yeah, best for you.* She even tried to justify her decision by telling herself that Cameron was some kind of threat because he was Katie's father, *her* Katie's father. Of course, she knew that it wasn't true. It was her perspective, clouded by guilt and need, that prompted her to have such irrational thoughts.

Before leaving to drive Cameron to a remote county library where he planned to meet with a folklorist, Julia made several phone calls from the privacy of her bedroom. The first was to Louie Marconi, the owner of Louie's Downtown Garage in Manhattan.

Louie's voice was cheerful when he realized who was calling. "Hey, Miss Sommerville. You want the Cavalier out today?"

"No, Louie. I'm calling because I need your help. I'm going to sell that car, and I'm wondering if you might be able to put up a couple of For Sale signs around the garage for me. Prospective buyers can contact you."

"That car runs good, doesn't it?" he asked.

"Yeah, the last time I had it out, anyway."

"How much you want for it?"

She'd checked an online car value site, considered the car's exterior flaws and come up with a figure. "Do you think we can get two thousand dollars? I'd cut you in for ten percent."

"Sounds fair."

"What are the chances of selling it?"

"Good. In fact, I bet I'll have that vehicle sold by this afternoon. I got a waiting list of people looking for a car that runs for a measly two grand."

"Great. I'll check in with you later."

She experienced a pang of loss when she hung up the phone. A major security blanket had just been yanked from her grip. But she needed the money more than she had to have a car for the few times she used it.

Next, she called the super of her building and asked him if a two-bedroom apartment was available. He told her that nothing was vacant now, but he'd notify her of the first unit to come up for lease. When she asked what the rent increase would be, she cringed. She'd really have to work on Ed to raise her salary. She hadn't had a bump in almost two years, so she was due. Last, she asked him about the location of the nearest elementary school and made plans to walk Katie by it over the weekend to acquaint her with the neighborhood.

Her next call was to Ed. His voice was guarded when he said, "You haven't changed your mind, have you?"

"No. I'll be back on Monday. But Ed, I need some time Monday morning to take care of a personal matter."

"How much time?"

She figured a couple of hours ought to be sufficient

to enroll Katie in school for Tuesday. She'd bring her to the office with her for the rest of the day Monday.

Julia's last phone call was the one that truly cemented her plans. She called the airline where she'd originally booked her open-ended ticket to Charlotte and scheduled a flight to Manhattan on Friday, for two. She would have Saturday and Sunday to introduce Katie to the city and her new, confined living quarters.

Those chores out of the way, Julia went into the kitchen to face her mother. She had asked Katie to keep their moving plans a secret for a couple of days so she could "prepare Grandma." Katie had reluctantly agreed.

Cora looked over from the sink where she was rinsing the coffee mugs. "You want breakfast?"

"No, I had a bowl of cereal earlier." She sat at the table. "Mama, I need to tell you something. Will you sit a moment?"

Cora's eyes widened. She approached tentatively and sat. "What's wrong?"

"Nothing's wrong, exactly," Julia said. "I've just made a decision that affects all of us."

Cora's hand fluttered at the neckline of her sweater. "What have you done?"

"When Katie was in trouble the other night, when she was at the ravine…" Julia paused, uncertain how to proceed though she'd contemplated this conversation for two days. Should she prepare her mother by trying to explain the sudden and overpowering thought processes that had caused her to offer this solution to Katie that night? Or should she just state the decision and help her mother to adjust.

She chose the latter, hoping for the best. "I told Katie that night that I wouldn't leave her."

Cora immediately jumped to an inaccurate conclusion. "Thank God, Julia. You're staying with us!"

Julia mentally scolded herself for her choice of words. "No, Mama. I told her I would take her back to New York with me."

Cora's face blanched. "You what? How c-could you do that?"

"I had to do something that night, Mama. She was going to jump. I had to let her know that I wouldn't leave her."

"But to suggest taking her from the mountain. You can't do that Julia. K-Katie belongs here. It's what Tina wanted."

"Tina wanted her cared for and loved, and I will do that just as you would. The place where she's raised isn't so important." She paused, gauged her mother's emotional state and added, "And, Mama, she wants to go."

"I don't believe it! This is Katie's home now. She has me and her school and Cameron..."

Julia ignored the all-too-familiar stab of pain in her chest. "Cameron is leaving, too, Mama. You know that. He won't provide the stability Katie needs for the future."

"But, I will," Cora insisted. "And so would you if you would just do the right thing for once in your life and stay here!"

Cora's implied accusation stung, and Julia fought the first flare-up of anger. Good God, she'd done the "right thing" her whole life while Tina had flitted from one place to the next, one man to another. Her mother was not going to lay the blame on Julia's shoulders this time. Julia had sacrificed enough.

She stood, replaced her chair under the table. "I'm sorry if you're upset with this decision," she said. "But it's made. Katie knows. She's happy with it. My life is in Manhattan. We'll visit as often as we can, but she's going with me."

Cora covered her face with her hands and wept. "I want you to ch-change your mind, Julia. Katie needs me." She looked up, her expression nearly causing Julia's knees to buckle. "And I need her. I really do."

"Mama, you have to make your own life, and you've started to do that. I'm proud of the steps you've taken, but you can't stop now. You have to realize that your life has worth and purpose on its own, not because of a nine-year-old girl." She placed her palm on Cora's shoulder. "It's best for everyone, Mama. You'll see."

Julia left the kitchen and headed for her car. As she drove up the mountain, she wondered about the words she'd just spoken. "It's best for everyone..." She prayed she was right and that time and distance would eventually lift the god-awful burden of her secret from her shoulders.

JULIA KNOCKED on Cameron's door before stepping inside the cabin. "I'm here," she called. "You ready?"

He came out of the kitchen, crossed the living room, placed his hand at her nape and drew her close for a kiss.

She stared up at him trying to think of what to say. Not surprisingly, nothing came to mind.

"Had to get it out of the way," he said. "Seems like we do a lot of dancing around until we get to the point where we're actually doing that. I decided to cut right to the chase this morning."

Was this Cameron, being fun and flirtatious? Julia watched him walk to a table and sort through notes before she came all the way into the room. "You're practical if nothing else," she said.

He grinned at her. "Oh, I'm something else. I'm thinking ahead to when we get back from the library today. We'll be alone, Julia. No interruptions."

"Cam…"

He studied her face a moment and then shoved papers into a briefcase. "I've seen that look before," he said. "I never much liked it. I think it means I'm not going to make love to you this afternoon."

She gripped the back of a chair. Her eyes darted to the winding staircase leading to the bedrooms.

He laughed. "Made you think about it, at least. It's okay, Julia. I'll just have to get my mind focused in another direction."

"Cam, I just can't. There's Katie…"

"Katie?" He made a great show of looking around the living room. "I don't see her."

"No, but it's complicated. You have a relationship with her. I do, too."

He snapped his briefcase closed. "My relationship with Katie is not nearly as complicated as the one I have with you."

She looked at the ceiling. If he only knew.

"How's she adjusting to the idea of going to New York, by the way?" he asked.

"Well. She's excited about it, I think."

He walked past her to get his jacket from a peg by the door. She grabbed his sleeve to stop him. "It's not that I don't want to," she said. "But aside from everything else, there's your arm to think of."

He took a quick, amused glance at his wrist. "Funny, but when I heard your car pull up just now, it wasn't my arm I thought of, at all. Other body parts demanded my attention, and half of them were yours."

She smiled. And she flushed and had every other emotional reaction a woman had when faced with the ultimate temptation—one she'd been thinking about for weeks.

He put his arm through a jacket sleeve and draped the other side over his shoulder. Before going out, he gave her a serious look. "I'm not giving up, Julia. This is going to happen between us. I'm just not sure when."

She decided now wasn't the time to tell him she'd made her plane reservations. If her damn conscience would ease up just a bit, she could certainly see the two of them climbing those stairs. He was out the door and headed to the Xterra before she realized he'd left. With a groan, she followed him out, slamming the cabin door behind her.

JULIA WALKED into the kitchen on Wednesday morning after taking Katie to school. Cameron's blunt statement that they were eventually going to make love had kept her aware of little else since. She believed his prediction because every cell in her body had come alive when he'd made it. She felt almost combustible, and the tension building inside her couldn't last forever without finding release.

Knowing her inhibitions were threatened whenever she was with him, Julia had avoided going to Cameron's on Tuesday. But he was expecting her today. She had to drive him to his doctor's appointment, and she'd promised to type up research notes he'd taken at the library.

Surprised when her mother wasn't in the kitchen at her usual hour, Julia poured cereal into a bowl and dribbled milk over the frosted bites. Carrying the bowl, she headed back to her room thinking she'd nibble while getting dressed. And maybe have a few extra moments to take care with her makeup. Her body tingled with the image of what could happen later, despite all her efforts to keep her relationship with Cam from ending up in one of the loft bedrooms of Josiah's cabin. She was only human, after all. Maybe she could ignore her conscience long enough to…

She halted halfway down the hall. Cora stood on the threshold to her room, a stricken expression on her face. Julia quickened her footsteps. "Mama, what's the matter?"

She didn't need an explanation. Not when she saw the envelope from Wayne dangling from her mother's hand, the two sheets of paper that had been stuffed inside braced in Cora's quivering grasp.

Cora stared, her eyes wide and glittering with the rage of betrayal. "What has happened to you, Julia? How could you keep this from me?"

Julia glanced over her mother's shoulder, noticed her bed linens had been stripped from the mattress and lay in a heap on the floor. Her first instinct was to strike out. "What are you doing in here? You have no right…"

Cora tightened her hand around the documents and waved them in Julia's face. "No right to change your sheets? It's lucky I did or I never would have discovered your little secret!"

Julia remained on the offensive. "It's not my secret, Mama. It's Tina's. She's the one who kept it from us for years."

"And your keeping it now makes up for her deception?" Cora backed into the room and lowered herself onto the bed. She stared at the paperwork. "This was in the package from Wayne?"

There was no point denying anything now. Julia released a long, pent-up breath. "Yes."

"Why didn't you tell me?"

Julia turned her desk chair to face Cora and sat heavily. "I wanted to. I debated it, but I needed time to sort out the ramifications of information like this."

Cora glared at her. "But Cameron's her father. And you've known for what—" she paused, her mind doing a mental check "—nearly two weeks."

"Yes."

"And you're taking his child away from him without even telling him? How could you consider doing such a thing? Katie isn't yours!"

Julia brushed a tear from her cheek. "But she feels like she is. She needs me. Tina gave her to me…to us, to raise. She wanted her with us. She could have tried to find Cameron, but she didn't. She didn't even tell us about him."

"She probably hadn't thought of him in years," Cora argued.

"Not even that night, when she left her child? No, Mama. She didn't want Cameron to know."

"Maybe she didn't know where he was. But she kept these records all these years. They prove that Katie's paternity was important to Tina."

"I think she kept them to use against Wayne," Julia said. "Tina knew they could be a sort of ammunition against that creep. She never meant to reveal the truth to Cameron or she would have, long before she walked into that pond."

"Even if that were true, it doesn't give you the right

to perpetuate a lie!" Cora thrust the papers at Julia's chest. "You're no better than Tina at this moment. You've chosen to play with people's lives."

"No. I've chosen to protect Katie. That has been my motive from the start."

"Who are you protecting her from, Julia? From that man on top of the mountain who loves her? From me?" Cora shook her head. "You're not protecting her. You're keeping her. You're laying claim to something that isn't yours, and when that something is a human being, that level of selfishness is unforgivable." She stood up. "You have to make this right."

"I am not selfish, Mama. Tina was, not me. I'm willing to give up my independence, my way of life, *everything* to shelter that child, to keep her safe, to love her. You saw what happened when Katie heard I was leaving. Is that what you want for her? To follow the destructive path her mother took? I'm Katie's salvation, and if you don't see that, then you're the one who selfishly wants to keep her."

Cora trembled. Tears rolled down her cheeks. "Of course I want to keep her here. I always have. From the moment she was born, I wanted her here on Whisper Mountain. But Tina kept her away and now you're planning to do the same thing." She walked to the door. "She's all I have left of Tina, Julia. You can't take her. Not now." She looked down at the documents still in her hand. "And especially not after this."

Julia rose and followed her mother down the hall. "What do you think Cameron is going to do? He'll take her to Raleigh when he's ready to leave the mountain, and he'll have no obligation to bring her to see you. But I will. I'll come back often, and you'll see Katie."

She skirted around Cora and stopped her in the living room with a firm hold on her arm. "Think about this, Mama. I'm promising you a long-lasting relationship with Katie. If Cameron takes her, you may not have that."

Cora's features pinched with determination. "But I'll have her until he leaves. What are you promising now? Another couple of days. It's not fair, Julia. It's simply not fair! I've given enough for one lifetime."

Julia opened her mouth to argue, but was stopped by the pain in her mother's eyes. She pulled Cora to her chest, and they stood in the middle of the room, their arms around each other. "Mama, I'm sorry. I didn't mean to hurt you, but what would you have me do? What do you think is best for Katie? Because, in the end, that's what's important."

She felt Cora nod her head. "You're right. Katie comes first. But she's only nine. She may not know what she wants."

Julia stepped back, looked into her mother's eyes. "I'll talk to her," she said. "Try to get her to open up to me. One thing I've learned is that Katie knows a lot more about what she wants than she lets on." She brushed her hand down Cora's rumpled hairdo. "She's her mother's daughter in that respect."

Cora's lips twitched in what Julia hoped was the beginning of a smile. "She is, isn't she?"

"We all want what's best for her," Julia said. "I'll see if she can tell us what that is." She crumpled the papers by squeezing her hand over Cora's. "Don't do anything till I talk to her."

JULIA DROVE Cameron to his doctor's appointment, waited while he was examined and then took him home.

She joined in his enthusiasm when he said he had only two weeks to put up with the external fixators before moving on to some sort of wrist immobilizer.

"That's progress," she said when she pulled in front of the cabin and shut off the Xterra.

He grinned. "A man's got to experience progress in some aspects of his life."

She smiled back.

"You coming in?" he asked.

"Sorry. I've got a few things to do before I pick up Katie at school." *Like becoming an expert in child psychology.*

"Maybe you can bring her here tonight," he said. "She'll be leaving with you soon, and I'd like to get in as much time with her as possible before she goes." He waited while Julia walked to the Toyota. "That goes for both of you," he added.

"Thanks, but I don't know that tonight will work. I'll bring her tomorrow for sure."

"Okay, but tell her I'm looking forward to spending time with her before you both fly out of here."

Julia went back to the store, helped out for a few hours while her mind stayed occupied with the conversation she'd planned to have with Katie later. When she picked her up at school, she didn't drive back to the store. Instead she went into town, stopped to buy a pint of ice cream and two spoons, and went to the circle across from the drugstore. She chose a quiet bench where they wouldn't be interrupted.

Katie licked the first helping off her spoon. "My favorite. Chocolate with fudge and cherries."

Julia smiled. "Gee, how did I know that?"

"I hope they have this kind of ice cream in New York," Katie said.

She had just given Julia the perfect opening. "I'm sure they do, but I'm wondering if you might miss some of the other things you've gotten used to on the mountain."

Katie looked up at her. "Like what?"

"Well, for starters, all those chipmunks you've begun to make friends with."

Katie considered Julia's example a moment. "Yeah, it hasn't been as hard to make friends as I thought it would be."

"And what about Mrs. Lunsford? You really like her, don't you?"

"Yes. But maybe I'll like my teacher in New York, too."

"Sure. You probably will." Julia took a bite of ice cream. "I should have told you this before, but you won't have your own room for a while when we move."

"I won't?"

"I'm going to try to find us a bigger place, but it might take time. And when I do, you'll have to adjust to having limited space for your things. And to not being outside as much."

Katie's brow furrowed slightly. "Oh. I like being outside. Cameron showed me all sorts of things about nature. And we painted pinecones and rocks."

"I know. I don't think we'll find many pinecones in Manhattan." She didn't want to influence Katie with only negative aspects of their new life, so she added, "But we have wonderful, huge libraries. And museums and theaters."

"That sounds good."

Julia let a few moments pass before she asked the question foremost on her mind. "Tell me something, sweetie. Are you going to miss Cameron?"

Katie nodded, dug the spoon deep into the ice cream.

"A little or a lot?" Julia asked.

Katie dropped her hand, leaving the spoon upright in the container. She stared down at her lap.

Julia placed her hand on Katie's shoulder. "Tell me the truth. It's important. I've got to know."

Her voice sounded small and distant when she said, "A lot." She turned her head to Julia. "I really like Cameron."

Julia put her arm around Katie and felt her tears in the tremble of her small body. "I know you do."

"But…but I would miss you if I stayed here."

Julia blinked back her own tears. "It's a tough one, isn't it, Pussy toes?"

Katie sniffed. "Yeah, it is."

Julia stood, picked up the ice cream container. She couldn't lie to herself any longer. It was time to do the right thing. "Let's go home," she said. "There's something I've got to do tonight that can't wait."

CHAPTER SEVENTEEN

JULIA PARKED at the house. Since an hour remained before Cora would close up for the day, Julia decided she would have dinner ready at six o'clock and then go to Cameron's afterward. She settled Katie at the desk with her homework and went to the kitchen. She peeled potatoes, put them on to boil and popped three chicken breasts in the oven. When she realized they were out of bread for Katie's sandwich for lunch the next day, she walked into the living room.

"I'm running to the store a minute," she said to Katie.

"Okay."

Julia entered the store from the back door, crossed to the bakery shelf and picked up a loaf of bread. She spoke to Rosalie, who was behind the cash register. "Where's Mama?"

"She's not here."

"Where'd she go?"

"I don't know." Rosalie began counting change in the drawer. "She said she'd be back soon, but she had to get somewhere before dark."

Before dark? Cora wasn't afraid to drive in the dark…unless it was to the top of the mountain. Julia pressed Rosalie for more information. "How long ago did she leave?"

"About fifteen minutes."

Shit. "Rosalie, I have to leave, too. Can I bring Katie here and will you watch her till one of us returns?"

"Sure."

"Thanks."

Clutching the bread, Julia ran to the house. She turned the stove off and bundled Katie into her jacket. "Dinner might be late," she said. "I have to run an errand and Grandma is out. You're going to stay in the store with Rosalie."

Katie gathered her school supplies and followed Julia. "Call if you need me," Julia told Rosalie. "Katie knows my cell number."

She reached Cameron's in less than ten minutes and immediately noticed Cora's Ford in front. Her heart slammed against her ribs. She climbed out of the car and ran to the steps.

Too late. Julia skidded to a stop outside the screen door. Cameron looked up from an easy chair. In his hand were the dreaded papers. Cora watched her through the door. She seemed to grow smaller as tense moments passed.

Julia stepped inside. "Cameron, I can explain."

His eyes, void of emotion, stared through her. "I don't see how."

She stopped just over the threshold. "I was coming tonight to show you the certificate."

"That's not the way Cora tells it."

Julia glanced at her mother. Cora looked away. "Mama didn't know. A lot has changed since this morning. I spoke to Katie."

Cameron stood, held up the papers. "Does she know about this?"

Julia shook her head. "I haven't told her."

"How long have you known? Since Katie was born?"

"God, no. I just found out a week ago Saturday. Wayne sent a box with some of Tina's things."

He rattled the papers in his grasp. "So you've kept this secret since then. During all those drives and appointments. Those times we…" He paused. "And you didn't think I ought to know?"

"I didn't know what to think," she said. "I kept going back and forth, trying to decide what was best for Katie."

His features seemed carved of stone. His back was rigid. Even the fingers of his injured hand curled into a fist. "Tina's dead, Julia. The man Katie thought was her father has disappeared from her life. What does it take to convince you? *I'm* what's best for her."

Julia's throat felt like it was stuffed with cotton. "I'm sorry, Cameron. But this decision was the most important one I've ever had to make."

"What decision is that, Julia? The one to play judge and jury? The one to keep secrets? The one to deny Katie her rightful father?"

"I wanted to protect her."

"Is that what you call it? I wonder what euphemism Louisa would have used when she robbed me of my child."

His words were a verbal punch to her midsection, and she clutched her abdomen. He was right. At this moment she was no different than his ex-wife.

He released a snarl of bitter laughter. "Just exactly what were you protecting her from? Did you think I'd hurt her? That I'd abandon her?"

"No, nothing like that."

"Then, God, Julia, did you think I wouldn't love her? How blind can you be? Can't you see I already do?"

"I know you care for her. That's what made this so hard."

"Care for her? I *love* her. The only reason I haven't put this feeling into words is because I didn't think I had the right to say them. But, Julia, I've felt a connection to that child from the moment I met her."

All of Julia's rationalizations seemed trivial when compared to his perception of her deceit. But she had to make him understand. "I thought if you knew, you might misinterpret your feelings. You had a relationship with Tina. You once loved her, and if you transferred those feelings to Katie, they wouldn't be real."

He shook his head and dropped the papers to the coffee table. "Now who's drawing conclusions? What Tina and I shared was wild and passionate, but it wasn't love. It wasn't anything like what I thought I…" He paused, rubbed his hand down his face. "I will appeal for custody," he said. "If you intend to fight that…"

"I won't." She saw her mother's relief. She drew in a short, ragged gulp of air and prayed she still had the fortitude to say what needed to be said. "I'll leave Katie here with you when I go back on Friday."

He nodded. "Is that what Katie wants?"

Recognizing the fear of rejection in his eyes, she said, "Yes. I talked to her today and I realized that living on Whisper Mountain is what she wants now. And once she finds out about you…"

The stiffness in his shoulders eased. "How will you tell her?"

Julia shivered in a blast of wind that suddenly swept through the screen door. She wrapped her arms around her chest. "We'll tell her together." She pressed her hand to her forehead and faced the truth that this would be the last thing she would ever do with Cameron.

"When?"

"Tomorrow afternoon when she gets home from school. I need time to prepare."

"That's fine. Tomorrow is soon enough."

Cora stood. "This is best, Julia. You'll see."

Julia paused at the door, took a last look around Josiah's cabin, especially at the winding staircase that once symbolized a promise. And then she turned and left.

CAMERON WAS EARLY on Thursday afternoon. He drove himself to the store fifteen minutes before Julia would leave to pick up Katie at school. Thankful to have a few minutes to prepare them both, Julia sat across from him in one of the booths in the snack bar.

"You won't have to drive her to school every day," she told him. "If you can get her here to the store, she can catch the school bus. It comes to the parking lot."

"I can manage to drive this far. Once the fixators are removed, I'll have more flexibility in my hand."

Julia traced her fingertip down the condensation on her Coke glass. "She'll need things before the first snowfall. Boots, a warmer jacket, earmuffs and mittens."

"No problem. I don't know much about girl's clothes, but I can pick up Cora and we can shop together. I'll make sure she has what she needs."

Julia nodded. "About food. You can ask her what she likes, of course, but green vegetables are a big no-no. Still, you should try to get her to eat them once in a while."

"Sure."

Julia breathed deeply, getting control of the momentary panic she was feeling.

Cameron stared at her emotionlessly. Perhaps he'd stopped hating her and now felt only disinterest. "Have you decided how you're going to tell her? About me, I mean?"

"Not exactly. I'm hoping for divine inspiration." She gave him an earnest look. "I just hope that what happened between us…"

He turned away.

She pressed on. "I hope our personal feelings won't be evident to Katie. She needs to believe that we're together on this, that we both feel this living arrangement is in her best interests."

He trained a cold gaze on her face. "Don't worry about me. I do feel that."

Her stomach twisted. His resentment was as strong as it had been last night; there was no reason why it shouldn't be. Her deceit was one day older, but its significance hadn't diminished.

She swallowed. "There's one more thing, Cam…"

"What?"

"I've never been a mother, so I don't know how good I'd be at it."

"You'd be fine," he said. "You just have a little trouble with the truth."

"Right. Anyway, I'm sorry if what I'm about to say sounds harsh, but I need to say it. If you ever feel like you can't cope, that you're not reaching Katie or she's not listening, I hope you'll call me, or Mama. Maybe we can intervene, take some of the pressure off you if things are starting to get out of hand."

His eyes seemed to bore through her. "Let me put this another way. You're saying that if I'm not a good father, I'll have to answer to you."

She felt her face heat. She hadn't meant to sound judgmental or threatening, but he'd definitely gotten the point. "I guess that's what I'm saying. Be good to her, Cam."

He leaned forward. "I'm not going to take offense at what you've just said, Julia, because I know those words came from your affection for Katie. So just let me say this. I've never been a parent, either, but I've decided to start out by simply cherishing Katie every minute and see where it goes from there."

It was a good answer and Julia was satisfied. "Okay, then, it's time. I'll go get her."

She slid out of the booth. After taking a few steps, she turned back and said, "But while we're on the subject of you being a good father…"

His eyes narrowed suspiciously. "Yeah?"

"I don't want to hear of you driving on slick roads with Katie in the car."

He actually chuckled. "I think I deserved that one. Now please, go. I'm getting more nervous by the second. Even without the pickles and ice cream phase, impending parenthood is a pretty daunting proposition."

HE WATCHED HER LEAVE and waited for the sound of her car engine to fade before he stood up from the table and crossed the room. He stared out the window at the falls tumbling from the crest of the mountain. He listened to it churn and boil over the rocks, gaining speed and power until it plummeted into the pool that had almost taken his life a month ago.

So much had happened since then. He'd put the city behind him and renewed his appreciation for the Blue Ridge Mountains. In an odd sort of parallel existence, the physical injuries he'd sustained on Whisper Mountain had mirrored the emotional ones he'd brought from Raleigh. The pain to his body and mind had seemed almost insurmountable at first, and yet both had begun to heal. He'd gotten over past love and experienced one so new, so hopeful… And now, just when he'd begun to accept the bitterness of his past, he found himself coping with the bitterness of the present.

He shook his head. There was no point in thinking about what might have been. He'd done that last night, through the long, dark hours. Julia had said she'd come to the cabin to tell him the truth. He didn't know if he believed her. Maybe she had. Or maybe she'd seen Cora's car missing from the store parking lot and sped up the mountain to stop her from revealing what Julia should have days before.

It didn't really matter now. Julia had had plenty of opportunity to tell him about Katie and had chosen repeatedly not to. He pressed his hand to the window-pane, welcoming the hard, cold reality under his palm. How could she have done this, he thought. *She knew I'd lost the child I'd longed for, and she was ready to deny me the one I already had.*

He turned from the window and tried to relieve a persistent ache in his wrist by massaging the joint through the gauze. Medication-free now, he supposed he would always experience some pain from the unexpected plunge he'd taken on Whisper Mountain. His lips curved into a bitter smile. Just as he'd fallen into the ravine, in the days following he'd fallen for Julia. And he knew the pain from that would be with him always, as well.

He sat in the booth again and waited for his daughter. This was life. There was pain, but thank God there was pleasure.

FIFTEEN MINUTES LATER, Katie bounded through the screen door of Cora's General Store, stopped long enough to determine where Cameron was, and ran over to him. "I knew you'd be here," she said. "Aunt Julia told me."

He slid over, making room for her to sit beside him and simply stared at her in amazement. Strands of her silky hair had come loose from a green ribbon and drifted around her delicate face. Her knit top, depicting three cartoon characters outlined in pink glitter, had smudges of paint on the hem. Cameron didn't know the characters but he figured Julia did. She knew, too, how to gather all that blond hair into the ribbon every morning and what detergent to use to get smudges from a T-shirt. These were things he'd have to learn.

"How was your day?" he asked Katie, suddenly feeling just a bit shy in her presence. She'd always meant a great deal to him. Now her importance in his life was immeasurable.

"Good. I saw your car. You aren't supposed to drive." She looked at Julia. "He's not, is he?"

"He can drive short distances now," she said. "And anyway, today's a special occasion."

"Why?" She turned toward Cameron. "What are we going to do?"

He smiled at her. "I'm not exactly sure."

Julia brought a small carton of chocolate milk to the table, tore off the attached straw and removed it from its plastic wrap. She stuck the straw in a tiny hole at the top of the box and handed the drink to Katie as if this were an everyday occurrence. He made a mental note. *Chocolate milk. Buy a lot of it.* "Let's go outside," she said. "We have to talk about some things, and I don't want to be interrupted. We can sit on the porch of the house."

Katie stood, looked at each of them and said, "Okay."

They walked across the yard to the house. Katie kept up a chatter about school. They settled on the porch, Cameron and Katie together on a swing and Julia in a chair opposite. After a moment, Katie said, "What things are we going to talk about?"

Julia folded her hands in her lap. "Really important ones. The other day your fa…Wayne, sent a box to Grandma."

Katie squeezed the carton between her hands. Milk nearly flowed over the top of the straw. "He's not coming to get me, is he?" she said.

"No. Nothing like that."

She lifted the drink again and closed her lips around the straw. But her eyes remained wary.

Julia looked at Cameron. He gave her what he hoped was an encouraging nod. He'd already decided to let Julia handle this and only contribute when she needed him to.

"The box had some items in it that belonged to your mother," Julia said. "Wayne thought you might want them someday."

"Okay."

"And your birth certificate was in the box, too. Do you know what a birth certificate is?"

Katie thought a moment. "I guess it's a piece of paper that proves you were born."

Julia smiled. "Pretty much. It provides certain details about your birth—where and when it occurred…" She paused before saying, "…your name and the names of your mother and father."

"Oh."

Julia glanced at Cameron. He mouthed the words, *You're doing fine.* She continued. "Anyway, there was a detail in the certificate that surprised all of us."

Katie looked up. "It's my middle name, isn't it? It's kind of funny."

"No, not that. Your middle name is lovely." She leaned forward. "You understand about dating, don't you? About how a man and woman decide they like each other and go places together?"

"Sure. Grandma is dating Oscar."

"That's right. Well, years ago, before you were born, your mother dated Cameron."

Katie's mouth dropped open. She shot a surprised look at Cameron. "You had dates with my mommy before you had dates with Aunt Julia?"

Julia quickly corrected the misconception. "Cameron and I never dated," she said. "I've just been taking him places because he hurt his wrist and can't drive."

Cameron smiled at the half-truth.

"You know the difference, don't you?" Julia said.

Katie nodded.

"Good. But Cameron and your mother liked each other, a lot. And when a man and woman like each other they hold hands and kiss, and sometimes they get married and have a baby. You understand all that, right?"

"Sure. Like Mommy and Daddy did, only they weren't really married."

Cameron flinched, looked at Julia. She blew out a breath. "Exactly. Sometimes people don't get married and they still have a baby. And if the mommy starts dat-

ing another man, then that baby has a real father..."
Julia emphasized by counting on her index finger.
"...and a stepfather." She pressed her middle finger.

Oh, boy. Cameron rubbed his hands along his jeans,
crossed his legs, uncrossed them.

Katie set her drink on the floor. "Like my friend
Jasmine Mancuso in Tennessee. She had a real daddy
she saw on weekends and another daddy who lived in
her house."

"Yes. Just like that." She reached across and took
Katie's hand. "Well, your birth certificate proved something none of us knew. The man you call Daddy is really
your stepfather. He lived in your house with you and
your mommy, but he wasn't your real father."

Katie's face pinched with appropriate confusion.
"He wasn't?"

"No. As I told you, before your mommy dated
Wayne, she went out with Cameron, and they liked each
other a lot."

Katie sat perfectly still, her mind obviously process-
ing all this information. She was so smart. Cameron
knew she was close to making the connection and he
didn't think he could take a breath until she did.

She looked up at him, and he had no idea what to
do with his facial muscles. Smile? Express shock?
Send her a look that attempted to express the insecu-
rity building inside him? She eliminated the problem
by asking, "Does that certificate say you're my real
father?"

He cocked his head to the side, shrugged his shoulders with a nonchalance he didn't feel and said, "I'm
proud and happy to say it does."

She stared at him a moment more, then reached down

for her milk carton and took a long sip. She licked her lips and said, "Wow."

Julia filled in the void of silence. "I know this is a lot to understand, honey. All this time you thought of Wayne as your daddy and now…"

She scooted forward. "Will I have to see Wayne again?"

"That's up to you," Julia said. "I don't know if he'll come to Glen Springs, but if you ever want to see him, maybe we can arrange something."

"It's okay. I don't miss him that much." She stared up at Cameron. "I don't want to hurt Daddy's…I mean Wayne's…feelings, but I love Cameron a whole lot more."

"I thought perhaps you did," Julia said. "You shouldn't worry about it. Wayne will understand."

Cameron drew his hand into a fist to keep from wrapping his daughter in a fierce hug. It was probably too soon. Katie would let him know when she was ready.

She remained thoughtful for a moment until suddenly her legs began swinging and her brow furrowed. "What happens now?" She looked at Julia. "Will Cameron come to New York with us and stay in our apartment?"

Cameron's heart beat double-time. He held up his hand when Julia started to answer. "Let me take this one," he said. He touched Katie's shoulder. "I want you to understand, Katie, that finding out you're my daughter has made me feel like the luckiest man in the world. And I hope you feel good about it, too. Now you have all these people who love you. Your grandma, your Aunt Julia and me. But I can't go to New York and Aunt Julia can't stay here."

He glanced at Julia. Her eyes were downcast preventing him from reading her expression. He wondered if she felt as bereft as he did. Did she wish his last sentence could somehow be reversed, that things could be different? But they had their own lives and so much had happened between them, bitter things. But good ones, too.

Katie's voice, soft and sweet, brought him back. "So where will I go?" she said.

"Your aunt and I have talked this over, and if it's okay with you, we think you should stay here with me in my cabin. I'll bring you down the mountain every day so you can go to school until I can drive all the way into town. And I'll be here every afternoon to bring you back home with me." He reached over and took her hand. "I want to be your daddy, Katie. In every way. I want to make you peanut butter sandwiches and help you with your homework and take walks with you in the woods."

He lifted his face. His eyes connected with Julia's, and he found her gaze comforting and encouraging. "I can't take the place of your Aunt Julia," he continued. "I wouldn't know how to begin. She loves you very much. And she can see you whenever she's on the mountain, and you can go to New York and visit her. But you're my little girl." He lifted his injured hand and placed it over his chest. "And you're here already in my heart. All that's left is for you to be here on Whisper Mountain with me so I can be a real daddy to you."

Katie withdrew her hand and walked over to Julia. Cameron held his breath. He didn't know what she would say, how she would react to what he'd just said. If she insisted on going with Julia, what would he do?

She leaned forward, placed a hand on each of Julia's knees. Her voice trembled when she said, "Will you be okay if I stay with Cam?"

Julia cupped Katie's face in her palms. "Oh, yes, sweetie. I'll be fine. I'll miss you, but I can call you, and we can e-mail each other every day. I'll see you on holidays." Her voice caught. She took a moment. "A little girl should be with her daddy, especially when that daddy loves her as much as Cam loves you. You're going to have a wonderful life with him, no matter if it's here on Whisper Mountain…" she gave Cam a pointed stare "…or anywhere else. And I'm going to think of you every day being happy."

Cameron let her words sink in. Smart Julia. She was even preparing Katie for their eventual return to Raleigh.

He had to strain to hear Katie's next words. "Are you still going tomorrow?" she asked.

Julia nodded. "I have to, honey." She wiped Katie's cheeks with the pads of her thumbs and Cam looked away. How could such happiness be entwined with so much heartbreak?

A moment passed before Katie turned back to Cameron. "Can I get my own e-mail name so I can write Aunt Julia?" she asked.

"Absolutely."

She smiled at Julia. "We can be Pussy toes and MoonPie, can't we?"

Julia laughed, almost like normal. "I can't think of anything better."

CHAPTER EIGHTEEN

CAMERON CAME OUT of the kitchen and slung the dish-towel he'd been using over his shoulder. He wiggled the fingers that stuck out from the orthopedic immobilizer he'd gotten from his doctor today. He still wasn't allowed to move his wrist, but he could take the thing off once in a while and at least feel fresh air on his skin. That was a little bit of heaven. As was the good report he'd gotten from the surgeon. Another month of wearing this contraption and he'd be ready for rehab. He could even use the keyboard now—awkwardly and for short periods.

Katie looked up from the computer. "I can dry the dishes tomorrow."

"Deal." He came closer. "Do you need any help logging on?"

She frowned up at him. "You've shown me three times, Daddy. I think I can remember."

"Of course you can." He went to the fireplace, picked up the poker and jabbed it into the logs a couple of times. A few cinders spit into the air, accomplishing nothing, but making the time pass.

"So what are you doing?" he asked Katie.

"Surfing. Answering e-mail."

He put the poker back in the stand and walked over to her. He had an excuse to stick his nose into her business now. He'd heard a message on TV that clearly advised parents to be aware of the sites their kids were checking out on the Net. He was not invading Katie's privacy. He was being a good parent. If he got a look at her e-mail messages that was just a perk of being a vigilant dad. "What are you looking at?"

"The Cartoon Network site. Wanna see?"

Not really. But he glanced down anyway. "Oh. Neat."

She waited a moment and stared up at him. "Aren't you going to ask about my e-mail?"

Perhaps he'd been a bit too obvious in his snooping the last two weeks. "Did you get one from Aunt Julia?"

"Sure. I get one every day. I've saved them all."

Cam pulled out a chair and sat. "How's she doing?"

Katie minimized the cartoon screen and clicked on her messages. "You want to read today's?"

He shook his head. "No, that's okay. It's meant for your eyes only."

She opened the latest entry. "I'll read it to you."

He shrugged. "If you want."

Dear Katie. I miss you. I hope you're having fun. Today the cat I told you about came back. He was on my fire escape. All I had to feed him was Dippin' Dots I'd bought on the way home from work. He seemed to like them.

Katie giggled, looked at Cameron. "Isn't that funny? She gave the cat Dippin' Dots. Do you know what those are?"

"Yeah. It's funny." He leaned closer. "How long has the cat been coming around?"

"A few days. Anyway, then she says, I interviewed a

violinist today. He was almost as cranky as Maude from the Hollow and he didn't even offer me cookies."

Cameron smiled. "Actually your Aunt Julia ended up liking Maude a whole lot."

"I know. She told me. She said Maude gave you Oreos."

"Does Julia say anything else?"

"Yep. She asks about you. She wonders if you got the fixators out. Yesterday I told her you were having them out today. Now I'll tell her you did." She swivelled the computer toward him. "Unless you want to tell her yourself. You just hit the Reply button, and…"

"I know how to do it. But I don't think she wants to hear from me."

"I'll bet she does. She asks about you all the time. You and the leaves. She always wants to know how the leaves look. Maybe we can send a picture. Do you know how to do that?"

"Yes, I do. That's a great idea."

"We'll take a picture tomorrow in the daylight. Do you want me to tell her anything else in my answer?"

He stood up, headed back to the kitchen. "No, that's okay."

He walked to the sink and looked out the window to the trees at the edge of his yard. *You're pathetic, Birch,* he thought. *Hanging on to e-mails sent to your nine-year-old daughter and scrambling for news from phone calls she makes at Cora's store.*

He went to the refrigerator, took out a ginger ale and held it between his injured arm and his chest. Then, with his left hand, he twisted off the cap with enough force to have wrenched the head off a rattlesnake. He took a long swallow. "Why don't you call her yourself?" Rhetorical question. He knew why. Hearing the phone slam in his ear wasn't exactly a confidence-builder.

He paced around the kitchen. *But she wouldn't do that. You're the temperamental one in this relationship. You proved that when you found out she'd been hiding the truth about Katie.*

He dropped the bottle cap in the trash. "Still, that was an unforgivable thing she did." He shook his head. "Even if she did it out of love."

"Daddy, who are you talking to?"

He smiled. "I'm talking to an idiot," he hollered back. "Unfortunately I'm the only one in here."

"Oh, Daddy, you're not an idiot."

"Thanks." He paced again, quietly this time. Was Julia's decision really so unforgivable? Hadn't he told his father to try to get past his resentment of Louisa? Hadn't he tried to do just that himself by coming to the mountain? What Louisa did was countless times worse than what Julia did, and Louisa would have kept the secret forever. And Louisa showed no remorse. In the end, that was more unforgivable than Julia's sin would ever be.

He walked out on the herb porch, sucked in a long, cool breath of cleansing Appalachian air. *Damn, Birch, you miss her. Nothing's been the same since she left. Your work, your love of the mountain, even your relationship with Katie seems strained and that's the last thing you wanted.*

"So what are you going to do about it?" he asked himself as he stood there, his chest swelling with the fullness of the mountaintop and his heart small and empty with missing Julia.

"Daddy?"

He turned at the sound of Katie's voice. "Yes?"

"I decided to send another e-mail to Aunt Julia, anyway."

"You did?"

"Yeah, and I want to tell her the answer to a question I've been thinking about."

He came across the porch and knelt in front of her. "What question is that?"

"I wonder who you really loved most, Mommy or her. I think it was Aunt Julia."

He flinched, his mind racing to finally accept the truth and his heart hammering to catch up. "You are one smart mountain girl, Pussy toes," he said. "So I'm going to give you my answer. I've never met a Sommerville woman who hasn't stolen my breath away." He looked into her beautiful blue eyes. "But will you do me a favor?"

"Sure."

"Let me tell her myself." He touched the tip of her nose and smiled. "I have a plan that I hope will bring Aunt Julia home and keep all three of us right here on the mountain where we belong."

On Friday afternoon, Julia lugged her laptop from the subway station a block from her office and walked toward the six-story brownstone building that housed the editorial department of *Night Lights Magazine*. She wasn't looking forward to the weekend. Caught up on her assignments, there wasn't anything pressing. No play openings or movie previews that another *Night Lights* writer wasn't already covering. She'd arranged to have a drink with a girlfriend later, but even those plans had been cancelled when her friend landed a better date, the male variety.

"Guess it's just me and the cat," she said after speaking to the doorman and proceeding through the revolving door. She checked her watch. 2:15 p.m. Katie would be getting off the bus at Cora's General Store in about forty-five minutes. Julia hoped to phone her for a quick update of her weekend activities before Cameron came to pick her up.

At least Katie was doing well. Cora consistently reported that she was happy with Cameron, and, as Julia expected, Cam was a great father. The three of them had been out for pizza a few times, with Cora still doing the in-town driving even though two days ago, Katie had reported via e-mail that her daddy's fixators had been removed.

Julia rode the elevator to the sixth floor, her mind occupied as it so often was with Whisper Mountain and the people there. She thought of Maude and Marcus, and Oscar and Linus Pope, even the kindly Mrs. Lunsford who'd been so good to Katie at school. And of course she thought of her family, the two she was connected to by blood, and the one she'd hoped would be connected another way.

She was thinking of Cameron when she went into the lobby of the *Night Lights* offices and walked toward the receptionist's desk. "Any messages, Sherry?" she asked.

"No, but there's someone here to see you." The young woman waggled her eyebrows in a suggestive way, leaned over her counter and spoke in a soft voice. "I think he's just the guy to make you forget the Mr. Right you left on the mountain. Look there."

Julia turned, gulped, dropped her laptop to the floor and gawked at Mr. Right himself, smiling at her from across the room. "Cameron, what are you doing here? Is it Katie?"

Appearing as casual as if they'd planned this meeting, he removed his right ankle from the opposite knee and stood. "She's fine."

"Then…what?"

"I've come to see you." He came close, picked up her laptop. "Can you come with me?"

"I guess."

"Do we have to take this?"

"No." She took the bag and slid it over the receptionist's counter. "Watch this for me, will you, Sher?"

He took her arm and led her out of the office to the pair of elevators. One opened and they stepped inside. At the fifth floor, the car stopped. Three women waited to enter. Cameron grabbed the service phone, and flashed his shirt pocket under his denim sports coat. "Maintenance, ladies. This elevator is making an odd sound. I'm checking it out." They jumped back. The doors closed again.

Julia looked under his lapel. "There's nothing there."

He hung up the phone. "Hey, it worked. And you're wrong, my heart's under there and it's hopping around like a Mexican jumping bean." He captured her face between his hands and kissed her. A great kiss, even considering the hard edge of his wrist appliance sticking into her cheek.

He grinned when he pulled back. "I figured I'd get that out of the way again so we can move forward from here."

He was back. The fun Cameron, although this time he'd added an edge of possessiveness that made Julia's body feel liquid and warm.

She leaned against the elevator wall. "So, I have to ask again, what are you doing here?"

"I brought you something." He took a folded piece of paper from the inside pocket of his jacket. "Read it."

The elevator doors opened and they walked into the lobby. While Julia read, Cameron went to the doorman and picked up a duffel bag. He tipped the guy and came back.

"This is a job application," she said. "For the *Vickers County Gazette.*"

He walked her outside where they stayed under the awning. It had started to rain. "I know. I told them about you. They need a features writer. Doesn't pay a lot, but you'd have quite a bit of leeway as far as assignments."

"But I have a job."

"I know, but it's here, and Katie and I are there."

She swallowed. "So what are you saying?"

He wrapped his hands around her shoulders. "I'm saying I want you to come home, Julia. I'm saying I'm sorry for letting you go. I need you. *We* need you."

She glanced down at his wrist. "You don't need me anymore. You're practically healed."

"Right. Okay. I misplaced the word *need.* It should have followed the word *love.*" His hands tightened on her arms. "I love you, Julia. If you love me, too—and I think you do—come back to the mountain with me."

If I love you? I've loved you in countless ways for ten years! Despite her yearning to shout those words, an instinctive caution trapped the stream of yeses that threatened to bubble up from her throat. "But you're leaving at the end of your sabbatical."

"Nope. After I got this application for you, I applied for the English Department Chair's opening at Riverton. I think I have a good chance of getting it. Pays a lot less, but I'll have Department Head's discretion to institute a few changes. Maybe even start a course in mountain lore." He smiled. "Besides, I don't need to pay a mortgage. I've already got a place."

She couldn't say yes, could she? She needed to ask what had changed his mind. Why he'd decided to forgive her? If he truly meant all this madness that was so un-Cameronlike? Or she could simply say yes. But that was madness, too, so instead, she took a deep breath, bought a little time and said, "I think I have a cat."

He laughed. "Okay. I like cats."

"I don't have a car."

"We'll buy the Xterra. You pretty much tore up the roads in that thing."

"I need to stay at *Night Lights* at least two weeks. It's only fair."

"I understand that." He pulled her collar around her throat. The rain had started falling harder. "Look, you missed Halloween, but you can give your boss notice and still make Thanksgiving."

She looked deep into his eyes and all doubt fled. All she saw there was love, pure and simple and lasting. She smiled. "Okay, I'll think about it."

He gave her a look that brimmed with confidence that bordered on cockiness.

She poked the duffel with the toe of her shoe. "What's in the bag?"

"Clothes. I thought I might stay a couple of nights. Katie's at Cora's. I'm a free man, for a while, at least." He stuck his head out from under the canopy. "How far is your apartment from here?"

"About six blocks. An easy walk."

He returned to the doorman. "Have you got an umbrella I can borrow? I'll make sure Julia brings it back on Monday."

The man handed over a large black one. Cameron

tipped him. "I could have bought a dozen new umbrellas for what these tips are costing me," he said.

"Welcome to New York."

"How long will it take us to walk those six blocks?"

"Ten minutes, maybe."

He popped open the umbrella, stuffed the duffel bag under one arm and wrapped the one with the umbrella around Julia. "We can cut that time in half if we run. And we do our best work in the rain, anyway."

She laughed and headed out with him into the drizzle. "What's your hurry, Professor?"

He drew her tight against him. "I've got to feed a cat, make love to a woman and propose marriage—not necessarily in that order. Those things take time."

* * * * *

Mediterranean Nights

Join the guests and crew of **Alexandra's Dream,**
*the newest luxury ship to set sail on the
romantic Mediterranean, as they experience
the glamorous world of cruising.*

*A new Harlequin continuity series
begins in June 2007 with*
FROM RUSSIA, WITH LOVE
by Ingrid Weaver.

*Marina Artamova books a cabin on the luxurious
cruise ship* **Alexandra's Dream,** *when she finds
out that her orphaned nephew and his adoptive
father are aboard. She's determined to be
reunited with the boy...but the romantic ambience
of the ship and her undeniable attraction
to a man she considers her enemy are
about to interfere with her quest!*

Turn the page for a sneak preview!

Piraeus, Greece

"THERE SHE IS, Stefan. *Alexandra's Dream*." David Anderson squatted beside his new son and pointed at the dark blue hull that towered above the pier. The cruise ship was a majestic sight, twelve decks high and as long as a city block. A circle of silver and gold stars, the logo of the Liberty cruise line, gleamed from the swept-back smokestack. Like some legendary sea creature born for the water, the ship emanated power from every sleek curve—even at rest it held the promise of motion. "That's going to be our home for the next ten days."

The child beside him remained silent, his cheeks working in and out as he sucked furiously on his thumb. Hair so blond it appeared white ruffled against his forehead in the harbor breeze. The baby-sweet scent unique to the very young mingled with the tang of the sea.

"Ship," David said. "Uh, *parakhod*."

From beneath his bangs, Stefan looked at the *Alexandra's Dream*. Although he didn't release his thumb, the corners of his mouth tightened with the beginning of a smile.

David grinned. That was Stefan's first smile this afternoon, one of only two since they had left the orphanage yesterday. It was probably because of the boat—according to the orphanage staff, the boy loved boats, which was the main reason David had decided to book this cruise. Then again, there was a strong possibility the smile could have been a reaction to David's attempt at pocket-dictionary Russian. Whatever the cause, it was a good start.

The liaison from the adoption agency had claimed that Stefan had been taught some English, but David had yet to see evidence of it. David continued to speak, positive his son would understand his tone even if he couldn't grasp the words. "This is her maiden voyage. Her first trip, just like this is our first trip, and that makes it special." He motioned toward the stage that had been set up on the pier beneath the ship's bow. "That's why everyone's celebrating."

The ship's official christening ceremony had been held the day before and had been a closed affair, with only the cruise-line executives and VIP guests invited, but the stage hadn't yet been disassembled. Banners bearing the blue and white of the Greek flag of the ship's owner, as well as the Liberty circle of stars logo, draped the edges of the platform. In the center, a group of musicians and a dance troupe dressed in traditional white folk costumes performed for the benefit of the *Alexandra's Dream*'s first passengers. Their audience was in a festive mood, snapping their fingers in time to the music while the dancers twirled and wove through their steps.

David bobbed his head to the rhythm of the mandolins. They were playing a folk tune that seemed vaguely familiar, possibly from a movie he'd seen. He hummed a few notes. "Catchy melody, isn't it?"

Stefan turned his gaze on David. His eyes were a striking shade of blue, as cool and pale as a winter horizon and far too solemn for a child not yet five. Still, the smile that hovered at the corners of his mouth persisted. He moved his head with the music, mirroring David's motion.

David gave a silent cheer at the interaction. Hopefully, this cruise would provide countless opportunities for more. "Hey, good for you," he said. "Do you like the music?"

The child's eyes sparked. He withdrew his thumb with a pop. *"Moozika!"*

"Music. Right!" David held out his hand. "Come on, let's go closer so we can watch the dancers."

Stefan grasped David's hand quickly, as if he feared it would be withdrawn. In an instant his budding smile was replaced by a look close to panic.

Did he remember the car accident that had killed his parents? It would be a mercy if he didn't. As far as David knew, Stefan had never spoken of it to anyone. Whatever he had seen had made him run so far from the crash that the police hadn't found him until the next day. The event had traumatized him to the extent that he hadn't uttered a word until his fifth week at the orphanage. Even now he seldom talked.

David sat back on his heels and brushed the hair from Stefan's forehead. That solemn, too-old gaze locked with his and, for an instant, David felt as if he looked back in time at an image of himself thirty years ago.

He didn't need to speak the same language to understand exactly how this boy felt. He knew what it meant to be alone and powerless among strangers, trying to be brave and tough but wishing with every fiber of his being for a place to belong, to be safe and, most of all, for someone to love him....

He knew in his heart he would be a good parent to Stefan. It was why he had never considered halting the adoption process after Ellie had left him. He hadn't balked when he'd learned of the recent claim by Stefan's spinster aunt, either; the absentee relative had shown up too late for her case to be considered. The adoption was meant to be. He and this child already shared a bond that went deeper than paperwork or legalities.

A seagull screeched overhead, making Stefan start and press closer to David.

"That's my boy," David murmured. He swallowed hard, struck by the simple truth of what he had just said. *That's* my *boy.*

"I CAN'T BE PATIENT, RUDOLPH. I'm not going to stand by and watch my nephew get ripped from his country and his roots to live on the other side of the world."

Rudolph hissed out a slow breath. "Marina, I don't like the sound of that. What are you planning?"

"I'm going to talk some sense into this American kidnapper."

"No. Absolutely not. No offence, but diplomacy is not your strong suit."

"Diplomacy be damned. Their ship's due to sail at five o'clock."

"Then you wouldn't have an opportunity to speak with him even if his lawyer agreed to a meeting."

"I'll have ten days of opportunities, Rudolph, since I plan to be on board that ship."

* * * * *

*Follow Marina and David as they join forces
to uncover the reason behind little Stefan's
unusual silence and the secret behind
the death of his parents....*

*Look for FROM RUSSIA, WITH LOVE
by Ingrid Weaver
in stores June 2007.*

HARLEQUIN®

Mediterranean N I G H T S™

Tycoon Elias Stamos is launching his newest luxury cruise ship from his home port in Greece. But someone from his past is eager to expose old secrets and to see the Stamos empire crumble.

Mediterranean Nights
launches in June 2007 with...

FROM RUSSIA, WITH LOVE
by *Ingrid Weaver*

Join the guests and crew of *Alexandra's Dream* as they are drawn into a world of glamour, romance and intrigue in this new 12-book series.

MN1

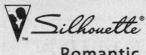

Silhouette®

Romantic
SUSPENSE

Sparked by Danger,
Fueled by Passion.

**This month and every month look for
four new heart-racing romances
set against a backdrop of suspense!**

Available in June 2007

Shelter from the Storm
by **RaeAnne Thayne**

A Little Bit Guilty
(Midnight Secrets miniseries)
by **Jenna Mills**

Mob Mistress
by **Sheri WhiteFeather**

A Serial Affair
by **Natalie Dunbar**

Available wherever you buy books!

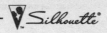

SPECIAL EDITION™

COMING IN JUNE

HER LAST FIRST DATE

by *USA TODAY* bestsellling author

SUSAN MALLERY

After one too many bad dates, Crissy Phillips
finally swore off men. Recently widowed,
pediatrician Josh Daniels can't risk losing his
heart. With an intense attraction pulling them
together, will their fear keep them apart?
Or will one wild night change everything…?

**Sometimes the unexpected
is the best news of all….**

 SSE24831

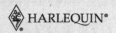
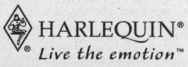

REQUEST YOUR FREE BOOKS!
2 FREE NOVELS PLUS 2 FREE GIFTS!

HARLEQUIN®-

Super Romance®

Exciting, emotional, unexpected!

YES! Please send me 2 FREE Harlequin Superromance® novels and my 2 FREE gifts. After receiving them, if I don't wish to receive any more books, I can return the shipping statement marked "cancel." If I don't cancel, I will receive 6 brand-new novels every month and be billed just $4.69 per book in the U.S., or $5.24 per book in Canada, plus 25¢ shipping and handling per book and applicable taxes, if any*. That's a savings of close to 15% off the cover price! I understand that accepting the 2 free books and gifts places me under no obligation to buy anything. I can always return a shipment and cancel at any time. Even if I never buy another book from Harlequin, the two free books and gifts are mine to keep forever.   135 HDN EEX7 336 HDN EEYK

Name	(PLEASE PRINT)
Address	Apt.
City	State/Prov.	Zip/Postal Code

Signature (if under 18, a parent or guardian must sign)

Mail to the **Harlequin Reader Service®**:
IN U.S.A.: P.O. Box 1867, Buffalo, NY 14240-1867
IN CANADA: P.O. Box 609, Fort Erie, Ontario L2A 5X3

Not valid to current Harlequin Superromance subscribers.

Want to try two free books from another line?
Call 1-800-873-8635 or visit www.morefreebooks.com.

* Terms and prices subject to change without notice. NY residents add applicable sales tax. Canadian residents will be charged applicable provincial taxes and GST. This offer is limited to one order per household. All orders subject to approval. Credit or debit balances in a customer's account(s) may be offset by any other outstanding balance owed by or to the customer. Please allow 4 to 6 weeks for delivery.

Your Privacy: Harlequin is committed to protecting your privacy. Our Privacy Policy is available online at www.eHarlequin.com or upon request from the Reader Service. From time to time we make our lists of customers available to reputable firms who may have a product or service of interest to you. If you would prefer we not share your name and address, please check here. ☐

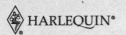

HARLEQUIN®

American **ROMANCE**®

**is proud to present a special treat this
Fourth of July with three stories
to kick off your summer!**

SUMMER LOVIN'
by
Marin Thomas,
Laura Marie Altom
Ann Roth

This year, celebrating the Fourth of July in Silver Cliff,
Colorado, is going to be special. There's an all-year
high school reunion taking place before the old
school building gets torn down. As old flames find
each other and new romances begin, this small
town is looking like the perfect place
for some summer lovin'!

*Available June 2007
wherever Harlequin books are sold.*

www.eHarlequin.com

HAR75169

COMING NEXT MONTH